WHAT WE LEAVE BEHIND

WHAT WE LEAVE BEHIND

A Novel

CHRISTINE GALLAGHER KEARNEY

SHE WRITES PRESS

Published 2023
Printed in the United States of America
Print ISBN: 978-1-64742-493-0
E-ISBN: 978-1-64742-494-7
Library of Congress Control Number: 2023900523

For information, address:
She Writes Press
1569 Solano Ave #546
Berkeley, CA 94707

Interior Design by Kiran Spees

She Writes Press is a division of SparkPoint Studio, LLC.

For Mom

and

For Michelle O'Hare (née Kearney)

"Disability only becomes a tragedy when society fails to provide the things needed to lead one's daily life."

—Judith Heumann, *Being Heumann*

PART I

CHAPTER 1
May 1947

Somewhere over the Atlantic, Ursula peered into a small square mirror. A shadow of her mother peered back. The plane jolted. Her right ankle wobbled and she lost her balance, somehow landing on her knees in the cramped cubicle. Clutching the dirty toilet seat, she threw up, and a red hair strayed across her cheek. She tried a deep breath to steady her nausea but was met with a familiar smell, the putrid stench of the unburied dead along the streets of Berlin. Her stomach threatened again, but she resisted. She flushed, stood, and washed her hands in the metal sink.

Back at her window seat, she pulled back the short accordion curtain. The water far below was indigo with brush strokes of jagged white. She had never been on a plane before, but now she glided through the air on the third leg of her journey on a DC-4 American Overseas Airlines flight out of Germany.

Ursula drew the curtain back across the window and shut her eyes to calm the blur of uncertainty. When Roger first proposed the idea of marriage, she had only half believed him. The end of the war had made many Allied soldiers giddy with promise. Before she met Roger, she was a secretary in G-tower, the imposing concrete structure meant to protect Berlin from Allied bombers and provide shelter to civilians during air raids. Like most women who had worked there,

she entertained numerous Allied proposals. Well, not exactly entertained. But Roger's maturity and earnest nature set him apart from
the others who courted her with less virtuous invitations. He pledged
to take Ursula to America, home to the state of Minnesota where he
had grown up and still lived with his family.

Her last conversation with her mother weighed on her mind, but
she tried not to linger on it. Reliving their talk just made her more
upset about leaving Berlin. Instead, she thought about the official
paperwork stowed in the small suitcase at her feet. She had read the
documents multiple times, shocked it had all come through. She had
been granted permission to move to the United States. She was grateful for the English she had practiced over the last few years while
working with the American military government. Those papers
were a small miracle: Military Exit Permit, Approved Marriage
Application (under the War Brides Act, Public Law 271), and Health
Clearance Form.

Then she thought about Roger. Roger Gorski, an American ser-
geant from Minneapolis, had fallen in love with her—a German
woman, the enemy!—and married her. American soldiers were
warned to be on their guard and not fraternize with German women,
but Roger had ignored the order. While she was not in love in the way
she thought she should be—was the piercing feeling that knocked
out all sense something that really happened?—Ursula was fond of
Roger. She felt safe with him. Under the Russian occupation, the
Americans were like saviors, and this was enough for her. She was
weary of running, weary of the struggle. Months, going on years, of
no heat, of no electricity, of little food. Any chance to move beyond
post-war life in Berlin would have been welcome, and Roger's proposal was better still.

As she drifted to sleep, she recalled an afternoon alongside

Roger on the crumbled streets of Berlin, clinging to his description of Minnesota's lakes, all ten thousand of them. Where he lived in Minneapolis, people could walk around pools left over from ancient, melted icebergs. The rounded bodies of water were linked together like the blankets she knitted, the yarn tracing well-worn footpaths—winding, looping, and intersecting.

He had described the pavilion with a café near his home. The boat club. The golf course, although Roger wasn't much of a golfer. "I could never quite get the swing right," he had said.

Instead of golf, Roger fished from a small boat he rented with his brother. "Pete always caught the biggest fish," he recalled, but that didn't bother him. "I wouldn't eat the fish out of Lake Harriet anyway. Too many boats and people."

Ursula would have eaten the fish. *How could he refuse food?* After years of rations, fish from any lake would be a feast.

As he'd told her these stories, she could not help but picture Berlin's green parks and lakes before they were destroyed. She had loved the lush green foliage, the chirps of finches and robins, and the way the sun dropped glittering diamonds across the water. Now Berlin was gray—the people, streets, and even the birdsong from the ragged trees was muted. Minnesota, as Roger described it, struck Ursula as quaint. She liked the way the name sounded when Roger said it, his American accent flat, but with a strange lilt. She would later learn because of that accent, Minnesotans were often confused with Canadians. But on that day in Berlin, to her, it was the sound of all America. Safe. Optimistic.

Roger had described his family—his widowed mother, brother, and aunt—as close-knit, and as the plane wobbled in the sky, she imagined being tucked comfortably into their fold. But guilt jolted her like turbulence. If her father had been at the airport to send her off, he would have begged her to stay. He would have told her she would be happier in Germany. And she might have listened to him, but her father hadn't been there and she was finished with everyone telling her what to think and do. Her mother, the Third Reich, and the Russians who had now taken control of the sector where her family lived. She could not endure one more minute of the oppressive, adamant voices.

A week before her departure, Ursula had found a tattered suitcase discarded in an alley and discovered a few skeins of yarn tucked inside. She thought this was a good sign, a chance to create something new. She had stuffed most of the yarn into the suitcase carrying her worn dresses, a nightgown, and a handful of photographs—one of her and Roger, her parents and one of her Aunt Kaethe. She'd rolled one skein into a neat ball and tucked it into the bag she was taking on the plane. Now, she reached for the knitting tools to distract from her troubling thoughts. As she moved her fingers over the stiff blue wool, fatigue overcame her and she fell asleep, not waking until the pilot announced their landing in New York.

At the airport, Ursula lingered for hours on a hard wooden bench in a waiting area while the American officials reviewed her papers. She calmed her nerves by reviewing a mental checklist, assuring herself all her papers were in order. She and Roger had made sure of it. As her mind ticked through the paperwork, it stopped on the Health Clearance Form. This form worried her the most, as it recounted the details of her recent hospital stay. In the end, it turned out to be just a terrible fever, nothing more. Still, it took a bottle of whiskey smuggled off the American base and a sympathetic doctor checking her exit paperwork to assure that the illness was overlooked.

"Ma'am?" A flat-nosed customs official gestured her forward and she stiffened, fearing the worst. Instead, she was approved for entry with a swift, decisive stamp. Her relief made her want to dance, to spin around with arms spread and toes tapping the ground. Instead, the doors swung open with the firm press of her hand and coughed her into a loud and hectic terminal. She was overwhelmed by the melee of suitcases, the click of heels on the hard, dark floor, and spring coats fluttering behind rushed travelers. Then she noticed carnations in women's buttonholes and froze. Her mother loved carnations. Ursula stared at a woman nearby.

"It's Mother's Day," the woman said, noting her gaze and smiling. She detached the faint yellow bloom from her coat and reached toward Ursula. "Here. Have mine."

She was self-conscious about her clothes—darkened with wear and punctuated by patched holes—but she was too worn out to say no. The composed American woman stuck the carnation through the buttonhole in Ursula's scratchy coat. She hoped the sick on her breath was not obvious. Then the woman stepped back and smiled.

"Happy Mother's Day!"

Ursula's eyes grew warm and unbidden tears welled and cascaded down her face. She had not returned to Zossen to say goodbye to her mother. She had manufactured excuses for not going. The journey from Berlin to their home in the south suburbs was difficult because the train service had only been partially restored. The nearest stop was fifteen miles away and the trek from it to the house could be dangerous. Her shoulders tightened with the memory of close encounters with Russian soldiers who roamed the streets leering at German girls and women. There were constant rumors of rape. But she could have made one more visit, one more chance to explain how America offered her the promise of a new beginning, one without Nazis and Russian occupiers.

She gently cupped her palm around the flower and let out a deep sigh. As she followed the stream of people in the airport terminal, she was strangely aware of the flower adorning her coat. Its delicate scent wafted around her head, soothed her, and masked the hours of travel and sick layered on like the rubble of war. Finally, after she struggled with her English to ask others for help, she found the departures board and saw her flight to Minneapolis. A new life awaited her.

Ursula's hand grazed the outside of the airplane as she stepped outside. The cool night air whispered on her face and she descended the stairs toward the Minneapolis airport terminal. According to the large clock just inside the terminal door, it was 2:05 a.m. She shuffled by passengers being greeted with shouts of welcome and warm hugs. Roger wasn't standing among the small group of people near the door. Worry ran through her. She looked up and down the long rectangular concourse. *Roger has to be here.*

Then, on a bench a few long strides away, he came into focus: his curled hair, broad shoulders, and the easy but confident way he rested in his body. Roger's eyes were closed, his head tilted forward in slumber. She shouted his name and ran toward him.

He jolted upright. "My goodness, Ursula! You're here. You made it," Roger said, startled awake.

"I looked at those people standing over there, and you . . ." she said while pointing a trembling finger toward the dispersing group as she collapsed on the bench next to Roger. He wrapped his arm around her shoulders and the fear unwound.

"You're really here," Roger said. He turned his head, taking in her every feature. "Gosh, it's so good to see you! I'm sorry I fell asleep. When I arrived at midnight, they said something about a delay. I thought about going home, but was afraid to not be here when you landed. So I sat down and must have drifted off."

"I have missed you. I have missed you. You don't know how much." She could not believe her fortune after all she had been through. A smile erupted on Ursula's face, but she started to weep. The stress of the journey unleashed.

"How was your first time on an airplane?" Roger pressed his back against the bench, but kept his arm around Ursula.

"The ocean crossing was, do you say mountainous? The plane went up and down." She made her hand into an airplane, then continued: "I tried to be a polite girl, but my stomach . . ."

"There was a rumor going around on base once that a general ruined his uniform on a flight over from the States," Roger mimicked the officer being sick, "Now, that is something to be embarrassed about."

"Poor man," she said but appreciated Roger's attempt to put her at ease.

"Oh, I bet he's fine. Besides, dear, you're tired. Let's get you home." Roger looked at his watch. Before they stood up, he brushed his fingers against the carnation in Ursula's lapel. "What's this? I can't imagine you brought this from Berlin."

"Mother's Day. It was Mother's Day when I landed," she said, too exhausted to explain the experience in the New York airport.

"That's right. I brought my mother flowers earlier today," Roger said, pleased with himself. Guilt strummed inside her. Even the most elaborate bouquet would not mend the fact Ursula had left her mother—her parents, her family—behind.

"Earlier today feels like a lifetime ago," she said, her body weak from the lack of sleep and the rough crossing over the Atlantic. But even with the fresh memory of turbulence and vomit, she had an urge to turn around, step back onto the airplane, and return home. To make things right with her mother.

"The car is parked nearby. We don't have far to walk," Roger said.

Ursula pressed herself against Roger's side. She could not let go now that they were together again. Her hand reflexively felt for the carnation, but it was gone. She looked over her shoulder and saw the flower on the hard floor.

CHAPTER 2

Over the course of her first week in Minneapolis, Ursula could not sleep through the night. Nightly air raids had left their mark, and even now the most innocuous of sounds startled her—a barking dog or a gust of wind in the trees. In the dull midnight silence, she flipped onto her right side to face Roger, sleeping deeply beside her. She watched his chest rise and fall as she thought about this home she hoped would eventually feel like her own.

She was getting to know the inside of the little white stucco house on Colfax Avenue in Minneapolis's McKinley neighborhood. It was a hand-me-down from Roger's brother Pete who had moved with his wife, Sally, and their two kids to the suburbs. They were looking for a better life, Roger had said. A bigger house, an expansive yard. Modern appliances. Pete and Sally had left behind odds and ends: old furniture, an assortment of kitchen tools, curtains in the bedrooms. She felt like she was occupying someone else's home, and it was normal to her. In the final months of the war, before the Allies rolled in, she had shared beds between her shifts in G-Tower and later, once the Germans surrendered, slept on cots in abandoned basements and stayed with friends if their houses were still standing.

Ursula detailed the contents of her new home as if counting sheep. The small living room contained a sofa so worn she raised her eyebrows at it, as if it was an affront to the American Dream. This was not the sparkling new America she expected. Before her arrival, she spent hours imagining grand homes filled with elegant furnishings and pantries bursting with food. When Roger gave her the short tour of the house, he seemed suddenly aware of its sparseness, aware she might be disappointed. Ursula did not think he had overstated his life, but she was surprised by its modesty after all she had heard from American soldiers of abundance and luxury.

She flipped over to her left side but it was no use. Giving up on sleep, she got out of bed and went to the kitchen. On her way, a brush against her calves startled her.

"Dummer Hund!" Ursula had roused Roger's large dachshund, Victory. She thought this creature was a silly, yet endearing, attempt on his part to make her feel more at home. "Sleep. You sleep," she said in English as she motioned for the dog to leave, but pleading eyes bored into her so she found a morsel of leftover dinner in the refrigerator and threw it to Victory. "Now go. You will wake Roger," she said in German. Victory gulped down the nugget, then slumped to the floor and closed his eyes.

At the counter, Ursula turned the knob with a gentle spin bringing the small radio to life. But all she found was static. It was too late for programming. Annoyed, she switched it off, then settled at the kitchen table and pulled a blanket over her shoulders. The stationery and pen she'd gotten out earlier were still on the surface and she, again, attempted to begin a letter to her mother. *Liebe Mutter*, she wrote.

Ursula had become a quick typist as a secretary to the quartermaster in G-Tower and now preferred working her thoughts out on a typewriter. Unfortunately, Roger did not own one. For perhaps the fifth time, her hand circled over the blank sheet of paper, her fingers wishing for round keys. The pen fell out of her hand, clattering on the table and breaking the silence. She yearned for the Allied broadcasts she had listened to in secret while wordlessly cheering for Germany's imminent defeat. She wanted night-owl voices to reassure her, to let her know she was not alone. She thought of the time a few weeks before when she had sat across from her mother at a similar table in Germany. She had hoped to change her mother's mind, to convince her to see a chance in a new American home to lead a better life, one that would be impossible in Germany.

Her childhood home, her *Elternhaus,* was a modest, coral-colored two-story that had managed to endure through the worst of the air raids. Allied forces had dropped waves of bombs and missiles south of their town onto Hitler's administration buildings and barracks. Through it all, their house—and the family—survived. But ever since she went to find work in Berlin, her strained relationship with her mother finally collapsed.

When Ursula had arrived at her mother's doorstep, she hoped *ersatz,* substitute coffee she had bought at the *Geschaft,* the black market, would ease their conversation. She knew it did not have the power to soften the news she had to deliver. On the battered, half-functioning train from Berlin to Zossen, she had repeated the news in her head. *I'm leaving soon for America. I have an opportunity to go to America.* The words' rhythms had distracted her from faces uneasy with hunger and soldiers' unwanted glances. It had seemed straightforward when she practiced the announcement in her head, but standing on the stoop of the coral-colored house, her nerves wound up like an accelerating train.

As she entered her *Elternhaus,* its familiar scent enveloped her: lavender, potato peel, and the persistent smokiness emanated from the fireplace. She could sense it even now in this Minneapolis kitchen thousands of miles away. Ursula's mother was waiting inside the doorway, and they had embraced. Then, when Ursula pulled away, she noticed her mother had lost more weight. There was never enough to eat.

"I'm leaving. My papers arrived," Ursula had said, blurting the words before they froze in her mouth. Her rehearsed announcement sounded stark and even cruel when finally released.

"With that man?" Her mother had glared and shot a stiff breath through her nostrils.

"His name is Roger. Yes, with him." Ursula's voice had been unsteady.

As they continued talking, she had searched for a gesture of understanding but found none in her mother's placid face. Those soft features, deceivingly warm, could quickly flip from understanding and comforting, to unyielding. Unforgiving. There was strength in her mother that she found difficult to match, but they shared the same rich, chocolate-colored eyes, the same delicate hands. Red hair the color of geraniums billowed around Ursula's face, the color flattened by age on her mother's head. Ursula was taller than her mother by a few centimeters and possessed a youthful shape. She had her father's chin, rounded with determination.

She had wanted to explain everything to her father as he was often more sympathetic than her mother. She wanted to tell him about German women marrying American soldiers and departing for better lives. But he had been arrested by the Russians more than a year ago for speaking out against the communist regime. Her father's opinions had gotten him in trouble before. She admired his forthrightness—a characteristic that had made him an excellent journalist before he was fired for refusing to join the *Partei*. And now, in the midst of all their postwar uncertainty, he was imprisoned and no one seemed to know when he would be released.

"Men are different when they are at war," her mother had said of Roger, though she had never met him. "He could be another man in America, someone you won't recognize."

"The war is over. We have to make new lives now," Ursula replied, but her mother's suggestion about Roger made her uneasy.

"You can make your life here with your family." Her mother spread her arms, as if the whole family were at the table. Ursula pictured her father across from her in the empty, rickety seat and held down a sob.

Her heart clenched at the thought of her mother alone in the house, understanding the loneliness she had endured since her father had been taken. Aunt Kaethe planned to return soon from Berlin, and her mother had friends in the village. And she planned to visit as often as she could, what with the prosperity she would find in America. But still, she hated to think of her mother's solitude.

"I've been waiting my whole life for the war to be over. Now that it is, I don't want to wait anymore." Her throat had twitched with a frustrated sob. She had already lived many lives at twenty-two years old. Why couldn't her mother understand that she needed a new start?

"Waited your whole life? For what? You are a young woman! Your whole life is ahead of you." She shook her head. "The impatience of youth."

"But what will my future be if I stay? Berlin is destroyed. The Allies are running Germany, and to what end? The Russians will want to make us all communists, and yet here we sit drinking acorn coffee." Ursula took her cup to the open window and thrust the weak swill into the lifeless garden, the pathetic drink another reminder of Germany's bleak future.

"I don't know what the future holds, but I do know that you will be alone if you go to America," her mother had said and crossed her arms. "You need to think about this decision, Ursula. You may never return to Germany."

"I'll be with Roger!" Ursula had said to the open window, feeling her mother's stony eyes on her back.

"He is not family."

"There's nothing here." She motioned outside for her mother to understand.

"We're here." Her mother slammed her hand on the table.

Ursula turned from the window and watched as her crestfallen mother rose from the wooden chair. Without a word, she had kissed her daughter on the forehead and went upstairs. She thought about running after her, but instead glanced around the sparse and tidy home. She listened for a moment for noise from upstairs, but the house was silent. She looked around again. What could she take, if anything, that would remind her of this place? She thought of the small box hidden in the kitchen where her mother had kept keepsakes safe during the war. Ursula knelt in front of the cupboard, pushed aside the fabric curtain. At first, she saw nothing, then she groped around the edges of the shelf. The box was there, tucked high in the back. She pulled it free and opened it up. Inside was her mother's necklace with the delicate silver carnation pendant. Ursula took it out of the box, and placed it around her neck. She would return it on her first visit home.

"*Auf Wiedersehen*," she said, as she closed the door of the coral home behind her.

Now, in her Minneapolis kitchen, Ursula wished she could go back in time. Back to her *Elternhaus*, where she could hug her mother and feel the rise and fall of her chest against her own.

"I heard paper rustling. You can't sleep again?" Roger rubbed his eyes, then patted Victory on the head, "I see you have a late-night companion."

"You gave me a fright," she said as she came out of her trance. The overhead light made the room glow yellow. Roger opened the refrigerator, poured two glasses of milk, and sat down next to her. She took a sip of the thick white liquid. Roger gulped his glass in one take.

"Americans like milk. I learned that from the moving pictures," Ursula said as she recalled the Nazi reeducation films she saw in Berlin during the American occupation. Then she thought about the cow that had wandered into their town. They slaughtered it for meat. Keeping it for milk would have been frivolous, and besides, someone else would have killed it and taken it for themselves.

"How do you think the American boys got so strong?" Roger said, wiping the back of his hand across his mouth. Ursula passed her glass to him, and he gulped it down, too.

"You won the war with milk? Not guns and tanks?" She pulled the blanket over her shoulders, the pinks, and greens and yellows a mixed-up rainbow. The night before she had finished knitting it when she couldn't sleep, and was glad for the comfort it provided.

"Well, the guns and tanks helped, too," Roger said. "But enough war talk tonight. I'm going back to bed. I have a lot of work tomorrow." Roger yawned and set the empty glasses next to the sink. The cotton pajamas he wore looked new, white, and crisp. With her index finger, Ursula traced the hole in the seam of her nightgown, ashamed.

"Roger, I can't believe I'm here." The fog that had followed her since the plane had landed in New York had started to clear. She was more present in this room. In this new life. In America.

Roger paused in the doorway and said, "Yes, *gnädiges Fräulein*, dear young lady, it's like a dream. Except this dream came true."

She adored Roger for learning a few German phrases, but tonight the term of endearment made her cry.

"What is it?"

"When I told my mother my papers arrived she was furious. She wanted me to stay home, in Germany. What is worse is . . . I did not go back to say goodbye." She pressed a corner of the blanket to her face. She squeezed her eyes closed, trying to see her mother, but couldn't conjure her image. The outline of her hair would appear, her face colored in—the eyes coming into focus, then flit away like a butterfly caught in a breeze.

"Why didn't you tell me?" Roger returned to the kitchen and leaned against the counter. His face blossomed with concern. Victory followed and sat on top of his feet.

"You went through a lot of trouble to bring me here, and you did not need more trouble." Ursula pulled the blanket tighter around her shoulders.

"But I could have helped," Roger said. "I could have talked to your mom, told her you would have a good life here with me." He wiggled his feet free from Victory's underside. "You silly mutt."

"My mother does not speak English and your German is terrible."

Roger pretended to be offended, the skin on his nose scrunched together. "You could have translated for me. Your English is getting better every day."

"It would have been useless. My mother does not understand." She took a deep breath. She knew it was more than an issue of translation. Her mother could not understand why she wanted to leave home and family behind. But once Ursula had met Roger and glimpsed another life, she saw no other option. She could escape her war-torn childhood. She could leave the post-war bleakness of Berlin.

Roger shook his head as he stared at the empty glasses on the counter. He lifted one and traced its rim as if he was about to say something, but Ursula cut through the silence before he could respond.

"Promise when life is better in Germany, and we have money, we go to visit." She wanted to prove her mother wrong, to show her she could go back if she wanted to. She stood up, shooed Victory away and pressed her check against his chest. She needed to be near him, to feel his warmth.

"I promise," Roger said. We'll go together, as a family."

Ursula stepped back and squeezed his hands as if sealing the promise. The tears had dried to her face and felt crackly on her skin. First thing in the morning she would write to her mother to tell her the good news.

Spring sun made the simple white curtain almost transparent. Ursula was still in bed, unable to shake her dream about meeting Roger's mother. In the dream, Roger's mother told her to go back to Germany to be with the rest of the Nazis. Now, awake, her stomach churned with worry. How would she convince Roger's mother of her commitment to democracy?

"I won't be home for lunch," Roger said from the doorway. "And please don't forget to take Victory outside to do his business while I'm gone." He took a few steps forward and handed a cup of coffee to Ursula, who sat up and grasped it in her hands.

"I am sorry I forgot yesterday. I never, um, a dog in the house," she said, struggling to make Roger understand dogs were not permitted in her childhood home.

"I think poor Victory has already forgiven you," Roger said and motioned to the side of the bed where the dog pawed playfully at the coverlet.

"I have something to ask you."

"Of course, what is it?"

"I have thought about this, and . . ."

"What is it, Ursula?"

"You will not believe me when I ask."

"It can't be anything terrible, after everything we have already been through."

"Does your mother want to meet me? I have a sense that something is wrong." She wanted his family's approval. She needed it. Without knowing she was welcome, she feared being returned to Germany, a failed war bride.

"Don't worry about my mother," Roger said as he ran his hand through his unruly brown curls. This was a nervous twitch Ursula had first noticed in Germany. The closer they came to finalizing the necessary paperwork, the more often his fingers tossed his curls. At one point, she worried he would be bald before everything was properly settled.

"When we were in Germany, you said how close you are with your family. I thought your mother might come to welcome . . . to say hello," she said, proud of how clearly she put her thoughts forward in English.

"Don't you worry about my mother. She can be a nervous woman. She worries about me just like your mother worries about you." Roger looked at his watch. "I really need to go now, but on Sunday we'll go to Mass at St. Thomas, and then to her house for lunch. I'll let her know today."

"Please tell her not to worry."

"I will, but I'm afraid it won't do much good. Besides, I wanted you to rest, not be concerned with making an impression on her. You were exhausted when I found you at the airport."

"I actually found you at the airport," Ursula said, remembering his dozing chin with a smile.

"Either way, I just meant that I want you to be rested." Roger said and sat down on the end of the bed. Ursula scooted across the covers to be next to him. His features were softer without the frame of his military uniform.

"Well, I'm rested." She pulled her eyes open with her thumbs and index fingers.

Roger laughed, then said, "That's my funny girl." But his shoulders slumped forward as if he bore an invisible weight. "My mom is a difficult woman."

"So is mine." She thought about her mother's hand slamming the table the day she shared the news about America.

"You'll see for yourself on Sunday," Roger said, giving her a quick kiss on the forehead. "But now, I really must go." Roger stood up and hurried out of the room. She heard the door close and the engine buzz as the truck backed down the driveway.

"Yooooo." Victory's snout shot to the ceiling.

"You are hungry?" Ursula leaned toward the shorthaired dog, his tail wagging. "First, I will take you outside. No mess in my house."

She pulled a house dress over her head, gathered her hair in a knot at her neck and padded to the bathroom to splash water over her face. Victory's pawing turned to an insistent bark. She found the dog's leash on the back of a chair, attached it to his collar, and went to the front door. But before she could turn the knob, a knock made her jump. She hesitated, but cracked it open.

"Hello dear, I am your neighbor, Mrs. Ohlin. I thought I would bring you something to eat." A small and solid woman with short blond hair thrust a foil-covered dish away from her chest. "I am sure your arrival has been quite eventful. Can't imagine you'd be cooking much."

Victory's tail wagged. He seemed to recognize this neighbor.

"Hello," Ursula said, "yes, I . . . the dog." She motioned for Mrs. Ohlin to step back and Victory rushed to the yard to release his bladder, pulling her forward off the front step.

"He's small but strong, that dog," Mrs. Ohlin said, trailing behind Ursula. "I don't know what Roger was thinking when he brought that mutt home. It caused quite the stir in the neighborhood." Mrs. Ohlin's face was full of disapproval.

"Hmmm?" Ursula only understood a portion of what the woman had said.

"Dear, that dog, well, do I really need to explain?"

She shook her head even though she could not make sense of the conversation.

"Sorry, I almost forgot. This is my son Henry," Mrs. Ohlin said as a small boy appeared from behind his mother's legs. "He wanted to say hello too."

"Hello Missus." Henry's voice was quiet, muffled by the fabric of Mrs. Ohlin's dress.

"Good boy," Mrs. Ohlin patted Henry's head.

"Hello Henry," Ursula said, then turned back to Mrs. Ohlin. "You wanted to tell me something about Victory?"

"Oh, it was nothing dear."

"Thank you for saying hello."

"It's what neighbors do."

"During the war," Ursula said, then stopped herself. No one wanted to talk about the war. They especially wouldn't want to talk about it with her, a German.

"During the war?" Mrs. Ohlin repeated, then peered at Ursula. "I didn't think you'd want to talk about such things. I was just saying to another neighbor that I wouldn't expect you to bring it up, but now that you have . . ." She gestured toward the side of her house next door, where Ursula could see a swath of dirt surrounded by railroad ties. Small bits of green were beginning to sprout. "I gardened during the war," she continued. "Watched the seedlings grow into plants and weeded out pesky creeping Charlie and those dandelions, they certainly caused a headache. I grew plenty of vegetables for my casseroles so I didn't need to use up what others might need. We called them victory gardens, like your dog." She stared again at Ursula, even closer this time. "It was my small fight against the Nazis, you see. But not you dear, not you. I know you're not one of them. They wouldn't have let you in if you were, right?"

"Ja," she said and nodded, dismayed. *Does she think I was part of the Partei?* Ursula tried to respond. Her head struggled for the proper English, then her tongue worked to form those words into sounds. But nothing came out.

"Once the vegetables come up later this summer, I'll keep some aside for you. Just wait until you taste the sweet corn! You'll be an American in no time," she said.

"Ja," she said again. The idea of eating corn from a garden perplexed Ursula. Corn was for animals.

"In any event, I made you this chicken and vegetable casserole. I hope you like it," Mrs. Ohlin said, finally placing the dish in Ursula's arms. "Just put it in the oven for thirty minutes."

As if Victory understood the word dinner, he scampered back into the house. She tried to refocus on Mrs. Ohlin, tried again to put English words together into sentences. Her neighbor eyed her with concern.

"You seem tired, dear. We'll let you be," Mrs. Ohlin said with a smile Ursula recognized as Minnesota Nice. Henry fidgeted next to his mother then darted off the stoop. But before running to his own house, he lifted his right arm toward Ursula and his voice was no longer hidden behind his mother's skirt. "Heil Hitler!"

Mrs. Ohlin yelled as her son scampered off. "Get back here, son. That is uncalled for. How dare you say that!"

Ursula's breath caught in her throat. *How have American children been taught this hateful gesture?* She gave Mrs. Ohlin a quick nod, then closed the door and sat on the sofa clutching the dish, trying to catch her breath.

She remembered the first time she was forced to perform the Hitler salute, *Hitlergruss.* It was a few months before her ninth birthday, and she was about to start a new school year. She'd spent the summer reading the Grimms' Fairy Tales and writing her own versions of them. Maybe she could share them with her new teacher. On that day, her father arrived home with a bloody nose. Had he fallen, Ursula asked? No, he explained, he had failed to salute a group of Storm Troopers marching through their town and had to pay for his disobedience.

"From now on, we salute," her father had said as he pressed a handkerchief against his face. She didn't understand fully, but she didn't want to get a bloody nose like her father. The next week at school, everyone was saluting everyone else. That was the year everything permanently shifted beneath them; the year Germany slid closer to war.

Ursula walked to the kitchen, set the casserole in the icebox, and tried to erase the memory of her father's bloody nose and the lifted arms of her fourth-grade classmates. Then she found the can of dog food and gave Victory his breakfast.

A knock on the door later that evening revealed Mrs. Ohlin and her apologetic son.

* *

Sleepless nights, and the odd visit from Mrs. Ohlin, stirred up more distressing childhood memories. If she sat still for too long her mind returned to Germany. So, with uninterrupted hours in front of her she further explored the contents of her new hand-me-down home. A modest living room occupied the front of the house, with windows overlooking the tree-lined street. A wood-paneled dining room separated the living room from the kitchen, with enough room for a table for four, maybe even six. Roger mentioned a dining set he was hoping to bring home, pieces someone had never picked up from the shop. He just needed to fix a wobbly chair. At the back of the house was the kitchen with white metal cabinets, scratched Formica counters, and a white ceramic sink below the window framing a view to the backyard. Ursula turned the faucet on and off, on and off, and thought of her mother's kitchen, how it had a view of their garden filled with flowers and a handful of vegetable plants. Here on Colfax Street, the view was of a scruffy patch of grass and the garage with its peeling paint.

On the opposite side of the house, a hallway led to two simi-lar-sized bedrooms and the delightfully cheerful pink-tiled bath-room. Flowered wallpaper clung to the walls in the back bedroom, with corners peeled away that would need to be tamed with glue. Roger had chosen this room for them—"more privacy at the back of the house," he explained. The bedroom at the front had been converted into a nursey by Roger's sister-in-law Sally, its sunflower yellow walls were now the only hint it had once belonged to a baby.

A narrow and steep staircase led to the attic, where Ursula found tinsel, a few broken Christmas tree ornaments, and Happy New Year 1946 hats spilling from a box. She set one on her head and swayed her hips as if she had been at the party, but the dust induced a coughing fit and she gave up her imaginary fun. In the basement she found canning jars and lids, and she pressed her fingers against the convex *Ball* name in the glass. Nearby, the smell of earth sat in the air next to a few garden tools and a shovel—the promise of a garden.

Ursula froze when she found a stroller and bassinette tucked away in a corner. Her eyes traced the objects, both in good condition. Had her sister-in-law Sally left them behind on purpose? If she had, Ursula thought she should be grateful for them. Prices had gone up since the war ended. They would need to keep saving to afford everything for a baby, to fill up that yellow room with furniture. She covered the bassinette and stroller with an old sheet. For now, their emptiness brought to mind all the things she longed to be doing, but could not. Not yet.

On Sunday morning, the countdown to the day she would meet her mother-in-law was over. Ursula pulled four dresses and two skirt-suits out of the closet and laid them on the bed to decide which one would make her seem like a potential American. It was pointless. Everything she owned—which had filled only one suitcase and now barely made a dent in the closet and dresser—looked old. Looked European. Looked German. Could any of it be suitable for a meeting with Roger's mother?

Once she chose the light blue skirt and jacket with a white blouse that gathered around her neck in a bow, though, Ursula examined herself in the mirror on the front of the closet door and was pleased by what she saw. There she was, a woman who had made the best decision she could and given the circumstances, taken a chance on a kind and generous man. Unfortunately, despite her confidence, underarm sweat was already dampening the fabric of her blouse. She took off the jacket and folded it over her arm. She could not afford to soil it knowing she would need to cover her shoulders once inside the church.

"You look beautiful," Roger said as he peered in the bedroom. He was dressed in his Sunday suit: a modest brown coat and slacks paired with a white shirt and tie.

"I think the blue is nice, better than my black dress," she said, placing her handbag under her arm to see how it looked. The metal clasp dug into her skin.

"The blue is perfect," Roger said. He walked to Ursula and tried to put his hands on her hips, but she stepped back.

"What if she thinks . . ." She readjusted her handbag under her arm, then remembered the sweat and lowered the bag, ". . . I was part of the *Partei*?"

"Where did you get that idea?" Roger laughed.

"From Mrs. Ohlin when she told me about the dog . . ." Ursula rubbed the fabric of her coat with her fingers to calm her nerves. She shouldn't have mentioned the neighbor. They could deal with her another day. Today she needed to concentrate on making the best impression she could on Roger's mother. But Roger was still looking at her with a quizzical expression and Ursula thought again about Mrs. Ohlin's visit.

"The dog?"

"She said, umm, how do you say this? Something about neighbors did not like the dog?"

"He does bark when he's outside, I suppose that's a nuisance—" Roger stopped and his forehead creased with understanding. "My god, if they can't understand by now that a dachshund isn't a symbol of the Nazis then we'll never build peace!"

"Oh," Ursula said. She was embarrassed, but now Mrs. Ohlin's comment made sense.

Roger slapped his hand against his thigh. "How absurd, how absolutely absurd."

"Perhaps we call him Vic." Ursula shrugged.

"Why?" Roger moved his hands through his curls.

"If the dog reminds our neighbors of the war, and his name is Victory, will they think you wanted Germany to win?"

"That is convoluted. Convoluted! If my neighbors are that dumb…" Roger's face flushed, but Ursula did not know if from embarrassment or anger.

"We don't need to waste any more breath on Mrs. Ohlin," Roger said. "Let's go, I want to get to church before mass starts. They don't like it when you're late." He thudded out of the room. She heard him open the front door and step outside. She paused to wipe the damp from under her arms with a handkerchief, said "*bis später*, see you later" to Vic, and hurried out to join her husband.

When they arrived at St. Thomas Catholic Church, Ursula gripped her blue coat firmly in her hands. She had wanted the tree-filled walk through their pleasant neighborhood to ease her mind, but she was still nervous and upset. How could a little dog cause so much trouble in the neighborhood?

She pulled on her jacket as they passed through a vestibule of the rectangular stone building as Roger guided her in the side door leading to the front pews.

"Mother insists on sitting at the front because she likes to see the altar without the backs of heads getting in her way," Roger whispered.

Before she slid into the pew next to Mrs. Gorski, she paused to will her new mother-in-law to look up, to express some form of welcome. Mrs. Gorski was kneeling, a black-beaded rosary dangling from her hands and a cloud of grey hair obscuring her bowed head. A silver cross adorned with a tiny figurine of Jesus swayed at the bottom of the beaded loop and banged against the pew. Ursula felt the eyes of other worshippers examining her as, shoulders hunched, she followed Roger into the pew to claim their spots. Once seated, she leaned forward to see past Roger to Mrs. Gorski. Her rose-colored lips were still moving in prayer, the beads slipping slowly through her fingers.

Mass began just as Mrs. Gorski made the sign of the cross and the beads disappeared into a small purse. The congregation stood. Ursula reached for Roger's hand and squeezed. He squeezed back.

The priest processed up the long aisle to the sound of the organ. From the altar, he called everyone to prayer. The Latin words reminded her of home, and she was relieved to find she could follow along without feeling out of place. Her lips moved in unison with the other parishioners but her mind focused on Mrs. Gorski. Annoyed with herself, she wondered how she managed to be tough in Berlin but found the same toughness difficult to summon now. Why was she so nervous about meeting Roger's mother? Why hadn't she insisted on an earlier get-together? She questioned her ability to navigate the new circumstances, people, and relationships.

At the end of mass, a bubble of voices echoed against the stone walls. She watched Roger as he kissed his mother's cheek and said, "Mom, I want you to meet—"

But before Roger could finish, Mrs. Gorski pivoted, striking up a genial conversation with the couple seated behind them, ignoring Roger. Had Mrs. Gorski even noticed her?

Roger touched his mother's shoulder and whispered something to her, then said to Ursula: "Let's go to my mother's. My aunt will be there. I think you'll like her."

"Is everything all right?"

"Let's go." Roger pushed past Ursula, stumbling over the kneeler she had left down. To keep up with him, she flipped the kneeler upward, and hurried outside where the sun forced her to squint. Where had he gone? Her eyes adjusted. In front of her, Roger paced around a newer Ford, pretending to admire it. Ursula knew he only liked trucks. She hastened to his side.

"Shouldn't we wait for your mother?"

"No, she's catching up with some friends. She'll meet us at home."

She reached for Roger's hand but he pulled it away, then brought it back again, tethering his fingers around hers. More people streamed from the side door. Ursula was still confused and wanted to go back into the church and meet Mrs. Gorski properly. But she also did not want to cause a scene so she followed Roger as he began to stride down the sidewalk.

What had happened in the church? Did Roger's mother just want to chat with friends or was she purposefully avoiding meeting the war bride her son had brought home? She resolved to clear up any potential concerns Mrs. Gorski could have. If it was about her being from Germany, she could explain that. If it was about marrying Roger, she could explain that, too. She wished for her own mother's strength in the conversation to come.

Roger's mother's home sat a block off the wide and green Victory Memorial Drive. To Ursula, it looked like the other homes in the neighborhood: white, stucco, one-story with an attic. A narrow concrete pathway led them to the back door. It was unlocked. Roger poked his head inside and called for his aunt Rose, but there was no answer.

"She must still be at church," Roger said, fingers now curled in his belt loops.

"Church?" She was confused, wondering why she wouldn't have seen Rose at St. Thomas.

"Oh, Aunt Rose attends the Lutheran church—my uncle is Lutheran."

"Oh, I see."

"Have a seat in the living room. Would you like anything?"

"Water?"

"Sure," Roger said. He seemed at ease in the house like it was his own.

She walked into the living room and stopped. One wall was covered in photos of a close and happy family. "It's so wonderful to see you all together."

"Mother is proud of us; she's been adding photos of us to this wall for many years." Roger handed Ursula a glass, then left her at the wall of photos, saying he wanted to find the Sunday paper.

She took a sip of the water. Her mouth was dry from nerves. If she could not change her own mother's mind, then how could she convince Mrs. Gorski of anything at all, much less that she wasn't a Nazi and was becoming a good wife to Roger?

Ursula heard a ruffle of paper, the back door slamming, then two voices.

"When you said you were bringing her to meet me, I thought you meant you would be stopping by the house," Mrs. Gorski said. Her voice shot through the thin walls.

"When I see you on Sundays, I always come to Mass first. Please keep your voice down, Ursula is in the other room," Roger said. Their voices hushed, and she could no longer distinguish words. She paced the living room, leaving a dark path in the midnight-blue wool carpet. The water sloshed in the glass. The resentment she had imagined emanating from Mrs. Gorski at the church was real. It was now rattling from behind the kitchen door. Ursula had the sudden sensation of planes overhead. Then they were in her body, rumbling just beneath her skin. The air raid siren was in her ears now, then it all fell to silence.

"Ursula," Roger said. His voice broke through and Ursula returned to her senses. To Mrs. Gorski's living room. Water pooled at her feet on the floor. She had dropped the glass.

"I am sorry, sorry, sorry," Ursula said. She stooped down but had nothing to tidy the mess. Roger threw a handkerchief over the spot and pressed his foot into the floor. How foolish she had been.

"You must be Ursula," Mrs. Gorski said. The irritation on Mrs. Gorski's face was unmistakable, but something else lingered in her eyes.

She forced an eager smile and clasped her sweaty hands in front of her. "It is so nice to meet you." She stumbled over the English words.

I'm not taking Roger away, Ursula wanted to say, but there was too much weight in the room for a heartfelt conversation. As suddenly as she appeared, Mrs. Gorski disappeared to the kitchen.

"I hope I have not upset her," Ursula said, lowering her voice. "I am sorry for spilling the water."

Roger was still toeing the mark with his shoe. He finally lifted his head. "Mother is going to make lunch. I said you might be able to help." His voice was sheepish and his eyes didn't meet hers.

For a moment, her vision clouded and she again imagined threatening planes overhead. She felt stupid for imagining America as a perfect place, for believing Mrs. Gorski would welcome her as if she were family. She felt even more stupid for believing she'd married a man who wouldn't hide behind his mother. But she couldn't tell Roger, not here, in his mother's living room.

"I can. I can help." Ursula's voice creaked from her throat and she threw her shoulders back and wiped her damp hands on her skirt. She knew how to keep her opinions to herself. Her life had depended on it during the war. The Gestapo were always listening, ready to throw any disobedient German onto a watch list or into prison.

Ursula pressed her hand against the swinging kitchen door. *I will not freeze. I will not freeze.* Then she watched as her two feet led her inside, the flowery linoleum softening the space. She followed the line Mrs. Gorski's finger drew in the air to the sack of potatoes on the floor next to the sink.

"Wash, peel, and cut," Mrs. Gorski said, then she returned to the living room, leaving Ursula alone in the kitchen. She exhaled. Another woman—another mother—telling her what to do. A mother she wanted to impress, just like she had wanted to impress her own mother. She had failed with her own mother, but perhaps she could do better this time. She reached for one of the dirt-covered vegetables. She didn't dare ask for an apron and hoped she wouldn't stain her Sunday clothes.

After a dozen potatoes were washed, the cold water on her hands an unexpected balm, Roger's Aunt Rose came through the back door.

"My God, what are you doing washing dirty potatoes in that lovely outfit?"

Aunt Rose was smaller than Mrs. Gorski, slight in a way that made her seem delicate. She wore a pink skirt-suit set off by short boyish graying brown hair and a strand of white pearls around her neck. Rose found an apron and helped Ursula into it, then pulled a second apron over her own head and whispered, "You are ever so kind to help my sister, but don't mind her. She's a grump. I'm Roger's Aunt Rose, if you hadn't figured that out."

"It is wonderful to meet you and thank you for your kindness," Ursula said, as the corners of her lips turned up. Aunt Rose spoke clearly in a way she could follow. She was intrigued by this woman who was already so different from Mrs. Gorski.

"Roger told me all about you in his letters," Rose said as she started peeling the washed potatoes. "I'm so happy he found someone so young and as vibrant as you seem after what happened."

"Hmm?" Ursula stopped and looked at Rose.

"He didn't tell you?"

"Tell me?"

Rose paused, the peeler in her hand hovering above the sink. "Oh gosh, well, Roger was seeing this girl for years, and after he was drafted, she left him for another man."

"Were they engaged?" She picked up a potato and scrubbed it hard, afraid to hear the answer. She did not like learning so much intimate information about Roger from family members.

"No, Roger wanted to wait until the war was over. He was scared, like we all were, of the men not coming home," Rose said, her voice heavy. "But then that woman broke it off before he was deployed."

Ursula thought back to her early conversations with Roger. "When we met he said he was unlucky with women, but I thought he was telling a joke. The Americans liked to tell us jokes." She now wondered how many of those jokes were truths. Roger had said he had courted other women, but none were serious enough for him to marry. *Why did he not share this with me?* A pain surged between her eyebrows above her nose. She dried her hands on her apron and rubbed her forehead with her thumbs.

"Well, this won't make you feel better, but I think you should know," Rose said, putting down her peeler and turning to face Ursula. "Roger's mother loved that woman. Felicity, her name was. Mary talked about their wedding, about all the children they would have, about what a wonderful daughter-in-law she would be."

"Oh gosh." Ursula's stomach flipped and she dug her fingernails into the potato in her hands.

"It's water under the bridge now," Rose said with a matter-of-fact nod. "Felicity is married off to someone else, and now you're here. Roger is happy from what I can see, and that's what matters." She shook her head. "Honestly, I don't know why my sister can't let Roger go. Pete left the house to marry Sally and that wasn't a problem. But ever since she lost Val—Mr. Gorski—Mary has held onto Roger. It's making us all miserable!"

"Where I come from, we call men like that *muttersöhnchen*."

"I'm afraid I don't know what that means, dear."

Ursula paused, unsure how to translate the word, then tried: "It means a mother who cares much about her son."

"I see," Rose said, the peels falling from the potato in her hands into the sink. "Roger cares about his mother too, I wouldn't blame it all on Mary."

"I notice he does not want to talk much about her." Ursula wiped a stray hair away from her face with the back of her hand.

"I'm sure you love him despite his shortcomings," Rose said. "God knows we're not perfect, and if being overly concerned with his mother is Roger's worst trait, then I think you'll be all right, dear." The older woman placed a gentle hand on Ursula's shoulder.

She relaxed under her touch. She wanted to trust Rose.

"These are too many potatoes for lunch." Ursula gazed into the sink, and Rose's eyes followed. It was heaped full with their peeled work.

When they finally sat down to lunch, the potatoes were nowhere to be seen. *All of the hard work for nothing.*

Roger leaned in and said, "Mom hates peeling potatoes."

Ursula felt duped, like she was left out of an open secret. She promised herself she wouldn't become her mother-in-law's minion. Next time she would stand her ground.

CHAPTER 3

That evening with Vic asleep at her feet, Ursula penned a short letter to her mother, only the second one she had written since arriving in America.

> *Berlin was in pieces. There was nothing left of the city I knew. I wanted the constant running and struggling to end. I'm sorry . . .*

When she wrote, "I'm sorry," it felt useless, even though she meant it. She was sorry for leaving, but she could not stay.

As she wrote, Ursula found there was so much she couldn't say. She left out the sleepless nights, the Heil Hitler salute from Henry, the potatoes she washed and peeled in some kind of test. She left out the fiancée, Felicity. Ursula did not want her mother to feel vindicated in all she had said about Roger and moving to America.

> *The journey was long, but when I finally saw Roger at the airport in Minnesota, I felt better. This place is more beautiful than I imagined. I just knew it would all work out.*

She crossed out the last sentence knowing an "I told you so" would not help their relationship. If she ever wanted to re-gain her mother's trust, Ursula needed to show her the woman she wanted to be, the woman she hoped she was becoming. For now, she could only do that through letters.

"Who are you writing to?" Roger sat down across the table from Ursula and spread open the evening edition of the *Star*.

"My mother."

"I know you left on difficult terms, but I'm sure she appreciates these letters from you. Please send her my love. Let her know I think about them."

"She will like that," Ursula said. She wrote a few sentences on his behalf. It could only make her mother feel better about her choices. Then she put her pen down and looked at Roger, whose eyes were already buried in the paper. "Any news?" she asked.

"Naw, nothing exciting," Roger said and turned a page. Ursula wanted to talk about more than the news. She wanted to ask him about Felicity, but she hesitated.

"Your aunt is a kind woman," she said instead. "I understand why you are close." It was true. Aunt Rose seemed truly kind, and Ursula had been refreshed by her thoughtful welcome.

Roger looked up, nodding in agreement. "After my father died of the heart attack, Aunt Rose helped all of us, even though she had her own family to look after."

"Did they have a good relationship, too, your father and your mother?" Ursula wanted to know what Mr. Gorski was like. If he was an involved father like her own. If he doted on his children and his wife.

"My father was quiet, a tough nut to crack as some would say," Roger said and sat his chin on his knuckles, a faraway look on his face.

"A tough nut—that's how you say it?—even for your mother?" Ursula had never heard this phrase before.

"Yes, even for my mother."

"Hmm," Ursula said as she pulled the cap off the pen and drew circles on the corner of the newspaper. "I cannot imagine this."

"Roger," Ursula said, locking eyes with him. "Rose told me something today about a woman named Felicity. That you were engaged, but she—how did Rose say this—called it off?"

Roger's face tightened. He sat up straight and drew his arms across his chest. To Ursula he looked like a statue, so still. And so quiet.

"Will you please explain?" she finally added.

"There's nothing to explain. We were engaged, then the war started, and then we were no longer engaged. It was years ago now," Roger said, his face still tense.

Ursula thought this wasn't much of an answer. Not from the man she thought had been totally open with her. "But why keep this from me? When we met you said you never had any serious girlfriends."

"When we met, I didn't think I was looking at my future wife," Roger said.

Ursula tried to make sense of this, but tears welled. "Were you in love with her?"

"I think you need to be in love to get in engaged," Roger said. He stood up and went to the sink, his back to Ursula.

"So, you were in love with her?" She wanted to see his face, to get a read on what was happening inside his head. For Ursula, with young German men at the front during the war, she had barely dated, much less had a chance to fall in love. Roger was the first man to catch her attention in a serious way. To know he had already been in love stung, as if another woman had already taken a piece of Roger. It was a part of him Ursula would never get to have.

"And then she left me, and then I left for the war. And it's now in the past." Roger turned on the faucet and filled a glass with water.

"If it is over, then why are you so upset now?" Ursula said, her stomach flipping. She did not know if she wanted to hear the answer, but she wished she had not pulled the curtains shut so early that evening. She wanted to see his face reflected in the window above the sink. Vic stirred at her feet with a sleepy whimper.

Roger took a long draw of his water. "She was the first girl I ever fell in love with, but she wasn't in love with me like I was with her. It was embarrassing, Ursula. We announced our engagement, and then she said 'maybe we should wait until you get home' and the night before I was deployed, she called to say she couldn't do it, that she was breaking it off." He set down the glass and pivoted so his rear was against the counter. Ursula noticed tears in his eyes and suddenly felt sorry for him.

"I am sorry this happened, and on the night before you left for the war . . ." Ursula said, shaking her head. She extricated her feet from under Vic, then stood and walked toward Roger. As she neared, he reached out and pulled her close. Ursula heard his heart thumping hard in his chest and she wrapped her arms tightly around him.

"Promise you won't leave me," Roger said, his voice so quiet Ursula thought she had conjured it. It was unlike Roger to be so vulnerable, to open up like this.

"I promise, I promise I will not leave," Ursula said. The words curled out of her mouth like steam, and their lips came together. But then she pulled back. "Promise *me* something, too?"

"Hmmm?" Roger said, relaxed now.

"That I never have to peel another potato for your mother again."

Roger laughed, then kissed her forehead. "That's funny! But it reminds me, too. She asked me to thank you for that when we left.

She makes casseroles on Sunday afternoons for the homebound from church. All those peeled potatoes were a big help."

"Oh?" She stepped back, feeling stupid for misunderstanding everything.

"She's started doing that every Sunday. I think it's good for her, gives her something to do," Roger said. He reached to pull Ursula back in, but she resisted. Roger could have explained why his mother needed help in the kitchen before sending her in there. He could have explained what happened with Felicity instead of letting her hear it from Rose. He could have explained it all.

"I feel lost Roger," Ursula said.

"I didn't mean to . . ." Roger paused, as if he didn't know what to say, then seemed to realize all she was saying. "I guess I thought the Felicity thing might upset you, and it happened so long ago. And the potatoes, those damn potatoes! I simply forgot. I was nervous about you meeting my mother, and then she reacted so poorly. I'm sorry, honestly, that's all it was."

"You promise?"

"I promise."

CHAPTER 4
June 1947

The mail carrier strode down the street, his satchel full of letters. Ursula watched impatiently at the end of her sidewalk, hoping for a letter from home. She could hear Vic barking from inside the house. His favorite perch was on the back of the sofa in the front window, where he could be a lookout and warn her about squirrels, birds, or any other neighborhood dangers. It was sweet in a way, but she cringed knowing he was trampling the knitted blanket she draped across the top of the couch, his nails long enough to pull at the loops. She loved how the blanket made the living room more inviting, more like it belonged to her.

"Shhh, Vic, shhh," Ursula said, waving her hand toward the window hoping he would obey. It was useless, Vic ignored her and his sharp yap punctuated the quiet morning. Mown grass stood at crisp angles. Bees buzzed at the geraniums in the flower boxes hung from the front windows of the home Ursula was beginning to make with Roger. Monarch butterflies caught in the light breeze, paused on the updraft, and were carried away. Her heart was as light as their wings. Ursula had not expected a reply so soon, but the mailman was extending a thick envelope toward her.

"Looks like an important letter for you, Mrs. Gorski." He presented it with a flourish.

Ursula clenched her jaw when she heard the name. It was hers, but it reminded her of the other Mrs. Gorski, and how their relationship was still strained.

Familiar handwriting adorned the envelope, careful and loopy letters. Ursula pressed the paper to her face, hoping for the scent of her mother's rosewater perfume, but it instead it smelled of canvas from the mailman's bag. She tore open the flap, pulled out the pages, and was startled to see a letter from her father folded inside the longer one from her mother. *Could it be? Is it really him?* Her hands shook as she quickly unfolded news from home.

My dearest Ursula, you will never know how much I have missed you, thought about you and yearned to hear your voice. If it weren't for you and your mother, I would have lost all hope of staying alive. For reasons I will never fully understand, the Russians allowed me to leave. Despite everything we've been through during the war, the awful details are more than I can bear to burden you with, but perhaps someday I'll share them with you. It took me weeks to find my way home, walking, hopping trains, and hitching rides. I arrived home to find your mother and Aunt Kaethe in moderate health. They were shocked to see me, as you can probably imagine. When your mother explained that your papers were approved for America, I knew you had left. My heart dropped. I never thought I would make it home from that awful place, and now I have to hope that I will one day see you again, my only daughter. I am regaining my strength and will look for work, if I can find any. Give my best regards to your new husband. In my absence, may he treat you with the respect and care you deserve. All my love, Your father.

Ursula's eyes filled with tears, but she was also full of joy for his homecoming. And guilt, too. So much guilt. *Why didn't I stay to help my family? How could I be so selfish?* Ursula shook with sobs, her heart torn between family obligations and the desire to build a life of her own. Through tears, she read the letter from her mother.

Greetings Ursula, I have your letter open next to me which means you have gone to America and arrived safely. We are occupied with your father's arrival and will be for weeks and months to come. He wanted to write to you himself, so I will not repeat the story. Paper and ink are hard to come by, as you know. Next time you write, it would be helpful if you could include blank sheets.

Ursula stopped reading. She doubted her mother would ever approve of her decision to leave. But to ask for stationery indicated some form of acknowledgement, a recognition that Ursula could be useful to her. It was also an opening to stay connected.

She read the remainder of her mother's letter, though she processed little of it. The heat from the summer sun mounted, and even in her purple cotton dress, she was warm. She wiped the sweat from her forehead, then watched a meandering line of ants crawl across the sidewalk, making homes out of tiny grains of sand they carried one at a time. Ursula thought about her own life, how she took one step and then another. *That's all you can do.* She read her father's letter again and watched an ant crawl over her toes on its way home. She imagined herself doing the same and running into her father's arms. But that couldn't happen. She would need to learn to live with regrets, to live with the realization that giving up one future meant building another.

CHAPTER 5
July 1947

A well-connected woman who worked with Ursula in G-Tower helped make the arrangement for Roger and Ursula to marry in Berlin. She had introduced them to her cousin, a priest. They had filed the required application for marriage with the American military government. Surprisingly, the author of the War Brides Act had failed to omit ex-enemy spouses from the legislation, creating a loophole that would allow them to marry. Allow her to escape Berlin. But even with a priest arranged and the law on her side, Ursula was worried. What if the law changed? What if someone found a new rule that would keep them from marrying? Roger, if he had been anxious, did not show it. On a snowy December day, a month before Roger was scheduled to depart Germany, they became husband and wife. In the quiet moments afterward, they promised each other a grander wedding in Minnesota.

Now, from the back of St. Thomas church, Ursula gazed down the long aisle at Roger's square back. She glowed from the inside out, the promise of a beautiful wedding a reality.

Ursula inspected the light-blue skirt suit for any sign of dirt from the potatoes but found none. Rose had loaned Ursula a pair of shoes, and Roger had bought her the small pearl earrings she squeezed onto her lobes. With her mother's carnation necklace strung around her neck, she was reminded of home. She styled her red hair so curls framed her face, then swept the rest into a French roll. Roger didn't have a fancy suit, so he chose to wear his military uniform. Ursula was glad. Roger in uniform reminded her of their early days in Berlin together, when their relationship was new and exciting. But there was also a solidness to it that made her hopeful about the future they would have together.

Ursula shifted her gaze to the gap in the church's front pew. Mrs. Gorski refused to attend the wedding. She disagreed with the marriage and was still hoping Roger would marry an American. When Roger had told her about his mother's decision, Ursula was furious and hurt. But disappointment would not overtake the day. She came too far for Mrs. Gorski to dash her dreams. When Rose learned of her sister's stubbornness, she graciously stepped forward to be a witness. Pete, Roger's younger brother, also came through at the last minute after Roger made a moral case for rebuilding Germany one international marriage at a time. Pete wanted peace, even if the way forward was unexpected. Roger had confided his brother's support for their marriage the night before, and Ursula thought Roger's argument was clever. She was also not surprised Mrs. Gorski was too set in her ways to be swayed by such arguments.

As Ursula waited for the ceremony to begin, her mind traveled back to a late night in the remains of a bombed-out house after a gleeful party on the American base. Shadows obscured Ursula's raised skirt and Roger's trousers at his ankles. He pressed against her. Ursula's lips caught in his. The remains of war faded away to something else she couldn't name. All Ursula wanted was to suspend that moment. No rubble. No rationing. No worries about the future. Just a man, a woman, and their desire.

The organist accidently hit a high note as she spread sheet music in preparation for the bride's processional. Ursula blushed as her lustful thoughts flashed and then faded. She looked down at the white satin pumps on her feet and then back at Roger, who stood still at the front of the church unaware the space between her legs burned. As a distraction, she looked into her small bouquet and inhaled the sweetness of the roses.

And then, the organ bellowed with authority. The processional music started, and she slowly walked up the aisle. Right foot. Left foot. Right foot. Left foot. A measured procession into an unknown future. She pressed toward Roger—hope in human form—her feet pretending to know her heart.

Ursula wanted the church wedding to nestle her comfortably in Minneapolis as if she had never lived anywhere but in this Midwestern city. She knew what was expected of her after the ceremony faded: a child. But she didn't feel ready for the chaos a baby would bring. She needed time to orient herself in Roger's orbit and she needed to shake off the sheen of uncertainty the war had glued to her skin. As a teenager, Ursula had not wanted to participate in the League of German Girls, but it was compulsory. Wednesdays and Saturdays were stolen. Children were pulled out of classrooms to learn obedience to the regime. All the lessons centered on a single truth: She should be dedicated to motherhood above all else. A teacher had once told her, "German girls are strong. They are made to have lots of children."

Here, in Minneapolis, though she could let go of the League's lessons, she still wanted motherhood. She would need to find a new way to that future, though. So, while Roger remade old furniture at the upholstery shop where he worked, Ursula did her best housekeeping and cooking. In Berlin, she had learned from *Die Frau* how to transform rations into satisfying meals. She now relied on those skills to satisfy Roger.

When Ursula wanted a break from cooking and cleaning, she knitted on the stoop hoping for letters from home. She wondered about her father's recovery and how her mother was coping without her. When the postman approached, she looked around to see who might be watching—the Berlin look, a habit so deeply ingrained she hadn't noticed until the postman asked her, "Is something the matter, ma'am?"

In her past life, the Berlin look had kept her safe.

Today, Mrs. Ohlin sped over as soon as the postman was gone. She was always peeking out at neighborhood happenings from behind her curtains, but this time Ursula's Berlin look hadn't noticed her in the window.

"Don't let him think you're a bored housewife," Mrs. Ohlin said. She had grown more comfortable with Ursula and opined on almost anything that caught her attention.

"Pardon me, but I don't understand, Mrs. Ohlin," Ursula said. She was still trying to learn the cultural nuances of this new place, and Mrs. Ohlin's dubious advice never failed to frustrate her.

"Oh, nothing, dear, it's just that you look in all directions when the postman gets close, as if you have something to hide." Mrs. Ohlin's face contorted into a mischievous smile and then she said, "You should also be mindful of that dog. When you're not home it yaps and yaps. I can't expect my children to sleep with that racket."

"Oh, I did not know . . ."

"Of course you wouldn't know, you're not home when he's making all that noise," Mrs. Ohlin paused, as if she expected Ursula to do something about it right then and there to silence the already silent dog. Then she shrugged and turned back to her house. "I have to go. I'm getting lunch ready for the kids."

Ursula was glad to see Mrs. Ohlin's knee-length skirt retreating across the grass. The woman was just like Frau Schulz, the mother of one of her schoolmates who gleefully informed on neighbors whenever she got the chance. Frau Schulz joined the *partei*, sang the songs, and replaced her family photo with one of the *Führer*. No one could be trusted, especially Ursula and her family. Ursula hated the idea of being fodder for neighborhood gossip. The stakes were different now, but it was a disconcerting reminder of the past.

Ursula stood up to find Vic. Maybe a walk would settle her mind. Besides, she could not leave him alone in the house if Mrs. Ohlin was going to complain about every yip.

"Vic?" The dog was asleep on the back of the sofa, the blanket like a nest around him, strands of yarn lose from where his nails caught the loops. He opened his eyes when Ursula approached with leash in hand.

"Time for a walk," Ursula said. He stretched, tail wagging and jumped off the sofa in two bounds. "Good boy."

On the sidewalk, with Vic's nose sniffing and snorting close to the ground, Ursula's head was far away, remembering. As a young girl, her thoughts had scared her. *I hate Hitler.* She imagined having said that out loud and the consequences of words tumbling out in the world made her shudder. The Gestapo took away citizens who talked back. The pettiness of the offenses against the regime juxtaposed with possible deadly consequences were confusing to Ursula.

Ursula walked south on Colfax, then turned east on 29th street toward Fairview Park where she could think more clearly with the Minneapolis skyline in front of her. The fully-formed city reassured her: bombs would not fall from the sky to destroy this place.

Children, children, children. The League of German Girls teacher's voice rang in her head. Her future had belonged to Germany. She passed the loop of Vic's leash over her arm and rubbed her palms against her neck. As a red-headed Catholic girl she had avoided the worst acts of the regime. Those crimes had now been discovered by the rest of the world and were now spread across the upper folds of the *Star*. Ursula would skim the first few paragraphs, then stop. Then, ashamed at her own callowness, she would try to read again. As a girl, Ursula kept her thoughts to herself, just as her parents had taught her to do. She ignored the League of German Girls who instructed them to inform on their parents, but she also never spoke up to object to the lessons. But now the war was over, and she had to confront the cost of growing up in a country the world despised.

"Let's go Vic," Ursula said to the dog in German. She tugged at his leash. He lowered his leg and a tree glossed with his mark.

When their walk took her to the top of the hill, Ursula pondered who worked in the city. Were there women like her in those buildings? Women who knew how to type and understood what it meant to have a job? Women who wanted to start a family but needed more time? Perhaps even women whose childhoods were marked by war but were now living unexpected lives. She sat down on a wooden bench and Vic splayed in front of her, panting in the sun.

Ursula's thoughts turned to a more practical—or perhaps it was silly—direction. She needed a new nightgown but was too embarrassed to ask Roger for extra money to buy one. He managed their incoming and outgoing money, giving every penny an assignment. Ursula worried he could not spare her a few cents in those meticulous calculations, but she was tired of making tattered clothes last. She had mended the hole in the seam of the nightgown from home, but each day another one appeared. Even the useful instructions she had studied in the pages of *Die Frau* were no longer sufficient. Instead, she wanted to earn her own money to buy whichever nightgown she wanted. It had been so long since she had something nice, something new.

On her last visit to the house, Rose had left Ursula a thick Sears catalog with pages and pages of nightgowns and every other item required of the American Dream. The sheer variety of the items for sale astonished her. She burst out laughing when she came across an electric shaver. Wasn't a normal razor enough? Every afternoon she opened to a new page and admired the colorful pictures as she imagined her way into a new life. The dog-eared catalog pages displaying those nightgowns were waiting for her at home. She mulled now over the choices: blue or yellow. The blue gown had lace and she knew it would look pretty with her hair, but the yellow one seemed like it would last longer. The yellow one was also a few pennies cheaper.

"Vic, we cannot sit on this bench all afternoon. We have things to do," Ursula said, tucking a red strand behind her ear. "And of course the yellow would look well on me, too. I've worn that color many times before." Perhaps it was a bit odd to share her feelings with a dog, Ursula thought, but he did not protest. They left the bench, the skyline a reassurance behind them.

CHAPTER 6
August 1947

At the butcher down the street Ursula was determined to order something new: an ingredient from a recipe she read about in the *Ladies Home Journal* Rose had given her. Conversational English came easier to her now, but it had taken Ursula an entire afternoon to translate and comprehend the correct measurements and ingredients.

"The same ma'am?" The butcher rested his palms on the counter.

"No, today I would like . . ." Ursula hesitated. She could not remember the word for spatchcock, even though she had looked it up earlier in her German–English dictionary. She tapped her pointer finger against her forehead as if it would help. Nothing, the word had disappeared.

The woman to her right interrupted, speaking a grammatically correct German Ursula hadn't heard in months.

Ursula gasped at the tall brunette, both surprised and grateful.

"Fraulien, why do you speak German?" Ursula asked. She had a sudden urge to know everything about this woman.

"I'm from Britain and took German in school. I was recruited for the war efforts. I translated documents during the war, but now I rarely have the chance to speak with anyone. Such a waste," the woman said, seeming to enjoy the chance to have German words on her tongue.

"Will you help me order? I was reading about this recipe for chicken, and I think my husband will like it," Ursula said. She was now delighting in her native language, too. How lovely to have words flowing effortlessly from her mouth.

The woman nodded, rattled off instructions, and then the butcher set a chicken wrapped in brown butcher paper on the counter.

"He says it comes to ninety cents," the woman said in German, and Ursula reached into her purse for a few coins, counted them confidently, and handed them to the butcher.

"Maybe we could have coffee?" Ursula said. The prospect of making a new friend elated her. She wanted human interaction, less time talking to the dog. Although she had to admit Vic was a good listener.

The woman looked at her appraisingly, as if assessing who Ursula was beyond someone who needed chicken for her dinner. "Would you like to join me and the other war brides? We are taking a citizenship preparation class at the Miller Vocational High School. The other girls are so nice. You should hear some of their stories!"

"How did you know I was a war bride?" Ursula asked. Ursula had read about the other war brides in the newspaper. Most had come from Allied countries—Britain, France, and even Australia. She had also read that German war brides were helping with the process of what officials were calling denazification. If women like her could be integrated into America, the evils of the Reich could soon be left behind. She also learned she was one of fewer than fifty German war brides to arrive in America in 1947. Only fifty! This surprised Ursula, and worried her a bit, too. Could the Americans change their minds and send her back if they thought denazification had failed?

"Mein Liebling, word gets around in this neighborhood. Mrs.

Ohlin, one of the women I see in here picking up meat, had mentioned that a war bride lived next door to her."

"Mrs. Ohlin is my neighbor!"

"That explains it then." She leaned in and lowered her voice. "You know they say—that war brides are stealing men from American women. Not that Mrs. Ohlin said anything like that." She laughed as if the notion was preposterous. Ursula thought about her neighbor and didn't think it preposterous at all.

As Ursula mulled this over, the woman laughed again. Goodness, this woman seemed happy! And goodness, how she could talk! Then she turned to face Ursula in a formal way. "And what am I thinking, I didn't even introduce myself. My name is Beatrice. Bea for short. Here's my number. It's a party line so keep trying until you get through. Classes are on Tuesdays and Thursdays. Maybe we'll see you next week. And not that it matters to you, but my husband George fell for me fair and square." Bea laughed yet again, then made the victory sign with her fingers. She waved to the butcher as she left, the door chiming behind her.

Ursula held her breath in excitement, then stepped outside. She wanted to see which way Bea turned. On Bryant, only one street away from Colfax!

That evening at dinner, Ursula and Roger ate the chicken she had prepared earlier that afternoon. She was satisfied with the browned meat spread out before them on a platter. If she made the recipe a few more times, she could perfect each step.

"I met another war bride today. Her name is Bea. She's English. She lives in the neighborhood. She told me about a school for war brides." The words tumbled out of Ursula's mouth.

"I think I might know Bea. What's her last name?"

"She didn't say."

"She might be the wife of one of our customers who lives in one of those nice, bigger houses near the park. When he was in last, he mentioned something about his wife wanting a fabric ordered from England." He trailed off, then shifted his eyes back to Ursula. "What kind of school is it?"

"To help us become citizens and find work," Ursula said.

"Hmm, good for your citizenship, but you don't need to work." Roger took a bite of chicken, then another. "This is delicious."

"A recipe from the *Ladies Home Journal*," Ursula said. She dug her knife into the tender meat. Roger hadn't noticed she oversalted it. She forked another piece, and decided she needed to say what had been on her mind ever since she sat in the park looking at the tall downtown buildings. "Roger, I worked through the war. It's what I know."

Roger sat back and lit a cigarette then offered the box to Ursula. She turned it down with a shake of her head.

"I didn't bring you all the way here so you would have to work. Your work is here, at home." Roger tapped the loose ash onto the empty plate and motioned around the kitchen.

Ursula got up, grabbed the ashtray from the sideboard, and slid it across the table toward Roger.

"I'll try the school. Improve my English. Then look for a job," Ursula said. Improving her English should have been reason enough for Roger to agree to the school.

"Take the classes. It will probably do you some good to get out of this house. We can talk about a job later."

"But I want to work. I have been working since I was a girl." Ursula knew her insistence would surprise Roger, but she felt like a piece of her life might slip from her hands. Work had been her survival tool during the war and after, when every other part of her life was uncertain. What else would she have to give up for this American life? This kitchen could not, would not contain her.

"It embarrasses me, the idea of you sitting at a desk. It will look like I can't take care of my family," Roger said and lit another cigarette. Ursula knew he would smoke more if they kept arguing.

"Since when do you care about what people think of you?" For a man who was prepared to defy his commander to marry her, Ursula was unnerved by his desire to suddenly conform. America was supposed to be the land of the free.

"You worked during the war because you had to. American women did, too. But now American women are back at home, and you've found a home here as well. Now you can focus on becoming a mother, an American mother," Roger said.

The tension grew between them, and she said: "Roger, I want to become a mother. I do, but I need more time. I have a lot to learn."

"You've been here for four months, that's plenty of time to settle in. And you can learn about life here as you go."

Ursula pushed her plate to the side, then moved the platter in front of her to gather the chicken to one side of the plate. They would have leftovers for tomorrow.

"Is it your mother?" Ursula asked. Here in America, the defiance Roger had displayed in falling in love—in marrying her—had faded to a new, different type of stubbornness. It was now all about extreme loyalty to his family. His mother mostly.

"What?" Roger pushed himself back from the table but didn't get up.

"Would she be upset to find out I worked—will work?" Ursula corrected herself.

"Why do you bring my mother into this?" Roger pressed his left hand against his forehead.

"Because you want her approval," Ursula said louder than she had expected to. To her, Roger wanted to have life on his own terms, yet he also wanted to find a way to please his mother. This balancing seemed to leave Ursula out of the equation entirely.

"I don't need my mother's approval," Roger said. He looked down, then under his breath said: "She is the one who should be grateful to me for helping her stay in her house."

"What?" Was this why he counted pennies? To help his mother? Ursula's hesitancy about asking Roger for money for a new night-gown was validated and she realized she should trust her senses. When she felt something was wrong it wasn't just about cultural misunderstandings or words lost in translation.

"She was in—is still in a difficult position with my father gone. So, I help her out with the mortgage each month. And I guess you're right." He sighed and looked directly at Ursula. "Maybe you should take the classes, find a job. We can put that extra money aside. It wouldn't hurt."

"Roger, if I work, I want to save the money I earn for my family," Ursula said, emphasizing 'my'. If Roger could help his mother, she could help hers, too.

"You can work and attend school until you become a mother," Roger said, ignoring Ursula's concern about her family in Germany. He got up from the table, and went outside to smoke another cigarette.

Ursula shuddered and stood up. If becoming a mother meant giving up her only way to help her family, then she did not know if she wanted this supposed "American Dream." She had given up her German citizenship to come to America, and the prospect of becoming an American still excited her. The idea of becoming an American mother excited her even more. She could raise a child differently, in a new place in peacetime. By giving birth to a child in America, she

could reconcile her own childhood. Somehow atone for her igno-
rance. But she didn't want to give up a piece of herself for that dream.

Ursula stacked the dirty plates into a pile, balancing them in her
hands as she went to the sink. She did not like how Roger's vision
of her looked less like what Ursula knew and more like what the
Reich had expected of women. Motherhood above all else. And now
motherhood might come at the cost of helping her family. A part of
her missed the postwar chaos, the will to endure under extreme circumstances. During that time, her life's purpose was to survive, and
she had little time to think about anything else. The tumult brought
immediate needs into focus while obscuring the future.

The water in the sink had cooled, so Ursula turned on the faucet
to finish washing the pots and pans. The hot water that flowed out
was a luxury. When she imagined America, she had not imagined
arguments with Roger or the way his mother would treat her with
disdain or ignore her. She had not imagined the hours on her own,
bored and irritated because she did not know yet what she wanted.
*Are endings easier than beginnings? Did I really expect life to be perfect
in Minnesota compared to Berlin?* If she could figure out how to spend
her days, maybe she could start to answer those questions.

CHAPTER 7
October 1947

Roger was still in his makeshift upholstery workshop in the back of the garage when Ursula arrived home, bundled against the autumn chill. The light was on, so she walked up the driveway toward him, squeezing by the truck he had left out in the driveway. Ursula had taken the streetcar from her office in St. Paul. She had gotten a job as a secretary for Brown and Bigelow, a publisher of stationery and calendars. Aunt Rose had helped. She had made a few calls through her church group, put in a good word, and landed Ursula an interview. Then they'd practiced together for the interview so Ursula could easily answer questions in English. It worked, and she was hired on the spot. Roger was still not pleased with the idea of Ursula working, but the growing nest egg kept him from complaining. They had made a deal. Ursula would reserve three quarters of her earnings for her family in Germany but the remainder would be kept for her and Roger.

"You're working late," Ursula said. He liked to take home special projects, the furniture he wanted to perfect. He was meticulous, hoping the attention to detail would bring in referrals.

"Hello, beautiful. How many letters did you type today?" Roger said as he nailed batting to the base of a sofa frame.

The initial shock of togetherness they had experienced upon her arrival in Minneapolis had worn to a comfortable companionship. Though their relationship was still dotted with cultural misunderstandings, they navigated them with frustration or humor, depending on the temperature outside and the amount of money in their pockets.

"More than yesterday," Ursula said. She had learned her way around the typewriter in English with plenty of mistakes at first, but she was now up to fifty words per minute. If she kept practicing, she would be nearly as fast as the other secretaries by the New Year.

"Your hands must be tired."

"They feel all right, just stiff from this cold. But yours must be tired! Look at all those nails you had to pull!" Ursula took off a glove and pulled her palm across the goldenrod-colored velvet folded on Roger's workbench. "Gosh, this is beautiful. Such high quality. A new project?"

"You'll never guess for who." Roger stood and gave Ursula a hug. He smelled of wood shavings and musty cloth.

"Who?" She tucked her face into his shoulder.

"Glyde Snyder, the director of Schiek's Singing Sextet!"

"Oh?" Ursula stood back and looked at Roger with admiration. She had heard of the singing group from the women at work. One of the secretaries had even gone to their show. It was a big deal.

"Word from the bird." Roger slapped his hands together.

"*Wunderbar*," Ursula said. His American phrase made her laugh, but she comprehended the sentiment and secretly hoped they might get to hear the Singing Sextet sing. Ursula loved music. She missed the concerts in Berlin before the war when her parents would take her to hear the philharmonic at Christmastime.

"It certainly is. My handiwork will be in the home of a Twin Cities' celebrity." Roger set his hands on his hips, his face covered with a satisfied grin.

"This calls for a celebration," Ursula said. She wanted to hold onto the excitement. In addition to Roger's good news, she had nearly forgotten her birthday was in a week, followed by her six-month anniversary in Minneapolis. She only realized when she looked at the calendar earlier that day at work. "I'm going to make us something nice for dinner."

"I would like that, but I need to finish this," Roger said, then squatted next to the sofa. "I'll be in soon."

For a moment, Ursula watched Roger nail new batting to the frame. His movements were precise, the nails equally spaced across the fabric. *Oh, how my life has changed.* Then she opened the side door to the kitchen to start dinner. Within fifteen minutes, Ursula had a porkchop sizzling in a pan, potatoes boiling, and peas blanching.

Roger whistled as he took off his work boots at the side door. Ursula had started tidying the kitchen but abandoned her task when he kissed her neck. She leaned in and shimmied her shoulders, loving the nuzzle from behind.

"Let me finish getting things ready," Ursula said, pulling a serving dish from the cupboard.

Roger stepped into the dining room, tuned the radio, and the static chirped between voices and music.

When the food was arranged, Ursula untied the bow at her back of her apron, pulled the loop over her head, then paused, clutching the fabric in a ball in front of her belly. Only a few months ago the prospect of becoming a mother scared her, in spite of how much she wanted it. Working had eased Ursula's worry, though. The extra money gave her hope of figuring out a way to make all of this work—a baby, helping her family, Roger's obligations to his mother. Ursula could not call this place home yet, but typing and being in a roomful of secretaries had given her a new sense of purpose. It was confidence that she could conquer the challenges she faced. Confidence that she would be a good mother, one different from her own. When Ursula was a mother, she would be supportive and loving. With her baby, there would be hope for the future.

"This looks delicious," Roger said, motioning for Ursula to sit down when she came into the dining room. He pulled out her chair, and then took a seat across the table. The pork chops, peas, and potatoes graced a gold-edged platter, a wedding gift from Rose.

"Roger, you had such good news today about your new furniture order," Ursula said as their forks clanged on their plates. "But did you know that today is important for another reason?"

"Hmmm?"

"Next week is my birthday, and my six-month anniversary in America is coming up too," Ursula said. She set her fork down and grasped her small glass of beer, preparing for a toast. "Sometimes I feel as if I am living someone else's life."

"Well, I'll be," Roger said. He leaned forward and, a curl fell over his forehead and covered his eye. It gave him a playful look, like the American men in the movies. He brushed it upward, a gesture Ursula had come to think of as pure Roger. "How could I have forgotten your birthday? And time flies, six months already?"

"You know that after you left Germany, I never thought I'd hear from you again," Ursula said, her voice softer. A few other women who had worked in G-Tower were abandoned by the American soldiers who had promised to marry them. After Roger left Berlin, she wanted him to follow through. She didn't want to be abandoned like an old war relic.

Roger swallowed a mouthful of food, then smiled. "Ursula, you know that if I could have stayed on so we could come here together, I would have. They shipped me home! What was I going to do? Beg my commanding officer to let me stay? You knew I would send for you as soon as I could."

The curl fell over his forehead again. This time, after pushing it back, he reached for Ursula's hand and held it tight.

"After so many years of hardship . . . well, it was difficult for me to imagine you would still want me. Other girls I knew were left with empty promises," Ursula said.

"You shouldn't have doubted me for a minute," Roger said. He stood suddenly and extended a hand toward Ursula. "Let's dance like we did the first day we met."

Ursula rose and came around the table to accept his hand. A spark ran up her arm when they touched, it was like the one she'd noticed on their first evening together, the one that kept reassuring her Roger would offer something beyond Berlin, even if in that moment she could not name it. Now, in tandem, they rocked from foot to foot to the jazz from the radio.

"You had come to me looking for a job, and instead I invited you out with me and my friends. Remember that night? I couldn't take my eyes off of you."

"Oh, I remember," Ursula said. "But all I was thinking about was how I was going to make money to pay my rent. You were a distraction," Ursula said, squeezing his hand.

"You razzed my berries," Roger said. He dipped Ursula low and kissed her.

"I know. I had you on the hook," Ursula said, trying one of the phrases she had overheard two women using at work.

"You sure did," Roger laughed. "Where did you learn that?"

"Oh nowhere." Ursula winked.

Bing Crosby crooned in the background as they circled the living room, dining room, and kitchen. They twirled and teased, dipped and kissed. Then they left their half-eaten dinner on the table and danced into the bedroom.

Roger unzipped Ursula's dress. Her back tingled from the cool rush of air on her exposed skin.

"Roger, I think I'm ready," Ursula said. Soon they were tangled and warm, full of excitement for each other, for the possibility they could suspend themselves in this state of love. The gap between them narrowed, then disappeared. She decided she could embrace the American dream. To be a wife to this man who could both build solid furniture and spin her around the room. And then, to become a mother like the one she wished she had.

CHAPTER 8
April 1948

Graying piles of snow crowded the sides of streets across Minneapolis. The largest of the heaps would remain until June. The winters were not unlike the winters in Berlin, so Ursula acclimated easily to the snow and cold of the frozen months. She was saddened, though, by the echo of the winter in her empty womb. Her menstrual cycle was intermittent, another casualty of the war. They said it was the lack of food. She had enough to eat now, and had put on weight, but she still didn't have a regular cycle.

"These things take time, my dear," Roger had said.

They had only been trying to get pregnant since October, but to Ursula, each period was a sign of failure.

From her perch on the sofa, Ursula watched as Roger tugged at his coat, pulling it around him. He didn't seem to mind the cold if he was bundled up.

"I have a few deliveries to make, but I'll be home later. Could you maybe make the chicken I like so much?"

"Ja," Ursula said, then immediately regretted it. Her abdomen was tight with cramps and she just wanted to sit on the couch and cry. Instead, she would have to leave the house for the butcher. She should have suggested they just have pork chops because they only needed thawing. There was another painful squeeze across her belly, then a reverberation down her legs.

"Thank you," Roger said as he kissed Ursula's cheek. "You are getting to be quite the home cook."

"You can thank your Aunt Rose. She keeps her magazines for me." There was a pile of them on the coffee table in front her, and Ursula remembered seeing an article about "women problems" in the *Redbook* tucked among the *Ladies Home Journals*. May it would have some solution for these horrible cramps.

The side door slammed shut as Roger left, and moments later a few letters slid through the slot on the front door. Ursula stood to receive the mail, and her stomach sank when she saw the familiar handwriting. Another letter from her mother. The last few had been troubling. They were having difficulty finding food again, and the Russian soldiers were still causing trouble. Her thumb slid under the flap, but she hesitated and set the letter on the coffee table. It could wait for a moment. She reached instead for the *Redbook*, but the words on the page swum and she quickly closed the magazine. The un-opened letter was a bomb in front of her so she finally tore it open. A few paragraphs in, she froze.

> *Aunt Kaethe has had trouble with some Russian soldiers. She tried to run away and then she tried to fight back. I heard her yell, and I sent your father to help, but he came running back like a coward. I confess I've lost respect for him. You are lucky to have escaped this chaos.*

Ursula could not breathe. She'd had close calls with leering Russian soldiers after the war but managed to avoid them or hurry into a crowd where they wouldn't bother her. The rumors about the Russians were rampant and undoubtedly more than just rumors.

She'd heard they would rape any German woman they could get their hands on. She ran to the bathroom and threw up, then she wailed, pounding her fists on the bathroom sink. *How could they? And Father . . . how could he have run away and left her there? When will all of this end?* The admiration Ursula held for him was abruptly tarnished. Ursula thought he was stronger than that, but now she knew the Russian camp had changed him. Who had her father become?

Ursula slumped to the floor, her back propped against the bathtub. Tears streamed down her face. She wished she had been there to help her aunt. She wished she were there now to hug her, pull her from the depths of pain she must be in. And then she was relieved it had not been her with the Russian soldiers. The urge to throw up ended in a dry heave. At the sink she stared in the mirror. Her cheeks were flushed and her eyes puffy. Her red hair had come loose from its knot and wildly framed her face.

Ursula went to her typewriter, a Christmas gift from Roger from the Sears catalog she so admired, but she was frozen with fear and anger. She needed to move, deciding instead to scrub the bathroom floor. She had seen her mother do the same when she was too angry to speak. In the kitchen she put the kettle on to boil, took the bucket from under the sink and shook in Bon Ami. With her cleaning bucket ready she treaded to the bathroom and, on her hands and knees, pressed the hot wet rag into the small white hexagonal tiles, rubbing the surfaces smooth. She washed and rinsed and washed and rinsed until the floor sparkled an hour later.

Now that she had shaken off some of the fear and anger, she sat back down at her typewriter. She dumped her guilt for her leaving and her grief for losing the image of her father she cherished. She dumped her frustration with being unable to get pregnant, with the ways the war itself had ravaged her body. Exhausted, she stopped and tore the pages to shreds. Then she stood and retrieved the letter in the living room. She did not want Roger to hear more bad news from Berlin—it would just make him worry more about her. In the bedroom, she tucked the letter in a shoebox alongside the others from home. As she closed the lid, she whispered, "Forget about this news. You've had to forget many things to survive."

Back at the typewriter, Ursula once again hovered her hands above the keys. It was difficult for her to comprehend how Berlin would be rebuilt, how the people would survive. Her throat tightened with sadness when she thought of the emptied zoo, tattered parks, and streets filled with crumbled buildings. *Aunt Kaethe* . . . Ursula quickly banished the image of her aunt being attacked. Her stomach lurched but she sat up straight, determined. From America she could help, at least with words of love and support. With a new sheet of paper inserted, she pressed her fingers to the keys then stopped when she heard Roger's heavy foot on the stoop and the squeak of the side door. Soon he was standing next to her, his cheeks red with cold.

"You're home early."

"Glyde Snyder invited us to Schiek's tonight to hear the Singing Sextet," Roger said. His eyes gleamed; his voice animated from baritone to tenor.

"That sounds like an extravagance we cannot afford." Ursula slumped away from her typewriter. She hated to dampen his spirits, but money was still tight and everything she had earned she wanted to send back, now more than ever. "And remember, I was going to make you chicken." Though she still hadn't been to the butcher. Why was everything so hard?

"He's treating us as a thank you for a job well done. I reupholstered nearly all the furniture in his house," Roger said, and propped himself against the doorframe. "All of those late nights paid off."

"Tell me that's not the way he is paying you," Ursula said, narrowing her eyes.

"Of course not. He paid me just as we agreed," Roger said. "When I delivered the last sofa and chair to his home on Lake Calhoun this afternoon, he insisted we come to the club. I had to say yes." Roger smiled.

"Oh, all right, I suppose it will be nice." Ursula relented, but she still wondered if she deserved to have fun while her family suffered. "We cannot get carried away."

Ursula pulled the half-written letter out of the typewriter and crumpled it into a ball. The dustbin beside her was already full of the pages she had typed earlier in her flurry of anger and frustration. Her mother would be upset by her wastefulness.

"Glyde said to arrive at six sharp." Roger looked at his watch, then down at the waste bin. He extracted the paper on top, smoothed it, and placed it neatly beside the typewriter. "I know how much your mother frustrates you. Leave your letter for now, you can finish it tomorrow."

"It was a terrible letter anyway," Ursula said under her breath. Her index finger traced the creased page where she had started again. *Liebe Mutter.*

"Put on your party dress and let's have some fun tonight," Roger said as he left the room. His easygoing logic grated but she also wanted to pull herself out of her dismal mood. She resented the bad news from home, but guilt strummed inside her with each resentful thought. She should be thankful to receive any news. Letters sometimes took weeks to arrive, if they arrived at all. Maybe there was a lost letter out there with good news? *Nonsense, this is all nonsense.* Ursula chastised herself for her wistfulness, as if it could make any of this better for her aunt.

In the bathroom, water tumbled out of the faucet into the tub, echoing in the small house. Soon, Roger would lower himself into the hot water like a large boy, scrubbing and whistling to himself. Just the thought of it made Ursula laugh. He always found a way to be playful. Closing her eyes for a moment, she convinced herself to let go of the grief of not being able to help her aunt, the grief of not being able to get pregnant. She could enjoy the night, or at least pretend to. She wanted to for Roger's sake.

As Roger pulled out of the alley and backed onto the street, the Cadillac's back tire logged in a pothole. The drifts of snow had started to melt and revealed cracks and holes in the pavement.

"These damn potholes!" Ursula said in German under her breath. In a city as beautiful as Minneapolis it upset her to see the streets marked with holes. It reminded her of the gouges from mortar fire in Berlin's streets.

"What did you say, dear?" Roger asked as he freed the car from winter's fading grip.

"Oh, never mind," Ursula said. She smoothed out her dress and reapplied lipstick in her reflection in the window. She had decided to wear her deep-pink dress. It was the color of the tulips, like a spring bouquet.

As they neared downtown, the buildings got taller and closer together. The Minneapolis skyline was different than Berlin's. It was small but inviting. Held so much promise. Tonight, it shone against the crisp blue sky.

At the restaurant, an elegant maître d' with a delicate moustache showed them to their table.

"Mr. Snyder will be with you shortly," he said in a snobby voice. Fake, Ursula thought. Like the voices of *partei* members, but their bravado was dangerous. She set her handbag on the side of the table and admired the white tablecloths, dark paneling, and long bar located opposite the stage. They were seated up front near the piano. Maybe she could relax, dance, and enjoy the evening after all.

"Gosh, this is fancy," Ursula said.

"Don't turn around, but I think that's the Dayton family," Roger said.

"The department store Daytons?" She wondered if her dress was elegant enough.

"Yes, those Daytons. Don't stare."

"Do you think if I went over there and asked them, they would give me a discount?" Ursula pivoted to get a look at them.

"Very funny. I need Glyde to have them over for dinner so they can get a glimpse of my upholstery work." Roger flashed a calculated smile. "Then you could buy yourself as many new dresses as you want."

Ursula laughed, saying she was only teasing. While she would love new dresses, it seemed in bad taste to ask for more business while being thanked for a job well done.

Ursula felt Roger's eyes run over her body and rest on her face.

"You look enchanting tonight," he said.

She blushed. Roger looked handsome, too, in his dark brown suit. "You look—" Ursula said, but before she could finish, a man who could only be Glyde Snyder interrupted her. An air of what Ursula could only think of as Hollywood surrounded him. A tight shave revealed a youthful face, but with the way Roger talked about him he must be in his forties. Pomade added structure to his parted brown hair, and set off his thin eyebrows. Then, the Hollywood aura was ruined when he started talking in the highest pitched voice of any man she had ever met. She almost laughed but stopped herself. She could not embarrass Roger.

"Roger! What do you think? Isn't it wonderful? Let me get you champagne. Oh, and this beautiful woman must be your better half," Glyde said in one breath as he swept his arm in the air to show off his domain. He was gone before Ursula and Roger could say a proper hello.

"That's Glyde, always in a hurry," Roger said.

A few minutes later two glasses of champagne arrived at their table.

"Roger, this is nice, but perhaps too nice," Ursula said, picking up the glass and taking a sip of the bubbly liquid. She wanted to appreciate the decadence, the flashiness of it all, but her thoughts kept returning to her aunt.

"You're one difficult woman when you want to be," Roger said, his voice warm.

"What's that supposed to mean?" Ursula said. She took another sip and concentrated on steering her mind to the present. It was almost impossible to square her life now with the life she left behind.

"Come on, Ursula, please enjoy the evening. Forget about whatever you wanted to tell your mother. It can wait. This is a treat!" Roger eyed the stage. The pianist started to play, the small orchestra tuned up, and the room was soon filled with the who's-who of the Twin Cities—judges, senators, doctors, lawyers, and anyone else who had saved for months to eat here. Ursula admired the glamorous women seated across from handsome men. They were adorned in pastel taffeta or cotton with tulle and their hair was sculpted into fancy updos or curled around their cheeks. Some wore elbow-length gloves.

A mix of emotions spun in her stomach. At times, she felt like she owed Roger her future, as if she was indebted to him for bringing her to America. She tipped the glass and finished the champagne, then gave Roger a weak smile. She wondered if they looked anywhere near as glamorous and handsome as the patrons filling the other tables.

They ordered the sauerbraten and the mint potato pancakes, one of Schiek's famous specialties. Their plates arrived, the sauerbraten swimming in gravy and the pancakes ornately stacked on the side.

"This isn't as good as my mother's sauerbraten," Ursula said. She'd hoped to taste something of home, but any hint vanished before she could swallow.

"Your mother isn't a chef here," Roger said.

"You're right about that," and Ursula forked potatoes pancake into her mouth. These are better, she thought, cheering up. Then the band started playing, and she found herself humming along.

"Let's dance," Roger said.

Ursula could not refuse him. She loved to dance. She set down her fork and followed Roger to the dance floor, swallowing her mouthful. For a few moments she forgot about her aunt, the distressed city, and her old life. They circled the dance floor with a few other couples who had chosen to abandon their dinner for a moment. There was a tingling between her legs as Roger's lips lingered on her neck.

"Roger, please! Not in front of everyone." Ursula pulled back, embarrassed, as if others in the room could see their desire. Roger stepped off the dance floor, hurt. Ursula watched him walk away and then followed him when she realized the song was over and she was standing alone.

"Please don't make a scene," Roger said. "Glyde was very generous, and I don't want to appear ungrateful."

Back at their table, a waiter had refolded Ursula's napkin and their champagne glasses had been refilled. All around her, diners chatted with their companions and sliced into steaks cooked just as they ordered. The discontinuity between what Ursula knew about her family at home and this upscale supper club was more than she could process. She unfolded the napkin and set it carefully back in her lap.

"Ursula, what's upsetting you? You've been acting strange ever since I came home," Roger said.

"My family is out of food again," she said, her fingers tracing the pattern on the stem of her glass. Before they left the house, she had promised herself she would try to enjoy the evening. She knew she should not share the horrifying news of her aunt being raped. How would she even begin that conversation, especially in this glamorous place?

"I was upset. I'm still upset. What if they starve and I never see them again?"

"Ursula, you worry so much. They won't go hungry." He patted her hand. "The American government is still involved over there, helping get food and supplies in as Berlin is rebuilt. And you will get to see your family again. As soon as we have enough money, we'll travel to Berlin."

"You promise?" She loved that he cared about her family, that he cared so much about her.

"Yes, I promise. I love you, Ursula. I want the best for you. I want the best for us."

Ursula swallowed. "Maybe this will never work . . . an American and a German."

Roger spit out the champagne he was drinking. "If I didn't think an American and German could be together, then I wouldn't have convinced you to come to America to be with me."

"But . . ."

"The second I saw you on base, I knew I wanted to get to know that determined redhead. You were so focused on finding work. Most of the girls that came on base just wanted to find an American husband." Roger sketched his index finger over the creases of Ursula's palm.

"But what if, what if people think . . ." Ursula tried, but could not say it out loud.

"Ursula, if you're trying to say what I think you're trying to say . . . you are not, never were, the Third Reich."

"I worked in Berlin's Air Defense Center!"

"But you weren't a Nazi. You were a German citizen trying to stay alive. You would have been punished, even sent to prison, if you had said the wrong thing to the wrong person." Roger took her chin in his hands, turning her head so he could look straight into her eyes.

"But I should have done something," Ursula said, letting out sigh. All of her effort to hold back her thoughts and emotions failed and she was suddenly exhausted. A minute ago they'd been dancing and now she was back in G-Tower, following orders from men she knew were evil. It was as if the war had taken a hold of her and never let go. Even though she had crossed the Atlantic, a piece of her had somehow stayed in Berlin.

"What could you have done?" Roger asked, rubbing his temples. "I was deployed to fight against the Nazis. I had the Allied countries behind me with their weapons, intelligence, and strategy. It still took years."

Ursula knew he was tired of this argument by the furrow in his brow that left deep wrinkles above his eyes. They had argued in Berlin before they were married about what it would mean for them to be a couple and how it would look in America. Roger was never as concerned as Ursula. Like now, he always took a more nuanced view during those conversations.

"I saw one of the higher-ups, Göring. A horrible man." His face flashed in Ursula's mind. "He gave us a speech to increase morale.

Friends who worked on his estate said he asked to be carried around like Caesar."

"What has gotten into you tonight?" Roger was shaking his head.

"My parents are hungry and I could be there, helping them," Ursula said.

"Oh Ursula, you can't blame yourself for leaving."

"But I am so far away . . ." Ursula said, a tightness in her throat. She did not want to cry, not here.

"Let's not ruin a perfectly nice dinner. We can talk about all of this tomorrow. We will figure out a way to help from here. I promise." Roger sounded sincere, but Ursula was still unnerved. What could they possibly do to help?

For the remainder of the evening, they danced and talked about the music, wondered about the Daytons, and watched Glyde float around the room like a celebrity. They ate sliced beef tenderloin and Wiener Schnitzel, along with fresh broccoli spears and au gratin potatoes. When the dessert arrived—double chocolate cake—the plate was barely on the table when Ursula stabbed her fork into the spongy middle.

"This is delicious." Ursula forced a smiled, her teeth covered in chocolate frosting.

"If I knew cake would cheer you up, I would have ordered that first," Roger said.

She ached to tell him about her aunt. But if she was being truthful, she did not want to burden him with this intimate information about her family. She kept the news a secret.

CHAPTER 9
October 1948

Over the summer, the Americans airlifted in food and supplies after the Russians had blockaded Berlin. On the radio, Ursula heard of soldiers dropping bars of chocolate from planes, and imagined children's heads turned upward, hands outstretched for the luxury. More than ever, Ursula wished she could package the hope she found in America and drop it over her parents' home like chocolate.

From across the ocean, though, Ursula could do little other than to finally reply to her mother's letter. That done, and with summer over, Ursula decided to follow through on attending the voluntary citizenship classes. She didn't have to enroll as part of the citizenship process, but she wanted to. But she had put off enrolling for a year because she thought it was more important to work, to build up savings. Each time Ursula had seen Bea at the shops in their neighborhood, she explained she wasn't ready yet. How she was busy with her secretarial work, cooking, and keeping the house tidy. Besides, someone had to walk Vic. She couldn't explain her more complicated doubts. That it was the best way for her to be useful to her family. That becoming an American meant she would lose a piece of herself and be left with a still unanswered question: *Who am I meant to be now?*

As a child during Hitler's rise and then the war, Ursula had swung between feeling indifferent, apolitical, and enraged by it all. In Berlin, she had grown up surrounded by the Nazis and their sympathizers. They shared the same air, classrooms, trains, streets, and toilets. Beyond their party affiliation, these were Ursula's neighbors, shopkeepers, fishmongers, postmen, and in the early days, friends. The changes she saw in Germany as a child seemed positive at first. After years of unemployment, fathers of classmates had gone back to work. Families had more food on the table. People were taking weekend holidays to other parts of the country, or simply enjoying day outings in the nearby countryside. It was all part of the Third Reich's "Joy through Strength" program.

The optimism was contagious enough for millions of people to turn a blind eye to growing anti-Semitism. In the homes of Ursula's friends, ubiquitous Führer trinkets proliferated on living room mantels that became Hitler shrines. Before, she'd only seen the face of Jesus create such adoration, and his image only appeared in churches and the homes of the devout. Many Germans had eschewed their devotion to God and placed it in the Führer. This distortion disturbed Ursula's parents and they warned Ursula to be suspicious of fanatical people. She trusted her parents, especially her father. After all, he was a journalist. It was his job to cut to the facts, leave behind the propaganda, and discover the truth. As Ursula grew and saw the world through maturing eyes, she knew her parents were right in resisting fascism. She also knew these beliefs could put her whole family in danger.

In a step toward the future, toward the woman she wanted to be, even if that woman was undefined, Ursula enrolled in the classes sponsored by the Minneapolis Board of Education. They were held on Tuesday and Thursday mornings at the Miller Vocational School, a multistory Art Deco building on 3rd Avenue South. The registrar helped Ursula select classes in English, history, government, and geography. Although not a requirement, she registered for home economics so she could learn to cook like Betty Crocker, who had recently been named America's First Lady of Food. Maybe this would help Ursula become a better housewife. The final years of the war taught her how to survive. Now she needed to perfect the art of making a home. Roger would like that.

On the night before her twenty-fourth birthday, in her comfortable bedroom on Colfax Avenue, many miles and years from the fears that had clouded her youth, Ursula had a nightmare that Hitler had escaped to America and was trying to become a citizen. When Ursula realized he was plotting to take over this country, too, she screamed and woke up. Roger grunted and rolled over. The fear that permeated Berlin as Hitler came to power swept over her now, her new yellow nightgown cold and damp with sweat.

She got out of bed to change into her old one. It was dry but had split new holes. Back in bed, with the blanket pulled to her chin, she wished she could wake Roger. She wanted to tell him about the nightmare, about her fears, and how grateful she was to be in America, but it seemed too difficult to explain.

On Ursula's birthday, Rose insisted on taking Ursula to a late breakfast at her favorite Minneapolis diner. Ursula loved the diner's motto: Sit Long, Talk Much.

"These are the best scrambled eggs in town—so light and fluffy." Rose scooped a mouthful onto her fork. "I can never make them like this at home."

Ursula nodded. She had yet to master fluffy eggs, too. "It's so kind of you to take me out for lunch. You don't know how much this means to me."

"When I heard Roger was working all day, I couldn't let you spend your birthday alone." Rose spread more butter on an already-buttered piece of toast. "I know it's hard enough being away from family. You've shared with me before how difficult it is to be away from them on special occasions and holidays."

"It is," Ursula said, then hesitated. She rarely got time alone with Aunt Rose and wanted to ask her about Mrs. Gorski, but she worried about ruining such a nice morning. The long and narrow diner was full of sunshine, conversation, and the aroma of fresh coffee. Since the wedding over a year before, Mrs. Gorski had been polite, occasionally even nice. But she never mentioned the wedding, and acted like her absence from it never happened. When Ursula dutifully sat by Roger at church on Sundays, she bit her tongue, knowing if she brought it up, she would open the past. Roger had assured Ursula that his mother couldn't keep up her distant façade, that eventually she would relent, especially if they ever had a grandchild for her to dote on.

"Is there something you wanted to say, dear?" Rose dabbed her napkin at the corner of her mouth.

"I was . . . well."

"Your secrets are safe with me." Rose winked.

"Oh, it's not a secret, I suppose. I only wish Mrs. Gorski—Mary—would warm to me. Roger said she might, that she just needed time."

"You're not alone in that wish."

"No?" Ursula examined the older woman. Though Rose had always been nice, she always assumed her loyalty to her sister was unwavering.

"The whole family is upset with her, but she's too stubborn to be convinced that you're good for Roger, and that he's happy. And that you are happy too."

"I am trying." And she was. Trying to form a connection with her mother-in-law. Trying to be a part of the Gorski clan.

"It's complicated, I suppose. Mary has been through a lot, but that's no excuse. I'd like to think I know my sister well at this point in our lives, but even I'm stumped about what might make a difference."

"I don't know what else I can do . . . I am polite, helpful."

"From the moment you peeled those damn potatoes for her, I knew she was going to be difficult," Rose said, shaking her head in disbelief. "Please excuse the curse, but I still cannot believe she asked you to do that."

"You helped," Ursula said, grinning.

"I couldn't just stand there and watch; I would have been no better than Mary." Rose pointed her fork at the eggs on Ursula's plate. "You haven't tried them yet."

"I'm sorry, I've been talking too much." Ursula lifted the white and yellow morsels to her mouth and swallowed. "They are delicious."

"I knew you would like them."

The waitress stopped at their table and refilled their mugs with coffee.

"Do you have chocolate pastries?" Ursula asked. The waitress pointed to the glass display case near the cash register and Ursula got up to take a look. Chocolate sounded good, but she mostly wanted a moment to collect her thoughts, to decide what else she might ask Rose about Mary. What could she do to find a way in? To at least make their relationship more bearable? Ursula maneuvered down the tight aisle, shifting sideways as wait staff scurried back and forth between the kitchen and their tables. She eyeballed the chocolate donut. If she was a baker, she could bake her way into Mary's good graces. A woman in her citizenship class said she had won her mother-in-law over with an apple pie.

Ursula laughed to herself. Then she placed her order and returned to the table.

"What did you decide on?" Rose cupped the mug in her palms. She had set a small wrapped box between them.

"The chocolate donut looked good," Ursula said, then pointed at the box. "And what is this?"

"Just a little something for your birthday, and I've had that donut before. Good choice."

"Can I open it?"

"Of course you can open it."

Ursula untied the white ribbon holding together neatly folded brown paper. She lifted two light pink skeins of yarn from the wrapping. "These are beautiful."

"I thought you might need more yarn for your projects.

"I can always use more yarn." She rubbed the smooth wool between her fingers.

"You know, Ursula, this has given me an idea of something that might help you with Mary."

"Really?"

Rose nodded with a thoughtful look on her face.

"With how much you love knitting and crocheting, well, I heard Mary talking about a blanket drive at St. Thomas for families in need—new mothers, I think. Maybe you could make a baby blanket and donate it?"

"Hmm. You really think that would work?" Ursula hefted the pink skeins in her hands, imagining a baby girl nestled in the blanket she could make.

"I don't think it will immediately make Mary warm up to you, but she'll see you trying and maybe that will crack her. You know, just enough to thaw the ice."

"I'll think about it." The pastry arrived on a plate but Ursula no longer had an appetite for it. She was too busy thinking about her version of her fellow student's apple pie. Could a bit of knitting really make a difference with her mother-in-law? It seemed too easy, too simple.

"It can't hurt. And with it being October now, you could have one ready in time for the December blanket drive."

"I sure could," Ursula said, but the vision in her mind had shifted. Perhaps a few hours with her knitting needles could bridge the distance with Mary. But what came of it would be a baby blanket for someone else's baby and not her own.

CHAPTER 10
December 1948

On the snow-covered sidewalks outside, people gathered packages in their hands, early Christmas shopping underway. Ursula could not believe she would soon celebrate a second Christmas in America. Greenery punctuated with red bows spiraled the street lamps, reminding Ursula of the festive Berlin streets from before the war. She had not decided what to get Roger yet—a few new upholstery tools were on the top of her list, but were quite expensive. A new tie might have to do instead.

"Have you started your Christmas shopping yet?" Ursula gazed at Bea whose dress was taught against her belly. Outside of citizenship classes, they had coffee a few times a month. Ursula was grateful for the common ground between them. As war brides they shared similar experiences with their letters from home, homesickness and the ongoing challenges of making a new city their own.

"All my focus has been on this baby. I managed to start decorating the house, but I haven't the slightest idea of what I should get John. With my due date so close to Christmas—the 23rd—I just don't have my wits about me for much else apart from the baby."

"John will understand, won't he?"

"Of course, I just want him to feel special too."

"He will feel special when that baby comes," Ursula said wishing she were pregnant, about to give Roger his first child. It had been over a year now of trying to get pregnant. Frustrated, she tapped her finger against her chin, then took a long sip of coffee. The pink skeins of wool were still sitting in her craft basket at home, untouched. She had toyed with the idea Rose had given here of a making the baby blanket for the Christmas drive for mothers in need, but she could not bring herself to do it. Not even to thaw her relationship with Mrs. Gorski.

"Is there something troubling you, Ursula? You seem a bit preoccupied today. But I know as well as anyone how hard it is to be away from family at Christmastime."

"No, no. Nothing to do with Christmas. I was thinking about your baby being due, and what a wonderful present that is."

"Gosh, yes, I couldn't ask for a better present than this wee one," Bea said.

"I wish, I just wish it would happen soon for me."

"The war didn't help anyone become a picture of health," Bea said, taking a small sip of tea. Through their citizenship classes, they heard of other war brides who had difficulty having children. "I think it's more common than we realize."

"I thought my cycle would come back, be regular like the months of a calendar." Ursula exhaled.

"But you've had one, right? It hasn't completely disappeared?" Bea asked.

"Yes, I've had a few." Ursula flushed. She didn't like talking about it.

"And you're . . ." Bea mouthed, "having sex."

"Yes, of course we are. That's not the problem." Ursula looked around to see if anyone was listening, but the café was busy, and people were engaged in their own conversations. She did not want the intimate details of her life in the ears of strangers.

"If I've learned anything about you since we met, I know you can be stubborn. Go see your doctor. I would if I were you."

"Who would I see? I know nothing about the doctors in America, how they work . . ." Ursula wished she was in Berlin before the worst of the war when seeing a doctor was straightforward.

"I can give you the name of my doctor, if you'd like. She's wonderful." Bea smiled and ran her hands over her waist.

Ursula had never met a woman doctor. "She?"

"Yes. She told me she was brought in during the war but didn't want to stop working after the men came home. A few of the male doctors tried to force her out, but she's so well-liked, they couldn't remove her. Mothers threatened to leave. And if I had been a patient then, I would have threatened to leave too!"

"Really? I did not know you were so tough, fighting for other women to work."

"You make me sound like some kind of feminist." Bea laughed and wrote Dr. Hunt's number on a piece of paper and handed it to Ursula.

"Maybe," Ursula stopped and read the name on the paper, "Dr. Hunt will understand my situation better. I never liked the idea of taking advice from a male doctor. They only know what they've read in books."

"She will, I know she will. I bet you'll have your own tiny Christmas present this time next year. You'll see!"

"How's your family?" Ursula wanted to change the subject. Nervous sweat had appeared under her arms as she folded the paper in half and stuffed it into her coat pocket.

"They are very excited for me and John. It's a new chapter for our whole family, not just me. This little person will bring much-needed light to the world," Bea said and leaned in. "I don't know about you, but I felt like my life was on hold and now, the days are flying by. I just never imagined I could be so happy. And, you'll never guess what! I cannot believe I forgot to tell you. My mother is coming all the way from England to spend a few months with us when the baby arrives."

A lump rose up in Ursula's throat. She would not cry in front of Bea. She pressed her lips together and then took a big gulp of her coffee. The caffeine jittered her veins.

"What wonderful news," she said, her voice squeaked.

"What is it?" Bea straightened in her chair.

"Nothing, nothing at all."

"You look like you're going to cry."

"Before coming here, I did not know how much I would miss my family. I wanted to leave Berlin so badly that I did not think—" A few tears spilled down Ursula's face.

Bea moved her chair next to Ursula's and put an arm around her shoulder, "It's dreadful. I know how you feel. It's okay. Shhh . . ."

Ursula heard Bea choke back tears, too.

"I'm sorry. I didn't want to cry in front of you." Ursula covered her face with her palms, and said through them, "How embarrassing."

"Don't be daft. I'm a blubbering mess with this baby coming. Yesterday I saw a girl walking a cocker spaniel puppy and it set me off. I was sobbing in the middle of the street! My parents always told me I was too emotional to be a proper English girl. You're more English than I am. You Germans seem to hold back a lot. But how boring would we be if we were all so stiff?" Bea tilted her chin up and laughed.

"You? I cannot imagine you crying in the middle of the street. But I have surprised myself by doing and saying things I would not have done at home. See: I cried in public today. This place is changing me already," Ursula said.

Outside, a few inches of snow had piled up on the ground. A man ran to help a woman walking hesitantly with a cane over a high curb buried in snow.

"I should probably get going before this gets any deeper. I don't want to get the car stuck. Shall I give you a lift home?"

Ursula nodded.

They pulled on their coats. Bea placed enough money on the table for her half.

Ursula tucked her hands into her pockets to reach for her coin purse, but caught the piece of paper with Dr. Hunt's number between her fingers. She had briefly forgotten about it. The uneasy feeling from earlier caught in her stomach. Calling the doctor would mean telling Roger her predicament was more serious than she realized. She punched a hole in the paper with her fingernail. She wished she had dozens of pieces of paper she could punch and rip apart. The frustration vibrated in her fingers as she squished Dr. Hunt's number in her fist.

"Ursula? Are you ready to go?"

"Sorry, I was looking for my coin purse. Here it is." She dropped a few coins on the table and they treaded out into the snow.

CHAPTER 11
April 1949

On a cloudy Tuesday afternoon after citizenship class, Ursula tucked her belongings into a locker at the municipal pool halfway between the school and home. She had rearranged her work schedule to Mondays, Wednesdays, and Fridays. Ursula pulled on her modest black bathing suit and covered her thick red hair with a flowered bathing cap. This afternoon ritual had become common over the last four months—it was the only activity apart from rigorous house cleaning that helped Ursula clear her mind.

She paused at the mirror in the locker room. Sturdy legs pale from the long winter months were anchored by thick ankles and delicate feet. Ursula wished the war had thinned her ankles—a small vanity that might have come from suffering. The yellow hue in her skin had disappeared a few months after she arrived in Minneapolis, and now her limbs were brushed with healthy pink. Ursula's belly was slightly rounded from abundant American food and her arms stronger from laps swimming the front crawl. A quick check of her bum: it was rounder too.

Hands on her hips, Ursula whispered to herself: "Stop being so vain." A snort erupted from her nose and echoed on the hard surfaces. *I sound like my mother.*

The pool was quiet, so instead of stepping in from the ladder,

Ursula jumped in the deep end, surfaced for breath and started her trek across the blue. She was freed of the weight of her body and allowed her mind to wander. Since she had confided her frustrations about not getting pregnant to Bea, the woman had become a friend, someone she could confide in. Ursula had tucked the slip of paper with Dr. Hunt's number into her top dresser drawer. It had remained there over the winter nestled among her undergarments. She still wasn't ready to call. For now, her healthy body sliced through the water, and she was confident it would stop betraying her. She could— no she would—get pregnant without the advice of doctors.

After a few laps, she stopped in the shallow end and pressed her back against the tiled wall to rest. Near her, a mother guided her son through various movements in the water. Ursula tried to avoid staring, but she couldn't help it. This did not look as if the mother was simply teaching him how to swim.

"Have you never seen a child with polio before?" the mother said, her eyes still trained on her son.

Embarrassed, Ursula looked away. She had heard about the polio epidemic. It was impossible not to. The newspaper reported daily case counts in the summer when the virus surged. Tallies were kept, but she had never seen anyone recovering from the disease, at least not this close up. The disease predominantly affected children, and there were few children in her life. As close as she was to Bea, she rarely saw her now. She had been successful in her own quest for pregnancy and she was now happily cocooning with the baby and her mother who had made the long journey from England to Minnesota to help. She rarely saw her niece and nephew in the suburbs. But then she recalled family she had seen at the park: a couple whose child's arms were slung through banded crutches, braces a scaffold on the child's legs. And last week at SuperValu, Ursula had stepped aside as a mother pushed a wheelchair holding both her daughter and a small shopping basket full of groceries.

Over the next few weeks during her swims, Ursula quietly observed the boy as he strengthened his legs under his mother's instruction. Eventually, her curiosity got the better of her.

"Does this help?" Ursula asked the mother, motioning to the water. She had taken up her usual resting spot in the shallow end. The slick aqua tile pressed against her back.

"The doctors said it would. I'll do anything to help. He deserves to have a life just like the other boys and girls his age."

The young boy looked happy in the water, but his mother's face was a painting of exhaustion and distress. An abrupt sadness overcame Ursula. She wanted to be as far away as possible from the mother's sorrowful face. It reminded her of her own mother's sadness.

"I wish your son a speedy recovery," Ursula said. In truth, she did not know what to say. Her mind darted to Bea's baby. To her niece and nephew. *What will happen to them if they get sick?*

Ursula pushed off the bottom of the pool and started her crawl. As she approached the deep end, she let her legs drop for a moment and her body quickly sunk until she was nearly vertical in the water. *What a strange feeling . . . poor boy.* She kicked and brought her legs back to the surface.

The boy and his mother were gone by the time Ursula grasped the edge of the far end of the pool. The water was inviting when she had jumped into the pool, but now goosebumps patterned her arms and legs. She pulled herself out of the deep end, too unnerved to continue her swim.

CHAPTER 12
May 1949

Ursula's period had arrived again, and she finally lost trust in her body. She retrieved the small slip of paper from her underwear drawer and called Dr. Hunt's office for an appointment. If she ever wanted to get pregnant, it was time for her to take a doctor's advice. A week later, she sat in a waiting room, her stomach an ugly tangle. She was relieved when she finally heard her name called.

"Mrs. Gorski?"

Ursula nodded and followed the white uniform to a small room with a chair and examination table where she was left alone. She shivered, suddenly doubtful about going through with the appointment. She wiped her sweaty hands on her dress. If she confessed barrenness to the doctor, it would be part of the record. They would know of her brokenness, and Ursula wondered if this would be putting her in danger. German women were expected to have children. Those who had many earned the *Mutterkreuz*, an honor given by the regime. "German girls are strong and made to have lots of children." How many times had she heard this as a teenager in the League of German Girls? *How could I have conformed to the demands of the Reich with this . . . problem?* A warning sign flashed before her eyes. *Feind hort mit. The enemy is listening.* But no, she was in America. There was no one listening.

A gentle knock at the door revealed Dr. Hunt. She was tall and wore her dark-blond hair in a bob, a style left over from another generation that reminded Ursula of Aunt Kaethe. The similarities left her breathless. For a second, she felt her aunt in the room beside her, assuring her that all would be okay.

"What brings you here today?" Dr. Hunt seemed efficient, but her voice was pleasant.

"I want a baby," Ursula said, her polite English suddenly awkward and demanding.

Dr. Hunt motioned for Ursula to sit on the examination table as she opened a folder with a few papers. Ursula clutched her black handbag in her lap, the money she saved for this visit inside.

"That's wonderful. You've come to the right place," Dr. Hunt said with an easy smile.

"We have been trying, but nothing." Ursula looked down. Shame filled her, the warning to be a "tough German girl" sounded in her head. But she swallowed the lump in her throat. She was going to be an American. She did not need to be a tough German girl anymore.

"So, you haven't been able to conceive," Dr. Hunt said.

Ursula nodded, and then talked about her woman problems, and also about years of going hungry, about leaving her family behind. It spilled out of her. She couldn't help it.

"You've certainly faced some incredible challenges." Dr. Hunt took a step back to reach for a chair. "But now it sounds like you're adjusting to a calmer life."

"Yes, I am. Being in America, well, Minneapolis, has been a good change. I am grateful to be here. I simply wish . . ." Her voice trailed off. Her very presence in this office told the doctor what she wished.

"I understand how difficult this must be. There are many women— couples I should say—who are experiencing similar struggles." Dr.

Hunt settled in the chair and placed the folder on the nearby desk. "Will your husband be joining us? I forgot to ask my nurse if he was in the waiting room. Sometimes the husbands get nervous coming back here."

"No, he's working today."

"All right, well, that's fine. We can proceed without him, but next time make sure he comes along too." Dr. Hunt turned a page in the folder and made a note. Ursula tried to see what she was writing, but the doctor's penmanship wound in tight loops.

"So, you will examine me today?" Nervous again, Ursula shifted on the exam table.

"I think it's best to wait until your husband can join you. But I will talk to you about common causes of infertility, and then explain possible treatments," Dr. Hunt said, as she finished the notation.

"I don't want a test tube baby, please," Ursula said. She had heard about this new development on the radio and all she could picture was a scientific laboratory, small babies squeezed into tubes on the counter.

"Oh gosh, no, we won't do that at this point. That is quite experimental. First, we can test for female tubal occlusion." She seemed to notice confusion on Ursula's face. "That's a blockage of sorts. This is also an experimental treatment, but women are having some success with it on the East coast."

"A blockage?"

"Yes, sometimes the tubes can become blocked. We can resolve it with something called a 'rubin test'—its not always effective, but it could give you a chance at conceiving. I've had women come in for the procedure and conceive within months, but others have not had as much success with it."

"Oh, does it hurt? The procedure?" Ursula tried to process all the new information. "And do I need to worry? Experimental sounds possibly dangerous."

"It hurts to a degree, but if you focus on the possibility of a pregnancy, I think it helps. And yes, at the experimental stage we have fewer degrees of assurance, but given some of the success others have experienced, it could be worth trying," Dr. Hunt said. She flipped the pen in her hand. "We can also test for male sterility."

"What is that?"

Dr. Hunt lowered her voice and said: "The men around here don't like to hear this, but sometimes the failure to get pregnant can come from the male. They can be the problem."

"How?" Ursula never considered the fault may lie with Roger. Dr. Hunt was right to whisper.

"I won't go into the details now, but sperm counts and a few tests can help us get to the bottom of it. Your husband will need to come in for that, of course."

"Mmm, yes, he will," Ursula said. These new ideas were forbidden knowledge. A threat to the masculine ideal.

"Are you working?" Dr. Hunt asked. "Some doctors believe work is the problem, but I've worked most of my life and have children of my own, so don't mind them."

Their eyes met and Ursula smiled. They had a shared understanding. Ursula's hope shot up a notch. Bea was right about Dr. Hunt. This was a doctor who understood women's problems.

Dr. Hunt closed her folder and stood. "I also want you to increase sexual intimacy with your husband," she said. "At least twice a week, more if you can. Think more positively about the baby. Then, if the pregnancy doesn't happen, come back to me in the fall. Does that make sense?"

"It has been so long already," Ursula said. She didn't want to waste time and money on solutions that might not work. But at least positive thoughts were free, if she could muster them. Maybe all those women's magazines had been right. Maybe it was all in her head, as even Dr. Hunt's prescription centered on the idea.

"You must give yourself time. Pay attention to your cycle. Keep notes and bring them to your next visit. And always remember that it doesn't all fall on you. It takes two to make a baby." Dr. Hunt left the room, closing the door behind her.

At first it had been about winning over Mrs. Gorski. But now Ursula knew better. This baby, if there ever would be one, was not an easy fix to anything. Instead, Ursula knew now she needed to fulfill this part of her destiny as a woman. This would prove she was not broken, that she could create something beautiful and new.

Ursula scooted off the exam table and as soon as her feet touched the floor, she was airborne for a second in a joyful hop. Finally, someone understood her struggle. She paid and left the office. Instead of taking the bus, she walked home imagining what it would feel like to be pushing a stroller. What it would feel like to be a whole woman.

CHAPTER 13
July 1949

The summer heat had risen quickly after the cold spring. Mrs. Ohlin sat on her front stoop and waved Ursula over. She was glad it was Saturday. She had sweated her week in the office with the rising temperatures and humidity. Ursula left her sandals on the sidewalk and pressed her feet into the soft grass. She loved the blades against her soles, the way they slid between her toes. This morning, they were still wet with dew.

Jean, Mrs. Ohlin's youngest, was playing hopscotch by herself. "Watch, Mom!" she occasionally yelled, but otherwise seemed content tossing her pebble and jumping through the chalk-drawn boxes.

"I heard on the news that the blockade ended in Berlin—you must be so relieved," Mrs. Ohlin said.

"Ja, I have been worried about my family, but they have learned how to cope." Ursula intertwined her fingers and squeezed her palms together. Her worry about them was always with her, a constant premonition that they were in trouble.

"Did you hear that Ruth's little girl got polio?" Mrs. Ohlin gossiped about the neighbors on a regular basis.

"No, I had not heard that." Ursula hated to indulge her, but she also wanted to stay up to date on the neighborhood news. Her mind immediately flashed to the young boy at the pool, working so hard to make his legs work like those of other children. If the child had grown up in Germany in the war years, he likely would have been put in an institution. If he were old enough, he'd be sent to the Cripple Guard then surely killed at the front.

"I have to keep a close eye on my kids in the summer," Mrs. Ohlin said, watching her daughter lean over to pick up her pebble. "They are saying we need to expect another outbreak. I can't imagine Jean or Henry being ill."

"Yes, it would be devastating." She sat next to Mrs. Ohlin, then looked around. "Where is Henry?"

"He's inside, still sleeping," Mrs. Ohlin said, then looked at Ursula's feet. "Where are your shoes?"

"I left them at my house," Ursula said, pointing at her sandals. "I love the feel of the grass in my toes."

"You had better be careful. You don't know where you could get polio. I heard adults are getting it more now, too. And here I thought I only had to worry about Jean and Henry!" Mrs. Ohlin cast her eyes up and down the street as if expecting to see the virus sneaking around a corner.

"Mrs. Ohlin, I'm hardly going to get polio going barefoot." Ursula shook her head.

"But you must stay away from the pools. I know you like to swim, but people are catching it at the pool." Her voice grew louder.

"You cannot believe everything you hear, and even if more adults are catching it, the disease mostly affects children." Ursula did not feel particularly concerned and was still swimming at the indoor pool a few times a week. Though, now that she thought about it, the pool had been surprisingly deserted lately.

"That's how they say Ruth's little girl got it. From the pool! She's at the hospital now. Poor girl. Her life will never be the same," Mrs. Ohlin said.

"Mrs. Ohlin, swimming in pools does not cause polio, you have to come in contact with someone who has the disease. It transports through water, but the pools are treated to make them safe for swimming." Ursula was sure of her facts as she had read a story in the *Star* explaining the disease. After a lifetime of guarding against propaganda, she knew better than to be influenced by neighborhood gossip or public scaremongering. Besides, she wanted to keep swimming.

"Suit yourself. I told Jean and Henry they aren't allowed to swim this summer, and they are managing just fine without it." She nodded briskly, as if confirming the rightness of her decision.

"Where did you hear all of this, anyway?" Ursula asked.

"Some of the women at church were talking about it today," Mrs. Ohlin said.

Just more gossip, then, Ursula thought. "You shouldn't believe everything you hear," she said. "I'll bring you my newspaper so you can read the article I saw." She looked at Jean, who was humming to herself while drawing a second set of lines over her first hopscotch grid. She was also starting to turn pink. "It would be hard for Jean and Henry to go a whole summer without the pool."

"I just tell them it's for their own good, so they don't get polio. And you're obviously not my child, but I worry about you, too. You really should stay out of the pool."

Ursula nodded but remained silent. She and Mrs. Ohlin sat quietly, watching Jean. The little girl had given up on hopscotch and started skipping rope. Every three to four jumps the rope would catch on her feet. She was determined and would start again, twirling the rope, catching it at her feet, pausing, and then repeating the steps again.

"Look, Mom, I'm jumping rope!" Jean beamed, her face now red and glistening with sweat.

"Very good, Jean. Keep practicing."

"She loves it," Ursula said. She was glad to see Jean having fun, but still thought a cool pool would make her even happier.

"I better get going," Ursula said, and stood up. "Roger and I are off for a swim in Crystal Lake. I've never been before."

"Remember what I said about polio," Mrs. Ohlin said. "Lakes could be just as bad as pools."

"Of course," Ursula said then started toward her own house. As she walked, she couldn't keep herself from muttering under her breath. "Read the paper, Mrs. Ohlin. It's all just rumors."

"Did you say something, Ursula?"

"No, no, I was trying to remember my grocery list. Have a good afternoon." Ursula slipped inside her front door, allowing it to slam behind her.

Later that day, Roger was stretched out next to Ursula on his back, a magazine open across his chest.

"I could lie here all afternoon," Roger said.

Around them, Fairview Park was crowded with people on picnic blankets thrown under shady oak trees. It was mostly couples. A few families dotted the scene, but it seemed most mothers were keeping their children home like Mrs. Ohlin.

"Roger, do you think we should be worried about polio?" Ursula rolled onto her side. They had gone to their favorite beach at Crystal Lake but it was closed because of an outbreak.

"Naw. It happens every summer," Roger said, closing his eyes against the sun. "Parents are the ones who have to worry. I just wish they would keep the beaches open for adults."

"But I've heard of adults getting sick too." Ursula grasped long blades of grass in her fingers and pressed them together. "Mrs. Ohlin said . . ."

"You know she's just full of gossip, I don't know why you pay any attention to that woman. It's best to avoid her." Roger lifted the magazine as if he might actually read it, but didn't.

"I still don't understand why Mrs. Ohlin gets under your skin," Ursula said. "If being nosy is the worst thing about her then she's no different from the women in my neighborhood where I grew up."

Roger slid the magazine from his chest and rolled to face Ursula, "I think all her poking into our business is more than just being nosy." He looked at Ursula, and she could see something churning behind his eyes. Something he didn't want to tell her.

"What is it, Roger?"

He sighed heavily. "Well, it's not really important, but she's a cousin of my ex-fiancé."

"What!" Ursula sat up. "Don't you think you could have shared that with me sooner?"

"I've warned you about her." Now Roger looked smug, which irritated Ursula even more.

"You warned me? You think she reports back to someone, that she's some kind of spy? By all accounts, that woman Felicity"—Ursula had a hard time even saying her name—"has moved on and so should you."

Ursula stood up and plodded up the crest of the hill in the heat. She needed to see the city. From her perch at the top a breeze tangled in her hair, then Roger's voice shot up the hill.

"Ursula."

She stood quiet, just wanting to be alone. But Roger kept talking.

"I'm sorry. I should have said something. The Twin Cities may seem big, but everyone knows someone who knows someone."

Ursula froze. She wasn't worried about Felicity. She truly thought the woman had moved on, and they should, too. But the idea of gossip introduced a new worry into her mind. She still hadn't told Roger about her visit with Dr. Hunt. Did someone who knew someone know Dr. Hunt? Would Roger find out she had been to see her through the Twin Cities gossip mill? She tried to reassure herself. *People aren't like that here. This isn't Berlin during the war. Your visit with Dr. Hunt is private.* She took a few steps toward the bench behind her, the place in the city she always came to think. She slumped down and tilted her head toward the sky.

"Are you all right?" Roger sat down next to Ursula. She felt his eyes on her face but did not answer. If she told him now about Dr. Hunt, it might ruin what, until a few minutes ago, had been a pleasant afternoon. But if he found out from a stranger, she was doomed. He would be livid.

"Ursula, what has gotten into you today?"

She lifted her neck from its awkward angle and straightened her spine to face Roger. "I need to tell you something."

A grin erupted on Roger's face. "Are you?"

"No, I'm not pregnant." Ursula flicked a finger against Roger's chest. She loved that this was his instant thought, that he was thinking about their future as a family.

"Oh." The sun had gone behind the only cloud in the sky and Roger reflexively took off his sunglasses.

"But, I did go see a specialist doctor, one who might help us."

"A specialist?"

"Someone who knows how to help women who are having trouble getting pregnant."

"You didn't think to tell me? I would have liked to be there." Roger leaned toward her, eager to hear more.

"The doctor is a woman," Ursula said.

"What does that have to do with anything? Just tell me what she said."

Ursula was surprised at how interested he was, but she told him everything she remembered. She explained the potential blocked tubes, the special test that could unblock, even Dr. Hunt's instructions to relax. Her words dried up, though, when she remembered the doctor's comments about male infertility.

"And, there's one more thing."

"What is it?"

"Men can have infertility problems too."

Roger stared at her for a beat, then chuckled. "That is the darndest thing I've heard in the longest time!" He stood up, shaking his head. His hands were on his hips, the tortoise shell glasses dangling from his left hand.

"It isn't something to laugh about. Dr. Hunt said—"

"Who is this woman anyway?" Roger stopped laughing. A shadow crossed his face.

"Roger! She can help me, she can help us! I cannot go on like this. Each month I hope and hope and then nothing. How is a woman my age incapable of having a child?" Ursula put her head in her hands. She wanted to scream, but didn't want to draw attention.

"Then we'll keep trying," he said. "You've been working too hard anyway. I think you should quit like other sensible women do."

"Quit? And how will I ever see my family again? We've talked about this."

Behind them, the park was emptying, the shadows longer on the ground. The scent of grilled burgers wafted up the hill.

"I promised my mother I would stop by," Roger said. "She needs help changing a few light bulbs."

"But we're not done talking about this."

"There's nothing more to talk about."

"Roger!"

"I'll see you back at the house for dinner." A few quick strides had Roger down the hill. He stopped and grabbed the magazine off the picnic blanket and curled it in his right palm. Ursula looked back at the skyline. Maybe she should have kept the appointment with Dr. Hunt to herself.

CHAPTER 14
November 1949

With fewer citizenship classes for Ursula to enroll in, she asked for more shifts at Brown and Bigelow and her workload grew to five days a week. On Tuesdays and Thursdays after morning classes, she went directly to the office. The long days centered her mind and kept her from thinking too much about the struggle to get pregnant. Ursula knew Roger was still upset that she had gone to see Dr. Hunt. And now every week at work it seemed like a secretary got pregnant and quit to take care of her family. The few expectant mothers who wanted to stay until the baby arrived were coaxed into leaving by Dot, the office manager.

"It's best for your health if you go home to your family and get ready for the baby," Ursula had once overheard her say. Dot was a widow whose husband was killed during the war. She had no children and Ursula wondered if Dot was lonely. The woman wasn't mean, just cool and matter of fact. She did not participate in the office gossip or even lunch with the secretaries in the break room. Dot walked the floor, silently checking on their work, and was otherwise holed up in her office. The men in the print shop, their hands covered in ink, kept to themselves. The management—men in suits—thundered into their phones, paced their windowed offices, and smoked until clouds rose from the gaps at the bottom of their doors, an eerie masculine fog.

"Ursula, can you stay for an extra hour tonight? Eleanor left this morning and had unfinished work." Dot dropped handwritten letters in need of transcribing next to Ursula's typewriter. With a long breath, Ursula took the pages in her hands and watched Dot walk back to her office.

Ursula smoothed the frizzed hair near her face, then took the page off the top of the stack and started typing. She was tired. It was Thursday and she was ready to go home. She worried Roger would be irritated with her for staying late again. It was one thing to work more days and keep regular hours, but she was testing his patience. Ursula needed Roger on her side, needed him in his best mood. Next week she would have to see Mrs. Gorski at Thanksgiving, a holiday that still seemed strange to her. Ursula generally avoided her mother-in-law and was nervous about the dinner, but she knew she would have to endure as she did at all holidays: quietly and politely. At least Roger's brother and his family would be there. Unfortunately, Rose was going to have dinner with her daughters and, without Rose around, Ursula was almost defenseless. Rose was her anti-aircraft gun against Mrs. Gorski.

Ursula exhaled and re-focused on the loopy handwriting in front of her. *Is that a "b" or a "d"? And is that one an "a" or a "u"?* Whoever belonged to this handwriting had a habit of ambiguous letters. When she finally left for the evening at 6:30, Dot was still in her office on a phone call. She put her hand up to say goodnight as Ursula left.

Ursula had won over Dot because she was a hard worker. And even though winning over one difficult woman gave her hope, it still did not make her feel any better about Thanksgiving. Winning over her mother-in-law was an insurmountable challenge.

Ursula and Sally stood on the back stoop of Mrs. Gorski's house on Thanksgiving Day. The last time Ursula had seen her sister-in-law was at a Fourth of July picnic at Crystal Lake. Sally smoked while her kids, Elizabeth and Chris, played in the snow. Chris rolled snowballs and lobbed them at Elizabeth. For a moment Ursula wanted to join them. Maybe their energy and enthusiasm would sustain her through dinner with Mrs. Gorski.

"You know I miss that house on Colfax sometimes," Sally said. "We had good years there. So many memories. Painting the nursery before Chris was born. Putting up the tree for our first Christmas as a family." Sally slowly blew out a stream of smoke. "But when I was pregnant with Elizabeth, I knew we would be bursting at the seams. Our house takes me twice as long to clean, but the children have their own rooms." Ursula was always surprised by her sister-in-law's easy demeanor. She wished she could possess a few ounces of whatever Sally had that she didn't. Including her ability to have children.

"I suppose it must be nice. At least the kids do not have to share," Ursula said. She rubbed her hands together in the cold.

"I was hoping I would see you rounded and glowing by now," Sally said, surveying Ursula and taking another drag on her cigarette. "I thought maybe because we started our family there, you and Roger would do the same."

"Yes, well we are having a difficult time of it," Ursula said. She had an urge to share more with Sally, let it all spill out. But she held back all the intimate details of her life with Sally. She didn't know how much Sally talked with their husbands' mother, and she did not need Mrs. Gorski meddling in her life. Besides, would Sally even understand the predicament she was in? Sally seemed to have no problem having children. Ursula half expected Sally to start bragging about how she would fill another bedroom in her large house.

"Roger said you're working more hours? Maybe that's not helping?" Sally trained her eyes on her children. "Chris! Stop! Play nicely with your sister!" Chris had thrown a snowball at Elizabeth's face. She cried for a moment but dug her hands into the snow to form another ball and fight back.

"At least the work keeps me from being idle." Ursula rubbed her hands together again. She'd left her gloves inside. It was mild, but the air was damp. She suspected there was more snow on the way and shivered. Sally's questions made her nervous.

"And you're still taking your citizenship classes?" Sally did not wait for Ursula to respond. "And a home economics course, too, I hear. I would love to learn how to manage my house better. Look at those two wild kids. When Pete gets home, they act like such angels, but, boy, they're a handful." Sally shouted for Chris and Elizabeth to come in, then pressed the cigarette into the stoop, extinguished it with a twist of her boot, and kicked it into the snow. Ursula wondered how long it would take before Mrs. Gorski noticed the butts littering her backyard.

Inside, the house smelled of turkey, buttery potatoes, and sage stuffing. A mold of cherry Jell-O wiggled on the kitchen table as Mrs. Gorski walked to and from the dining room, setting out platters. The smells reminded Ursula of her first Thanksgiving with Roger not long after they had met in Berlin. He had invited her to the American base, and it was the first substantial meal she'd had in years. Rations were just that—rations. The empty feeling in her stomach had become normal, but growing accustomed to it was impossible. That Thanksgiving meal with Roger, a few other soldiers, and German women had given her hope and nourishment. If she stuck by Roger, she wouldn't starve. Today, while she wished for peace, she would settle for Mrs. Gorski being cordial.

Roger led grace, then heads lifted, and eager hands passed full dishes clockwise around the table. Roger stood to slice the modest turkey, its skin had browned and glistened. As his hands carefully cut away slices, steam rose in the air around his proud face. Ursula grinned, as if she was in an American movie come to life. The Thanksgiving she fondly remembered at the American base had only been a glimpse of what the holiday could be like at home with family. Ursula flashed her eyes at Roger who smiled, then quickly looked down as he cut the last slice. He put small slices on Chris's and Elizabeth's plates so they could go to a kids' table in the kitchen, then started the platter around the table.

"I know I say this every Thanksgiving now, but I'm grateful you're both home," Mrs. Gorski said, beaming at her sons. Ursula wasn't surprised to see her blink back tears. Holidays brought out the sentimentality in her mother-in-law. "I dreamed of the day when we would all be home around this table again. And, here we are. Many families will never be the same."

"I was at the Legion earlier this week and ran into a few guys who just got home. They told me it's still bad over there," Pete said as he lifted a slice of white meat onto his plate. "But who knows, it could be hearsay—you just never know these days."

Roger nodded but was concentrating on ladling gravy onto his mashed potatoes. Ursula hoped it was hearsay; she could not bear the thought of her family facing another crisis.

"I heard with the east and west split up, families are being torn apart! Some of the ladies at the beauty salon were talking about it," Sally said. She stopped eating for a moment, then sighed: "How awful for those people."

Ursula's chest tightened. They were talking about her family.

"We need to stay focused on building a democracy across Europe. Without it, we won't be able to fight the communists," Roger said. He gave Ursula a reassuring look. He had been there and seen the despair. He understood how bad it was. The tension in her shoulders softened.

"That's right, America needs to push democracy in Europe. We can't let the Soviets gain even more influence in the region. We need to show our power and strength." Pete crossed his arms over his chest.

Roger jumped in, his voice as strong as his brother's. "Pete's right, if we stand back and do nothing, the Soviets will continue to cause problems. Look what happened with the blockade last year—they blocked the roads and railways, the people in Berlin were starving and America looked weak."

Ursula wanted to speak up. This was her country they were talking about! But she was afraid of making the conversation even worse. She had been working so hard to avoid any difficulties with Mrs. Gorski.

Within moments, though, Ursula realized her mother-in-law did not feel the same. She jumped into the conversation, her voice as loud as her sons'. "Well, I don't think they deserve any of it! After everything America did, after all those lives lost. We should let the Soviets have the lot of them." Mrs. Gorski let out an angry huff. "To hell with Germany."

Sally gasped and looked at Ursula. The table came to a standstill, with forks hanging mid-air, bowls frozen in hands, and glasses halfway to lips. And as quickly as they froze, gravity brought what was meant to be a festive activity onto the table with a thud.

"Mom, that's not charitable of you. We can't abandon them," Pete said, his face earnest.

Ursula's shoulders tightened again. She was thankful for Roger and Pete, they understood. She wanted to say something and defend her family, but her words were trapped by shock.

"Why not? They deserve it for what they've done." Mrs. Gorski cut into the turkey on her plate. Everyone else had stopped eating.

"All those futures lost, those poor young GIs. At least my sons made it out safely."

"Mrs. Gorksi," Ursula hesitated. She wanted to steady her voice, but she could no longer contain her frustration. "You're talking about my family. My mom, dad, and aunt. My friends, too."

"Oh, you can just be quiet," Mrs. Gorski said, looking at Ursula as if she couldn't understand how this German woman had landed at her American table. "Roger never should have brought you here. He should have left you there with the rest of them!"

"Mom, take that back and apologize to Ursula," Roger said. He was furious and slammed his hands against the table.

"I will not," Mrs. Gorski said. A strange, self-satisfied quiet settled over her as she scowled at Ursula.

Ursula's body stung. She wondered how long Mrs. Gorski had wanted to say those nasty words to her face. She could have shared her feelings in private, but she had chosen to say them in front of the whole family. If Rose had been here, maybe Mrs. Gorski would have kept her opinions to herself.

"Mom, how do you think we're going to fight the communists?" Pete asked.

Ursula guessed Mrs. Gorski cared very little about logic.

"Pete's right. We need them," Roger said. Roger mouthed, "I need you" to Ursula. This time she did not feel assured like before. She bit her lip to hold back tears.

"Please excuse me," Ursula said. She stood abruptly, rushed up the stairs on her wobbly legs, and locked herself in the bathroom. In the privacy of the small space, she leaned against the sink and cried as she took the carnation pendant between her thumb and index finger.

A soft knock landed on the door.

"She didn't mean it. She's just upset," Roger said from the other side.

"What she said is unforgivable," Ursula said.

"She thought we would die over there."

"Well you didn't, you came home. And she does not need to treat me this way." Ursula balled up the tissue in her fist and tossed it into the wastebasket.

"Come back and finish dinner. I know how much you like stuffing. Remember how good it was at our first Thanksgiving?" His voice coaxed.

"I cannot go back to that table," Ursula said, dabbing her eyes with a fresh tissue.

"You can. I'll be right beside you," Roger said.

"Your mother humiliated me in front of your whole family," Ursula said. The makeup she had applied that morning had dissolved into dark streaks on her face. She turned on the cold tap and let the water run over her palms, then she splashed it over her face. She mouthed, "you're a tough German girl" to herself in the mirror, then dried her hands on the pink flowered towel and knitted stray hairs into place.

"I know. It wasn't right or fair," Roger said. The hinges rattled as he leaned against the door. "Come out, Ursula, I don't want to have Thanksgiving dinner without you."

"All right, but if she starts again, I'm going home."

Ursula twisted the lock and opened the door, ending her own personal blockade. Then she took a deep breath and remembered who she was. The more Ursula was forced to march and sing with the League of German Girls, the more resentful she became. She didn't like anyone telling her what she could or could not do, what she could or could not think. Not then, and not now. She no longer wanted to fear her own voice.

"That's my girl, the tough broad I fell in love with in Berlin. Come here," Roger said, pulling Ursula into a tight embrace. "We don't want to waste all of this good food."

Ursula silently followed Roger downstairs to the table. Mrs. Gorski managed a stubborn sideways glance, but did not apologize. Sally mouthed "I'm sorry" from across the table and Pete shook his head in embarrassment.

Ursula wondered how a Catholic woman could be so cruel. The woman she observed praying in church, those beads threading through her hands. The woman who brought meals to homebound parishioners on Sunday afternoons. The woman who wanted baby blankets for mothers in need. *What was all that piety for? Could she not share that compassion with the people in Berlin too? With her own daughter-in-law?*

Ursula had wanted to belong in this family to lessen her heartache. But now, as she placed a hand against her chest, a rapid thump echoed against her palm. Maybe Mrs. Gorski and her mother were right. Maybe she should have stayed in Berlin.

There were many times when Ursula wished she had spoken up, rebelled more, and resisted. Instead, she most often retreated inside herself to dream of another life. She was filled with guilt for her silence, but everyone she knew had done the same. Did that make it right? *No, but what could one person do?*

"Mrs. Gorski." Ursula pushed a piece of turkey onto her fork, then stopped and looked the old woman in the eyes. "I'm sorry this is so upsetting for you, but I am not leaving. Minneapolis is my home now, and we'll have to learn to share it."

PART II

CHAPTER 15
Late August 1950

Ursula lay in bed, half covered by a sheet patterned with pink roses. During the night, she had swept the coverlet to the floor with a restless arm. Ursula and Roger had made love the night before, and now the sheets were strewn around her legs. Since the conversation at Fairview Park the summer before, Roger had compensated for any doubt about their ability to get pregnant by initiating sex a few times a week. At first, as Roger's energy rose, Ursula's did too. She was more connected to him, and the bond between them grew. But, over time, constantly trying for a baby struck enjoyment from the act. To Ursula, it was as if Roger was trying to prove Dr. Hunt wrong. She also wanted to prove the doctor wrong, prove that they had just needed more time. But after so many years of barrenness, she had begun to lose hope of ever getting pregnant.

But this morning, she realized her cycle was late by five days. The thought that she might actually be pregnant made her giddy. They could finally stop their arguments about the topic. Sex could be about desire, not duty. And Ursula could forgive herself, forgive her body for its betrayal.

"Roger, I don't feel well," Ursula said and groaned. Sweat ran down her back. The hope she had was interrupted by an intense throbbing in her head. Temperatures were holding steady in the 90s, cresting to over 100 in the afternoon. She had been lethargic for a few days, with stomach cramps and a backache.

"It's probably this awful heat and humidity. If you hurry, I'll drop you off at the office. I have a piece of furniture to pick up in St. Paul," Roger said, wiping his forehead with a handkerchief. "And I think they might talk to me about a promotion today."

"Hmm. That's good," Ursula said, but didn't process what he was saying. She was trying to decide if she should tell Roger that maybe all of their effort worked.

"Remember, I mentioned it in July after I took in another client for them?"

"I think so." Ursula dragged her body out of bed. Her mind was foggy, but clear enough to decide not to tell Roger her period was late. No sense getting his hopes as high as hers were. In the bathroom, she found the bottle of pills in the medicine cabinet and shook an aspirin into her hand. A quick gulp of water from the faucet sent the white tablet down her throat. She splashed cool water on her face then donned her lightest summer dress, but the fabric was heavy and oppressive. The lightest touch against her skin chafed, and her copper-colored hair plastered on her neck.

When she arrived at the office, Dot had opened all the windows. The humid air was oppressive, and every electric fan was switched on high in an attempt to improve circulation. The day before, a secretary had fainted and been sent home. Corners of papers fluttered like flocks of geese. Anything that could become a paperweight—staplers, coffee mugs, coin purses—kept the white sheets from flying about the room. The women pinned their hair off their necks and dabbed sweat from their bare faces. It was too hot to wear makeup. The men abandoned their suit coats and wore short sleeves.

In the office kitchen, Ursula filled a glass full of water and walked back to her desk, waving at Dot, who calmly made notes on a piece of paper in her office. Ursula managed to transcribe a few letters, but her vision blurred for a moment. She was dizzy. Woozy. More water might help, Ursula thought, but her glass was already empty. When she stood up, her legs were unsteady and she held the edge of her desk to support herself. She slowly moved toward the kitchen for more water, but suddenly her knees buckled and she crumpled to the floor. She heard women frantically calling her name, asking if she was okay. Ursula could only mumble.

"Step aside, girls," Dot said. "Ursula, can you hear me? Let's get you upright." Dot, with the help of the other secretaries, moved Ursula so she was firmly propped against the side of a desk. Her back cooled against the metal with her legs limp in front of her. She opened her eyes. Someone put a glass of water in her hand and she took a gulp.

"I just fainted because of the heat. I'll be okay. I can get back to work," Ursula said to reassure Dot. No need for her boss to think she couldn't do her job. But she needed to reassure herself more. She could not understand why her legs were heavy, like the thick stacks of paper on her desk.

"I don't know how they expect us to work in this weather!" Ursula heard one of the secretaries say.

"If you think you're going to be ill, you should go home," Dot said to everyone, and motioned for another glass of water.

A hush fell over the room then was replaced by rustling paper and the clattering typewriter keys. No one wanted to challenge Dot.

"I'm going to be okay. I think I can get up," Ursula said, but her back still ached and the headache from earlier pierced. The aspirin she'd taken hadn't made a bit of difference.

"Let me help you." Dot offered Ursula an arm. With one hand on the floor and one hand firmly gripping Dot's arm, Ursula tried to stand up. But when she put weight on her legs, she collapsed again. Someone nearby gasped.

"Oh gosh, I don't know what's come over me," Ursula said. She leaned her head back against the metal, perspiration beaded on her forehead. She was a fool for being giddy this morning, for any hope of being pregnant. Her late cycle wouldn't cause her legs to collapse beneath her. No, there was something wrong.

"I'm calling the rescue squad. We need to get you to a doctor," Dot said and rushed to her office.

"I'll be all right," Ursula called after her, one last attempt to reassure herself and everyone around her. Her heart pounded like someone banging on a door. If she was stuck in the hospital, she would lose her job. Dot had no problem finding new secretaries to replace the ones who left, even for a few days. Ursula needed this money, it was her lifeline to her family in Germany. And whatever was happening to her didn't make sense. Her legs wouldn't be weak from a summer flu. Her thighs and calves ached like she had sprinted laps across the pool, an effort that always gave her a smoldering burn. But that burn was familiar, a buildup of strength, not the opposite. She reached for the trashcan to her left, brought it as close as she could to her face, and threw up.

In a small examination room at Twin Cities General Hospital, a doctor hunched in front of Ursula. His white coat so stark Ursula squinted against its brightness as she read the name embroidered on the chest. Dr. Anderson. His glasses sat crooked on his nose as he took Ursula's pulse, blood pressure, and checked her reflexes. Her legs did not respond to the thump he made on each knee. Through the pounding in her head, she sensed she needed her legs to move, that their lack of response was a sign of something terrible, but trying to understand why was like pushing through mud.

"What's wrong with me?" Ursula pressed the words from her lips.

"Just a moment, Mrs. Gorski." Dr. Anderson looked into Ursula's ears and eyes, his breath a combination of cigarettes and spearmint chewing gum. Ursula craned her jaw to the side and coughed. He took her temperature, and when he pulled the thermometer out of her mouth, he shook his head and muttered. "A hundred and two." Then he pressed his lips together in a stern line.

Ursula's senses narrowed in an attempt to focus, thinking only of her muttered temperature. That was a high fever. Something was wrong. Something was eating away at her body.

"Why didn't my legs move when you tapped them?"

"Mrs. Gorski, I have to ask you some personal questions."

"Why can't you tell me about my legs. They should move. Why aren't they moving?" This seemed like a simple question to Ursula. He should answer it.

"I need you to answer a few questions first. Could you tell me when was your last menstrual cycle?" He'd taken a clipboard from a nearby counter and had pen poised over paper.

Ursula stiffened when she heard the question. "Doctor, I am not pregnant." She hated the sound of the words out loud, a reminder of a milestone she could not seem to reach. She wished Dr. Hunt were here, a doctor who would listen, and understand her better.

"We need to eliminate all possibilities."

"Last month," Ursula said from a foot above her body. She was hovering outside herself, unable to connect to the feeling of paralysis that wound through her legs.

"I see. Have you been vomiting? How is your head? And where do you feel your aches and pains?" The questions poured out of his mouth. He pushed his glasses up on his nose as he waited for Ursula to respond.

Ursula could not get her brain to articulate answers. Her heart pounded again. The thump rang in her ears.

"Mrs. Gorski, please try to answer my questions."

"I've had a backache and cramps in my stomach all week. My legs are weak, and my neck is stiff." Ursula clasped her right palm on her neck. The touch of her own damp hand repulsed her, but it brought her back from where she'd been hovering above herself. Back to her body.

Before Dot had left the hospital, she had promised to contact Roger. He still hadn't arrived, and Ursula wished he was beside her.

"Can you touch your chin to your chest?" Dr. Anderson asked.

"I think so," Ursula said. She continued rubbing her palm against the back of her neck as if she could coax her chin downward, but it remained suspended above her collarbone, above the damp circles that had formed under her arms.

The doctor placed the clipboard back on the counter, then crossed his arms over his chest. "I'm afraid the symptoms you are having are signs of polio. But of course, there are other illness that have similar symptoms like meningitis or the flu."

"Polio?"

"Yes Mrs. Gorski, I'm sorry."

"But it's a disease . . . for children." Ursula blinked, trying to push back both confusion and pain.

"Adults get infected with polio too," Dr. Anderson said, as if he had heard this objection before. "We can perform a spinal tap to confirm." He unclasped his arms and took up his clipboard again, burying his eyes in his notes.

"I don't know what that means," Ursula said in German, then repeated herself in English. He finally looked up from his scribbles.

"It's a simple procedure that will give a definitive diagnosis."

"Maybe I have a flu? Like you said." Ursula floated again, inches from her frozen body.

"The symptoms are all very similar, but the weakness in your legs and the fact that you cannot touch your chin to your chest concern me."

Ursula opened her mouth to say something, anything, but the words evaporated with a surge of pain across her forehead. It curled and fell like a violent wave. A woosh echoed in her ears. She rubbed a damp palm above her eyes.

"Mrs. Gorski, are you listening?"

An anxious "yes" left her mouth.

"I'm going to prepare the spinal tap. I'll return in a moment."

Dr. Anderson left the room. The clunk of his methodic steps striding away was like a hammer against Ursula's head.

Once those footfalls faded, all was quiet. But then Ursula heard the distinct sound of Roger's voice—the calm inflection in his baritone washed over her. She tried to sit up and angle her body toward the door to make out the words, but she was too weak. It was as if she had been cut in half at the waist, her legs useless.

Soon, Dr. Anderson returned in a surgical mask and protective garments, a similarly-dressed nurse at his side. They looked like eerie life-size paper dolls, a horror come to life.

"Where is my husband? I need to see my husband!" The rasp in her voice unnerved Ursula even more. Sweat on her chest darkened the fabric of her dress, making it nearly transparent. From her reclined position, she muscled her arms over her breasts in attempt to hide them, modesty slashing through the mud in her brain.

"We need to conduct the spinal tap now, Mrs. Gorski," he said.

"But Roger, I want to see Roger," Ursula said, her voice weak but insistent.

"Dear, you can see him for a moment after we finish this procedure, but first I need to help you into this gown," the nurse said.

Dr. Anderson stayed in the room as the nurse maneuvered Ursula's weak limbs from her dress, unhooked her bra, and tugged her underwear away from her body. A child being undressed. Ursula wanted to scream at the doctor, tell him to get out. Let her have some dignity. The nurse helped Ursula into a fetal position, placing her legs tight against her chest. Ursula felt even more like a child, but the surging pain in her forehead kept her from saying anything.

"This will be quick and painless." The doctor positioned himself behind Ursula. The rattling of instruments on a metal tray splayed her nerves. Then, without warning, a pounding, as if a stake were being driven into her spine. Ursula yelped. The nurse's paper gown brushed against her face, and she grabbed a handful and bit down to keep the brutish noise inside her.

"Mrs. Gorski, we're finished now." The nurse coaxed the damp paper from Ursula's mouth. "You'll be able to see your husband in a moment." The doctor had already left the room. The pain from the puncture in her back was now radiating outward. Her body had transformed into a pin cushion—thousands of pricks pressed into her skin. *Where are the pins? How many needles had they used?* Breathless and disoriented, Ursula shuddered, which only heightened the piercing sensation.

A light knock on the door revealed another life-size paper doll in front of her. It was Roger.

"I came as soon as I got the call. I nearly ran someone off the road I was driving so fast." Roger was breathless. "Then I argued my way in here—they weren't going to let me through, said something about getting infected. They made me put on these." He motioned helplessly at the gown.

"I'm so glad you're here," Ursula said, her voice shaky. "You look odd wrapped in paper."

Roger chuckled, but it sounded forced. He walked closer, as if he was going to take Ursula's hand in his. "I'm here now. Everything is going to be okay."

"You can't get too close," Ursula said, suddenly thinking of Roger becoming ill. She pressed her eyes closed. Tears came without warning.

"Before they let me come in here, the doctor explained the situation." Roger looked down. The paper gown crinkled as he shifted from side to side.

"Polio. They told me that I might have polio," Ursula said, but the words sounded like they were coming out of someone else's mouth.

"But they haven't confirmed it. It could be a bad flu."

"But what if it isn't?"

Then, they waited, and Ursula and Roger worked through every possibility, every ailment she had over the last week, every cough and ache. It had to be something else. Finally, an hour later, feet shuffled outside the door and a nurse in protective garments entered the room.

"Your time is up, Mr. Gorski. We need to move your wife to the isolation unit," the nurse said.

And then the nurse stepped aside as Dr. Anderson came into the room. He glanced at Roger, then looked directly at Ursula. "Mrs. Gorski, I can confirm that you have poliomyelitis, more commonly known as polio."

Ursula froze, staring at the unsmiling, unblinking doctor.

"You are certain? Could it be something else?" Roger said.

She eyed Roger, thankful his voice worked, thankful he could speak on her behalf.

"I am certain. The spinal tap confirmed what I suspected." Dr.

Anderson now directed his comments to Roger, who was clenching and unclenching his jaw.

"Are there more tests you can run?" Ursula's voice returned. There had to be something else they could do. How could she go from looking forward to a weekend stroll with Roger at Fairview Park to lying in this bed with legs that wouldn't move? How could a few hours change her plans so quickly, in such a paramount way?

"You will be going into the isolation unit of the hospital to recover and until we can be sure you will not infect anyone. We will continue monitoring your condition to see where your muscles develop rigidity." Dr. Anderson's voice was serious. "We need to pay close attention to the effects of the disease over the next few weeks."

Before Ursula could ask any more questions, he left the room.

"How can this be? I don't understand what's happening to me." Ursula's body shook from the sobs.

"Mr. Gorski, I need you to step outside now," the nurse said. Roger gave a fearful nod to Ursula and crinkled away.

"My name is Betty," the nurse said, once Roger had left. "I'm going to help get you ready for moving to the isolation ward." She seemed nicer than she had been when the doctor was in the room. Ursula wanted to trust her. Be comforted by her. "I need whatever jewelry you have. And, I'm afraid your clothes will be burned. They have been contaminated. We cannot risk infecting others."

"Burn my dress? Everything?"

"Yes, everything, dear."

"But what about my wedding ring?" Ursula gazed at her hand. The thought of throwing away her wedding ring heaved another sob from her gut. It was being ripped away like everything she had lost during the war.

"I'll sterilize your ring and give it to Mr. Gorski," Nurse Betty said. She took it gently and placed it in a metal dish. "And I'll need that necklace, too."

With shaking arms, Ursula tried to unclasp her mother's necklace with the silver carnation pendant, "I can't."

Nurse Betty unlocked the chain from Ursula's neck, letting her hand linger briefly on her shoulder. "We do our best with these sentimental items. Now let me help you onto the gurney. You are being transferred to the polio unit."

Flat on her back on the gurney, Ursula's feet were bare. Exposed, achy, and depleted, she tried to move her legs against the weight of paralysis. How similar her legs had felt in the pool when she let them drop, the pressure of the water holding them down. How similar to the lifeless legs of that little boy whose mother pulled him through the water. *How could I have been so stupid? How could I have let this happen to me?*

Stark light bore down on Ursula as the gurney was pushed through the whitewashed hallway. Roger fixed himself to Ursula's side until they arrived at two doors. Ursula traced her eyes over Roger's face. His own eyes were watery with tears.

"I love you," Roger said. He looked like he was about to reach for Ursula's hand but stopped, the disease an invisible barrier.

"I love you, too," Ursula said, her voice a whimper. The memory of being separated from Roger after he had left Berlin hit her like a wave. She trembled as the gurney was pushed through the swinging double doors. And then Roger was gone, on the other side of the barrier separating the healthy from the afflicted.

On the afflicted side of those doors, doctors and nurses in white masks and gowns moved with speed and purpose. Patients mostly lay quiet, but sometimes moaned or cried out. The swish of machines called iron lungs provided an eerie rhythm to the commotion. From her bed against the wall opposite the machines, Ursula put her hand over her chest to feel her heartbeat. She could hardly look at the iron lungs. There was something about the futuristic metal tubes that seemed militant to Ursula. They controlled the people placed inside, held them at the cusp of life and death.

The nurses had settled Ursula between a young woman with the longest blond hair Ursula had ever seen and a man in his thirties, who despite being cloaked in a hospital gown looked stout and strong. The heat of the day had given way to a cooler evening, but this was the only comfort Ursula had had over the last twenty-four hours. The spasms in her legs were relentless. The pain reminded her of the feeling she had as a girl, when her bones and muscles length-ened, reaching toward adulthood. Except this pain was magnified a hundred times over. Between the spasms, Ursula directed her right leg to move. It stayed still. She tried her left leg. Nothing. Her legs were there, she could see them, but they no longer felt like her own. She tried again, willing her thoughts to translate into movement. Adrenaline surged. Fear spread. This loop played for hours until she begged one of the nurses to give her something that would make her sleep and to take away the fear and pain. But the nurses sped by, attending to other patients, other cries of pain. Pain that was appar-ently more urgent than hers.

At some point, Ursula finally fell asleep thinking about Roger. He had been so reassuring, so calming, when Dr. Anderson gave them her diagnosis. She drifted off wishing he could be with her now. But sleep didn't last, as Ursula jerked awake as another patient feverishly called for a nurse.

"I hate the sounds of those machines," the young woman next to her said. "And I don't know how you fell asleep. I cannot sleep with all these people yelling."

"Mmm." Ursula pressed her lips together. If she closed her eyes and focused on the whoosh of the machines, she was taken back to the rush of the creek she played in as a child. With her eyes open, she knew there was nothing innocent about the iron lungs.

"I thought I would be home by now," the young woman said.

"How long have you been here?" Ursula didn't want to talk, but she needed this information. The doctors had been vague about how long she'd be hospitalized. "We'll need to see how you progress" was all they said.

"I've been in this awful place nearly two weeks! They said I would be able to go home soon, but I don't believe them." The young woman rolled her eyes.

"Miss Rachel, you will go home when the doctors decide you will go home," a nurse said, stopping at the end of their beds. "For now, though, we'll need to do our next round of hot packs."

The nurse pointed to a contraption in the corner of the room. To Ursula, it looked like a cauldron from a Grimms' fairy tale and the nurse, a character come to life. Her crooked nose, small eyes, and thin face inspired a new wave of nervous tension in Ursula's chest.

"Oh gosh, the hot packs! I hate them." Rachel threw her head back into her pillow. Then she tried to raise her arms, perhaps to cross them over her chest, but they barely rose above the sheets. She let out a deep wail.

The wail triggered a spasm in Ursula that rose from her toes to her hips. Her legs jolted against the mattress. She clenched her jaw against the surge. Then a wave of repulsion broke over her. *How could I have become so pitiful? Do I look as helpless as Rachel?*

"Miss Rachel, this is my first and last warning—grow up! I don't have time for your complaints."

The nurse brought the cauldron to their beds. Ursula swallowed in fear, but her throat was dry and she coughed. All around her, nurses were frustrated by the constant requests of their patients—a glass of water, to be turned, to relieve themselves. Uninvited helplessness hung in the room. When her bladder filled would they come to help her? She would prefer dehydration to sitting in her own urine.

"What are hot packs?" Ursula pushed aside the disgust, the idea of soiling herself like a baby. This hot treatment—whatever it was—would have to be better than a bed dirty with excrement.

"You'll see," Rachel huffed. "I don't want to spoil it for you."

"Miss Rachel, do I need to warn you again?" The thin-faced nurse created a muzzle with her tone. Ursula clenched her jaw again, fearing she might lash out. She was angry now, but knew she had better keep her opinions to herself. She worried the next time she needed something—food, a drink of water, to relieve herself—she would be ignored.

"Mrs. Gorski, this treatment will help treat the muscle spasms."

Ursula grimaced. She didn't like yet another person telling her what to do, but she pushed aside her irritation. She needed to get better and maybe this treatment would help.

She examined the contraption at the foot of the bed. It was a metal tub with a wringer attached to the top, similar to the wringer-washer Ursula had at home. It emitted moist air that somehow compounded the awful fairy tale sensation from Ursula's childhood. But if this hot pack treatment could calm the muscle spasms, she would endure it. With a practiced motion, the thin-faced nurse plunged two wool blankets into the hot water with sturdy tongs, careful not to burn herself. Once the wool was soaked, she ran one piece and then another

through the wringer attached to the side of the tank. She placed a
length of steaming wool across each of Ursula's legs, and the heat and
the weight of the blankets set them on fire. She made fists with her
hands, and tried not to scream.

Spasms, hot blankets, spasms, hot blankets, a cruel undoing of
her mobility and a relentless undoing of her mind. Ursula wanted to
see Roger. Even to hear his voice would have been enough, but family
members were not allowed to visit. Ursula wanted to walk out of the
hospital into Roger's arms, as if the past twenty-four hours were just
a nightmare. She wanted to return to the life she was making. Start
her family, have the life she dreamed of when she came to America.

Through her first week in the isolation unit, Ursula was dogged
by disturbing and lucid dreams. In one, she wandered through her
empty childhood house, her parents nowhere to be found. In another,
she arrived in America, only to be turned away and sent home, back
to crumbled Berlin. The dreams gathered her anxiety, and sent her
mind spinning, her legs spasming. The moment the spasms subsided
she swore to herself she would not be able to endure another wave.
But then she did.

At the end of the second week when the spasms dissipated, the
wreckage of polio revealed itself. One leg was partially paralyzed. The
other was even worse.

As the polio transport vehicle pulled up a long drive surrounded
by lush mature oak trees, Ursula glimpsed the upper floors of The
Riverwood Polio Hospital. This would be her new, temporary home.
From her supine position on the gurney, her eyes lingered on the
vines crawling up the white stone façade, the tendrils clinging to any
piece of the stone on which they could find purchase.

Dr. Anderson had given Ursula the "all clear" to leave the isolation unit at the general hospital but explained extensive treatment and rehabilitation would be needed if she were to, even in the best case, walk again. A backache had led her to all this. It seemed impossible. The word "cripple" crossed her mind and she shuddered. She wasn't stupid. She had seen how children with polio were treated, how the mother at the pool looked embarrassed by her son's disease. If children were treated poorly, adults might suffer even more humiliation.

Roger had followed in his truck, which had a reupholstered sofa tied down in the back. When they drove around a bend in the road following the Mississippi river, Ursula glimpsed the aquamarine fabric in her periphery vision. The bright blue reminded her of the water at Lake Harriet, and the clear sky from the hill at Fairview Park. Would she ever again enjoy these comforts from her former life?

Now at her new home's entrance, the team wheeled Ursula into the crisp autumn morning. Still supine, she closed her eyes and breathed in through her nostrils, the air's freshness like a bath.

"I'm so glad you're out of that hospital. I've been—we've all been—so worried about you." Roger clasped Ursula's hands in his, his fingers warm and solid.

"Me too." While Ursula had been confined in the isolation unit, she had yearned to see him but also lived in the fear that when she did, he would only be able to see her illness. But now, this fear was blotted by the comfort of Roger's touch.

"They are going to help you get better here," Roger said as he let go of Ursula's hands and waved toward the building.

The medical technicians wheeled Ursula up a ramp to the entrance. From her angled position, Ursula noticed the worried look on Roger's brow, the one she assumed he'd worn since she was diagnosed. But compared to that day, his eyes were now calm and a smile remained steady on his face.

Inside at the reception desk, Roger handled intake forms while a nurse helped Ursula into a wheelchair. She introduced herself as Nurse Ballard, head of the women's wing. Ursula rested her arms against the cold metal arms of the chair. Her legs, while immovable, were freezing. The gown she had been transported in nearly exposed Ursula, the fabric thin and white. She wanted privacy after the isolation unit had taken away her humanity. Suddenly she was back in G-Tower in Berlin, right before the war ended. Sleeping on shared cots. Rationing showers to once a week. No privacy or the simplest of creature comforts.

"I can't stay here," Ursula said, the Berlin memory so strong it controlled her. "I want to go home, be in my own bed, eat in my own kitchen, bathe in my own bathroom."

"Mr. Gorski, could you come here please? Your wife is quite distressed," Nurse Ballard said, taking a few steps back.

Roger knelt down next to Ursula and rested a palm on her arm. "Ursula, you have to stay here. You're going to get better here."

"Take me home," Ursula said, covering his hand with hers. "Please take me home."

"Ursula, they'll help you here, they'll work on your legs, help you walk again. This is one of the best polio hospitals in the country." He sounded like the information sheet they'd given her a few days before. "You are lucky to have this care, this chance at getting better with the help of everyone here."

"But how many days? How many days did they say it would take?" If she had a specific number of days, she could mark her calendar and work toward her release.

"They didn't say."

"It wasn't on the forms, the papers you signed?" The possibility that her legs would take weeks, maybe even months to work again sent terror upward from Ursula's stomach. The fear lodged in her throat at the idea that she might never regain mobility.

"No, I'm afraid not," Roger said. He stood up and slung his hands in his pockets. "I can ask."

For the last two weeks she had been at the mercy of the isolation unit staff who were vague about what she could expect from the treatments and her ability to regain mobility in her legs. It suddenly occurred to Ursula that maybe the Riverwood doctors didn't know either.

"I'm sorry to interrupt." An erect woman Ursula somehow knew to be the one in charge—Superintendent Erickson—appeared at their sides. "Mrs. Gorski, I suggest you make a list of items you'd like to have with you during your stay. This should include clothing, shoes, books, any tools for hobbies like needle point or knitting. Oh, and I wouldn't include anything of much value because we cannot be responsible for those items." She held out a clipboard. "And also shoes that offer stability, that are good for walking."

Ursula nodded and took the clipboard with its attached paper and pen in her hands. A list. This was something she could accomplish. In block letters, she wrote: two skirts, two blouses, three everyday dresses. She stopped when she got to undergarments and stockings. Picturing Roger rooting around in her intimate drawer made her flinch. She especially didn't want him to find Dr. Hunt's phone number tucked in the back under an old brassiere. She brought her left palm to rest over her abdomen. All of that was lost now, anyway. She pressed her eyes shut and the room darkened. She gripped the pen again, her knuckles white from force and resumed writing. Comb and toothbrush. Bag of knitting projects (check next to sofa). Wedding ring. Carnation pendant necklace.

"That's all I can think of now." Ursula removed the sheet from the clipboard and handed it to Roger who read through the items.

"Superintendent Eriksson said nothing of value," he said, his forehead wrinkling. "I can understand why you want your ring, but, do you really need the necklace?"

"You know how much it means to me." With the pendant against her collarbone, she would have the strength to write to her mother about her life-changing news.

"I know, I know, I would just hate to see it go missing." The list fluttered in Roger's hand.

"I am not planning on taking it off. Just like I won't be taking off my ring."

Nurse Ballard appeared between them again, all officialness and efficiency. "We need to get Mrs. Gorski settled in her room. I don't want her to miss the afternoon treatments."

Roger folded the list in his palm and knelt again beside Ursula. "My bride, this is goodbye for now, but I'll stop by later with your things."

"You never call me that."

"What?"

"'My bride.'"

"Well, that's who you are, aren't you?" Roger grinned.

"I wish you could stay a bit longer."

"I'll be here on Sunday during family visiting hours."

"I love you," Ursula said, but the words caught in her throat. Tears streamed down her face.

"I love you," Roger said, kissing Ursula. He lingered for a moment drying her tears with his handkerchief. Then, he righted himself, tugged his suit coat into place, and left. Away to the life they had created together. Ursula held her eyes on the door while Nurse Ballard planted Ursula's feet on the metal rests of the wheelchair. Then she rested a gentle hand on her shoulder, an acknowledgement of Ursula's despair.

"Wait, I need to tell Roger something," Ursula said, grasping the wheels and pulling herself across the lobby. Nurse Ballard was close behind, and held open the large wooden door. From her perch on the landing, Roger's solid frame wavered on the driveway in front of Ursula. Ursula suspected he was crying. She recognized the tremble in his shoulders from the happy tears he'd shed the day they were married.

"Roger, Roger!" Ursula's voice reverberated within her chest.

He stopped mid-step and swung his head over his shoulder. She wanted to tell him not to forget about what they were working toward. That she would work hard so she could come home soon, that she could still be a good wife and hopefully a mother someday. But it was all too much to process, so instead she said: "Please don't forget to take Vic for walks. He loves going to our park where you can see the skyline."

"Don't worry, Ursula. He'll get plenty of walks. And you'll be home in no time! You'll be able to take him back there, too."

Ursula lifted her hand into a lifeless wave as Roger got into his truck and drove away.

CHAPTER 16
September 1950

As the elevator rose, Nurse Ballard told Ursula about the layout of the hospital. Women in the west wing and men in the east. The children had their beds downstairs in the large, windowed nursery. Ursula caught glimpses through side windows as she was wheeled down the hall. She saw old oaks enveloped in blankets of grass. Nurse Ballard continued with her introduction by telling her how the dense forest obscured the Mississippi River at the back of the hospital but they could still hear the river after a rainstorm.

"This is your room, Mrs. Gorski."

On one wall, two windows overlooked the hospital entrance and Ursula could see the curved U-shaped drive, the arch a path of possibility and change. The other two windows faced west to the old trees, lush green with hints of yellow. Two wood-framed beds shared the same wall as the door with a call button above each. Ursula admired the flowered curtain panels over the windows, cheery but not overdone. A narrow table on wheels stretched over the end of each bed. Ursula had seen books and potted plants set on top as they wheeled by rooms with open doors. She would be able to write letters from bed if she remembered to ask Roger for stationery and a pen. Each patient also had a wooden arm chair for reading. Ursula thought the space was well organized and to her surprise, well decorated. She had expected the Riverwood Polio Hospital to be more like the isolation unit she had come from—cold and intimidating. But this place was homey.

In the bed farthest from the windows a woman sat upright reading a book. Neat mahogany waves framed her face and touched her shoulders. A dash of lipstick reddened her round lips. Ursula had not thought to ask Roger to bring her lipstick and compact. She lifted a palm to her unadorned face and her eyes welled up again. *You are a tough German girl.* She lowered her hand into her lap and forced a smile.

"You're going to need this," the woman in bed said, an eager kindness on her face. She took a handkerchief from her pocket.

The nurse passed the white square to Ursula. Ursula nodded in thanks and pressed the soft fabric against her puffed cheeks. The cotton smelled of lavender, like her childhood living room. Delicate white flowers were embroidered along the edges. Ursula wondered if the woman had done the needle work herself, if this woman was as handy with thread as Ursula was with yarn.

The nurse helped Ursula into bed and brought it to an angle so she was upright.

"You can keep that," the woman said, after nurse Ballard left, gesturing to the handkerchief.

"I couldn't do that, miss, or ma'am." Ursula said, correcting herself after seeing a wedding ring on the woman's finger. She seemed just as kind as Minnesotans were promised to be, and when they exchanged names, the woman insisted Ursula call her by her first name. Phyllis. Ursula said her own name in the most American accent she could muster. She did not have the energy to explain her background, get into her history. At least not today.

"I cried my first day, too. I dampened enough handkerchiefs to send them to the laundry in the basement," Phyllis said. "And when I saw that bed empty, it only made it worse. I thought I would have someone to talk to in here. Needless to say, it has been a lonely few weeks."

"The isolation unit where I came from wasn't much better."

"Which one?"

"Twin Cities General."

"I was there too. What an awful place. Well, I'm glad you're here now. And what a unique name. You don't hear it that often. Ursula. Is that—?"

"German. I, it's a German name," Ursula said. She traced the embroidered flowers with her fingers to hide her anxiousness.

"My great-great-grandmother was from Germany. Don't remember where." Phyllis narrowed her eyes in thought, then shook her head. "But have you ever been to New Ulm? It's south of the Twin Cities. With a name like that, you'd fit right in."

Ursula thought she recognized the name of the town but did not know anything about it.

"Germans settled there years ago," Phyllis said. "For a long time they only spoke German."

"How do you know that?" Ursula tilted her head. Her curiosity grew with each new piece of information Phyllis revealed, as did her gratitude for Phyllis not seeming to care that Ursula was German.

"Family stories. But that was many years ago before my relatives sold off their farm and moved to the city. My grandmother's family if I'm remembering correctly," Phyllis said. She closed her book like she wanted to settle into a long conversation. Then she took a close look at Ursula. "I'm sorry, you must be exhausted. My husband says I could talk the leg off a wooden horse."

"Yes, I am tired," Ursula said. "I think I need to take a nap," She would have more than enough time to get to know Phyllis over the coming days and weeks. Her mind stopped at "months," unable to confront the notion she might have to stay here that long.

"You better do it quick because our afternoon therapy starts soon. They'll wake you up if you're sleeping. They run a tight schedule." Phyllis sighed, then laughed.

"Why are you laughing?"

"Oh, one afternoon I was sound asleep, and they tried waking me up, but it took them a minute. I was having a dream that I was walking around the grounds of the hospital. When I woke up, I told them I didn't need to go to therapy, that I could walk," Phyllis said, playfulness on her face as if she had outwitted the doctors. Ursula pictured Phyllis walking and guessed she was tall, and if they stood side-by-side, Phyllis would tower next to Ursula. She reminded Ursula of an American actress from a Hollywood film.

"I admire your cheerfulness."

"If I don't laugh, I cry," Phyllis said, her voice rueful. "Besides, the staff is helpful here. They want us to get better. We're going to walk again. You'll see."

"I hope so," Ursula said. She let her eyes close and drifted off to sleep.

Soon she was rustled awake by a rush of activity in the hallway. She heard voices of patients, nurses and doctors all mixed together. It must be time to begin afternoon treatments.

"How long you're in here is entirely up to you," Dr. Johnson said. He had introduced himself and now stood between the beds, his tall, slender frame like a turret as he explained what Ursula could expect. "What I mean is that we will work with your legs—do everything we can to help you get strong. But, and this is a big but, sometimes there is an element of will. You need to want to get better just as much as we will help you do that."

Ursula rubbed her eyes, still pulling herself up from sleep. "When I was admitted, they wouldn't give me an answer about how long I might be here. Can you tell me now?"

"It is, I admit, an individual experience. Each person comes here with a different level of paralysis. Much of your recovery depends on how you progress through therapy, and how your legs respond to the treatment." Dr. Johnson tapped his fingers against Ursula's bare foot as if he were testing her.

Ursula wanted to pull away. She even thought for a second that her toes had curled back from his touch. But they were lifeless, like the toes of a doll. The doctor continued his pep talk, but Ursula's attention was on her foot, how angry it made her to have no control over her limbs.

"Do you have any questions Mrs. Gorski?" Dr. Johnson looked down at her, eyebrows raised.

Ursula shook her head no, but she had hundreds of questions. Questions she'd been obsessing over for the past two weeks but had been too scared to voice. She couldn't stand the possibility of those cruel nurses in the isolation unit informing her she'd never be able to walk again. Never be a good wife to Roger, become a mother, or fly home to see her family.

"Well, if that's it, we'll get started on the hot packs. And don't go anywhere, the nurse will be here shortly," Dr. Johnson said.

"You caught me Dr. Johnson," Phyllis said, rolling her eyes at Dr. Johnson's back as it left the room. "I had planned to walk out of here at this very moment."

"That would be astonishing, but excellent progress," Dr. Johnson said over his shoulder.

Ursula wanted to laugh but was too exhausted. All she could think about was the timetable the doctor refused to give about going home.

Nurse Ballard soon was in the room, methodically wrapping their legs in what Ursula now knew was called a "Sister Kenny hot pack," named after the Australian nurse who had developed the treatment. Even after two weeks of the treatment in the isolation unit, Ursula could not understand how anyone grew accustomed to the searing heat. Her legs still felt like they were being cooked in an oven. But Phyllis managed to look calm as the blankets were placed. It astonished Ursula.

"I know these work, but how much longer?" Ursula unclenched her jaw. It had slammed shut when the boiled wool hit her legs.

"Ten more minutes," the nurse said over steam as she wheeled the cauldron into the hallway.

Ursula turned her head to Phyllis, whose face was placid. "I thought I'd left these blankets behind in the isolation unit," she grumbled.

Dr. Johnson had stuck his head in the doorway to check on their progress. "You'll become more accustomed to it, and once your legs are loose enouugh, you won't need the hot blankets anymore. Just think, every treatment is one treatment closer to going home." Then he was gone again, his steps echoed in the hallway.

"He's full of encouragement," Ursula said, surprised to find herself feeling less tense.

"He tries to keep our spirits up." Phyllis shifted under the weight of the blankets. "I can't fault him for that."

But if Ursula was honest, she did not want to talk about walking or not walking, hot blankets, therapy—any of it. Outside, what looked like a discharged patient rose from a wheelchair and was met by a man and two young children. Ursula wished she were the one walking out, straight into Roger's arms.

"Mrs. Sundberg and Mrs. Gorski, we must reapply the hot packs," said Ms. Ballard who announced herself with a gentle knock. "I know these blankets scald your skin—I'm sorry—but your muscles need to relax to prepare them for therapy."

Nurse Ballard lifted the cooled blankets from Phyllis's legs, helped her move to her stomach, then carefully placed newly steamed blankets over her calves. Then she returned to the tank, ran the second blanket through the wringer and replaced Ursula's, as well. Ursula took in a deep, frustrated breath. The steam from the hot wool permeated the sheets, walls, and fogged the windows.

"I'll be back once these have cooled, but please press the call button if you need anything in the meantime."

"Does this get any easier, Nurse Ballard?"

"I'm afraid not." She pressed her lips into a half smile and wheeled the water tank out of the room, taking some of the heat with her.

"It reminds me of coming inside on a freezing day in the winter. Everything tingles and hurts, but at some point, I lose track of whether I'm too cold or too hot. It's as if there is no temperature at all, only pain," Phyllis said.

"I know what you mean," Ursula said and grimaced. "What has the doctor said about your legs? Are they getting better."

"My muscles are getting a bit more flexible. But I'll tell you, when Nurse Ballard bends my legs nearly to my chest, I want to scream. It feels worse than having a baby, but at least with that, it was over after a day or two."

"I want to believe exercises will help," Ursula said. She flinched at Phyllis's remark about childbirth.

"During the worst of the pain I try to think about other things. Like my son's laugh or how my daughter likes to run across the grass barefoot. They have so much joy. It helps me forget about hot blankets."

"They sound like nice children," Ursula said.

"You'll get to meet them soon. Robert and the children come to the chapel for church on Sunday, and then they stay for family visiting hours. Will you join us for church?"

"No, thank you, but I would love to meet your family." Ursula had no intention of going to church on Sunday if she didn't have to.

"I would love for you to meet them, too." Phyllis reached for the book on her nightstand.

The wool had lost some of its heat, becoming heavy and soggy again. Ursula wished Nurse Ballard would return to take the blankets off. She wished she and Phyllis could be two women chatting over coffee at a kitchen table, not stuck in a hospital facing the unfathomable turn their lives had taken. None of this was fair. None of it. And no one—not a single one of the doctors she had seen—could tell her how long it would take for her to return to some version of her old life. To let the soles of her feet touch the floor and move effortlessly from the kitchen to the table, from the dining room to the living room, to outside where the grass under her feet sprang upward to tickle her skin. As Ursula thought about all those steps, every movement she never thought about before, a piece of herself floated upward, disembodied. From the ceiling she wondered who was below her, that woman in bed with the unmovable legs.

Unease pumped through Ursula's body. A wild animal let loose inside. It was excruciating not having answers. During her first exam in the afternoon, she hoped she would finally learn more about her prognosis. America had offered her the promise of a new beginning, one without Nazis and communism. She could have a family in the land of freedom and democracy, just like the transformation portrayed in the American reeducation films. And now Ursula was again being transformed, but into whom she did not yet know.

* *

Later that afternoon, in Dr. Johnson's office on the first floor, Ursula listened carefully.

"Based on how your legs are behaving now, and what we've seen other patients accomplish, I think you'll regain mobility," Dr. Johnson said. He tapped his pen on the chart on the desk in front of him.

"But how? I can't move them—they are there, but they aren't there." Ursula pressed her palms against her thighs, her skin tingling under the cotton of her dress. Even the fabric seemed composed of fibers making miniscule scratches along her shins, over her knees, and around her upper legs.

"You'll work with a physical therapist—Miss Miller has been assigned to you. She will help you to stretch your legs, to loosen those muscles. Once you've made enough progress, you will learn to stand first, then take steps with the parallel bars."

"How long will this take?"

"I wish I could give you a clear answer, but I can't." Dr. Johnson tented his fingers on the desk and gave her a serious look. "For most patients, it takes months."

"Months?"

"Yes, Mrs. Gorski, months. Now if you'll excuse me, I have to get to my next patient. Keep your chin up. You're in the best polio rehabilitation hospital in the Twin Cities."

"But—" She was trying to exist in this new body, where she was constantly uncomfortable. Weeks she could maybe manage, but months?

"Like I said, chin up." Dr. Johnson stood up and left the room, leaving Ursula alone for a moment before another voice was at the door.

"Mrs. Gorski, I'll take you back up to your room now to start our first muscle reeducation session."

It could only be Miss Miller, her physical therapist.

"Reeducation session?" Ursula had only heard the term in the context of denazification.

"That's a strange term, I know," Miss Miller said. Then, as she pushed Ursula's wheelchair across the lobby to the elevator, she explained she was a Sister Kenny–trained therapist, and part of the initial therapy involved methodically moving, lifting, and stretching polio-affected limbs. "We'll complete this part of your therapy in your room. Then, in a few weeks, we'll move to the therapy room."

Ursula thought about all she had read about Sister Kenny in the newspaper. She'd been impressed by this woman who had come all the way from Australia to share her innovative polio treatment methods, controversial as they were. Ursula never expected she would be on the receiving end of these treatments.

Once back in her room, Miss Miller helped Ursula onto her bed, and slowly raised Ursula's right leg so her toes shot upward to the ceiling. Ursula scrunched her eyes closed against the tension.

"I want you to push against me, as if you're trying to force my hand down to the bed."

"I can't," Ursula said, willing her leg downward against the nurse's strong grip but the strength had evaporated, stolen by the virus.

"Can you feel the tension in your muscles?" Miss Miller asked Ursula.

"Yes, it hurts," Ursula said. She held her breath for a moment and then let out a loud exhale.

"If you can feel pain, then you can try to push against my hand." Miss Miller repositioned her hand.

"I am trying," Ursula said and scrunched her eyes closed again to pour all her energy into moving her leg. To her surprise, her leg responded with a tiny movement.

Miss Miller cheered then did a small two step. Ursula burst into a huge joyful laugh.

"I cannot believe it."

"This is excellent work," Miss Miller said. "Sometimes that step takes patients a few weeks."

"Really? So, this is very good?"

"Yes, very good. Now we're going to repeat that movement a few more times and then we'll try again on the left side," Miss Miller said and once again placed her hands in position.

Ursula's leg responded again, and this time she didn't have to pour so much energy into the movement now that she knew how to engage the muscles. She marveled at Miss Miller's patience and her consistent and diligent approach. She marveled at herself, too. Maybe she actually had the power to change.

CHAPTER 17

The rehabilitation hospital maintained a strict schedule: breakfast at 7:00 a.m., followed by two rounds of hot blankets, then muscle reeducation, then lunch, then more hot blankets, then more muscle reeducation or occupational therapy. Life began at 3:30 p.m., when recreation was allowed before dinner. Some patients learned how to make jewelry in the basement classrooms, others like Ursula knitted and crocheted in the sunroom. The older men liked to play cards, especially poker. Television was only permitted after dinner for a few hours and for significant events. George Grimm, a columnist from the *Star*, often visited and entertained patients with stories. Every few months, Nurse Ballard told Ursula, there was a band on Saturday night, or guest performers from the opera or orchestra.

The first week at Riverwood had gone by faster than Ursula expected as she adapted to the rhythms of the hospital. When Roger had dropped off her things, she had asked Superintendent Erickson if he could stay a bit longer and she had agreed. They had sat in the garden, holding hands across the arm of the wheelchair, her legs covered with a blanket. She told Roger it was to stay warm in the cool September evening but it was mostly about keeping them hidden. With legs out of sight, she had the illusion of an evening on her favorite bench at Fairview Park, overlooking the city that had promised her opportunity. On that evening, she had asked if any letters had arrived from home, but none had. She could wait a while longer before writing to her mother, then. Roger had been uncharacteristically chatty. Glyde Snyder wanted more work done on his furniture. Aunt Rose sent her regards and would try to visit soon. His nervous cadences of news seemed designed to avoid talking about what was in front of them both. Her legs beneath the blanket.

A small radio on Phyllis's nightstand was switched on when Ursula returned from the first-floor therapy room. Ursula had moved from muscle stretching in bed to the room with more equipment, and Miss Miller said they might be ready to work on standing soon. Between the left and right legs being circled as if she were riding a bike, Ursula had spent the session thinking about that evening with Roger. She wished she had interrupted his nervous chatter and said more, but what was there to say? She was still trying to understand what was happening to her, let alone figure out a way to explain all of her fears to Roger.

Phyllis sat up in bed with a book, but she had closed it when the 4 p.m. news came on. Ursula listened to the announcer. "Stiffening United Nations forces Friday halted the five-day offensive of 80,000 Korean Reds on the north front. The United Nations security council Thursday refused to condemn American bombing practices in Korea."

The war news unsettled Ursula. "Phyllis, would you mind turning that off?" If she didn't have to listen, she wouldn't.

"Can I finish listening to the headlines?"

Ursula let out a deep breath. Phyllis's request was reasonable. How could she know how deeply unsettling any news of war was for Ursula, how easily the terror of Berlin might bubble to the surface?

Phyllis rotated the dial, and the voices faded. She adjusted her head so she was looking at Ursula, "How was the extra time with your husband this week?"

"Wonderful. I wish they allowed visitors more often, even if only for an hour in the evenings during the week."

"I had asked them about that during my first week here, but Superintendent Erickson said we need to focus on our therapy."

"I agree with her, but that hour with Roger has kept my spirits up all week."

"I passed by the window and saw both of you sitting out there. What a lovely couple you two make!"

"I do think of us as quite handsome together." Ursula blushed.

"I'm sorry for being so nosy, but I'm dying to know how you two met."

Ursula liked Phyllis, the way she probed out of curiosity, not a need of gossip like Mrs. Ohlin. If they were going to be stuck in the same room for weeks or months, Ursula thought it best they got to know each other. She cleared her throat.

"Roger was stationed in Berlin. I was looking for work and heard German women were able to get work from the Americans, so I went to the base and he was the first person I spoke to." She paused, thinking about that first conversation. "He promised to help me find a job, but then he asked if I would come to a dance at the base."

"And you obviously said yes!"

"I was hesitant at first because you never knew what these GIs wanted." Phyllis looked confused, so Ursula explained. "They all did not have Roger's moral character."

"I suppose I never thought about that," Phyllis said, scrunching up her nose.

"Roger said he would do everything he could to bring me to America. At first, I didn't believe him, but then we sorted out the paperwork, he bought my airplane tickets, and well, here I am," Ursula said.

"What a romantic story," Phyllis said, her face soft and open. "My husband and I were high school sweethearts. I played violin in the school orchestra, and he played cello. During rehearsals, I'd stare across the room, hoping he wouldn't catch me looking."

"Did he catch you?"

"Obviously, he did, but that was kind of the point." Phyllis opened her eyes wide. "After our spring concert senior year, he asked me on a date. That was after the bombing of Pearl Harbor, when all the boys wanted to join up, and he decided on the Air Force. He didn't see any action. He's an engineer, worked on airplane runway surfaces. And now with the war over he works for the Minnesota Department of Highways. Cars instead of planes."

"That's a very romantic story, too," Ursula said. She loved the idea of falling in love across stringed instruments. It seemed American somehow, like a musical. "Do you still play together? In the orchestra?"

"Oh gosh no. We stopped playing in the orchestra after we finished school. We were both eager to start our family," Phyllis said, her arms lifted to pretend play the violin, then shifted to make the shape of cradling a baby.

"You have a perfect life." Ursula stared at her legs. She tried to move them under the blanket, but after the week of muscle re-education they were limp with fatigue. She knew Phyllis's legs were little different, but at least Phyllis was already a mother. There was some perfection in that.

"Do you have any children?" Phyllis asked.

The question hit Ursula's chest like shrapnel. She wished she could better prepare for this question—she knew it had been coming—but it shook her every time anyone asked her.

"No, no I do not."

"I'm sorry."

"Me too."

Phyllis lowered her voice, "It's not your fault you know. Not any of it. There are plenty of women who suffer from not having children. And there are so many people—adults!—who have fallen ill with polio. Just look around our ward. But I do believe we have a responsibility to get better. We have to for our own sakes. For our family's sakes."

"What if it is our fault?" The words slipped out of Ursula's mouth, and she wasn't sure if she was talking about her childlessness or polio. Maybe both? She reached for the pendant at her neck, and pressed her index finger into the sculpted edges of the petals. If she had listened to her mother and stayed in Berlin . . . but no. It was pointless to think about a different life. A life in Germany. A life where her legs still worked. But if she had convinced Roger to see Dr. Hunt, maybe they would have had a child by now. So many lives not lived.

"We are here now. Our only duty is to get better. I don't know about you, but I'm walking out of this hospital on my legs. On my healthy legs."

"You sound like Dr. Johnson. Has he really gotten inside your head already?" Ursula said.

"I've been here nearly three weeks. And of course, he's in my head. He better get inside your head soon. It's the only way we're going to get better."

CHAPTER 18
Late September 1950

Ursula settled in the library after afternoon exercises. Most days, they left her exhausted, but today she was alert enough to read instead of taking a nap. She had decided against knitting because though the clicking needles kept her hands busy, her mind went all over. She dug into all the questions she still couldn't answer. How long would it take to finally walk again? How was her family doing? The previous Sunday Roger had forgotten to bring a letter that had arrived from Ursula's mother, and now all she could think about was how her family was faring in the East, now controlled by the Soviets. Ursula wondered about how Aunt Kaethe was coping. If her aunt could get through an attack by Russian soldiers, surely Ursula could find the courage to move forward with her rehabilitation.

She grabbed the newspaper from an end table and rolled up to the window where the light was better. Headlines jumped from above the fold, beckoning her, but all Ursula could think about was her therapy session. Today she had managed to stand with the support of parallel bars, but her legs were untrustworthy beneath her and she sank into her chair, unable to balance. It seemed the wheelchair assigned to her—the rubber and metal stuck together to aid her mobility—was the only thing she could depend on.

Ursula unfurled the newspaper, hoping to get lost in other people's problems for a moment. A cramp spread across her lower belly, and into her upper thighs. At first Ursula paid no attention to it—cramps appeared often now, in her calves, thighs, and legs. Often in her lower back or her sides, too. She straightened the papers in her hands. They were testing the polio vaccine on monkeys. She thought about the monkeys in the Berlin Zoo. When she had visited once before the worst of the air raids, they had babbled at her in the trees. She knew most of them had died from bombs and later starvation. And now, they were being used to combat this awful disease.

She flipped the page, but the cramp stung this time, a stabbing twitch. *No, no, no, no.* Her period. She had forgotten about her period. *What was the point of having a period at all if?* Ursula dared herself to say it: "if I cannot have children . . ." She still could not bring herself to ask Dr. Johnson what he thought, if he considered her progress strong enough to eventually try again for a child.

Ursula threw the paper onto the nearest table. She needed a nurse, a nurse she trusted—Nurse Ballard. She pushed her wheelchair to outside the library where patients crowded the hallway. Afternoon therapy was over and recreation had begun. A trickle, then a warm dampness. Ursula rolled faster, scanning the corridor. Each time she saw a person in a white uniform it was someone else.

"Mrs. Gorski," a voice said over her shoulder, "I've been looking for you. There's a telephone call. You can take it in my office." Superintendent Eriksson motioned for Ursula to follow.

Ursula was surprised. She wondered if it was Roger, with terrible timing. She guessed she had a few more minutes before the blood soaked into her dress. Where was Nurse Ballard?

Superintendent Eriksson's small office sat behind the lobby. The phone was off the hook, the receiver waiting on top of a stack of medical files on her desk. Before Ursula reached for it, she asked Superintendent Eriksson if Nurse Ballard was still at work.

"I'm afraid she's gone home for the day. Is there something I can help you with?"

"No, nothing. I can speak to her tomorrow." Another trickle. She needed this phone call to end quickly.

"Mrs. Ursula?" a familiar voice asked.

"Murphy, is that you?" Only one person she knew called her Mrs. Ursula, it was Murphy, her government teacher from citizenship classes.

"I heard you had some bad luck." Somehow, coming from Murphy, "bad luck" sounded nice, like she wasn't indefinitely stuck in a hospital. Like she wasn't paralyzed.

"How did you know I was here?" She wound the black phone cord around her left hand, nervous. She had forgotten about her citizenship classes in all of the chaos of the past month. Ursula was delighted he noticed she was absent from class. A wave of optimism came over her. It was a signal from her old life, before the hospitals, before the diagnosis, before she collapsed at work. Before her period demanded urgent attention.

"Word gets around. Anyway, I thought I'd drop your books off so you can continue your studies. I don't want you to fall behind. I know how much citizenship means to you."

"Gosh, you don't need to do that."

"It really isn't a bother."

"Are you certain?" Ursula didn't want to be a burden to Murphy. Her citizenship could wait until she was released from Riverwood.

"I am certain, and this will give you a nice distraction I imagine."

Ursula nodded in agreement even though Murphy couldn't see her. She heard him adjust the phone against his ear. "Murphy, that's very generous of you."

"It's no bother, Mrs. Ursula. I'll drop them off later this week," Murphy said, his voice warm.

"But I have to get permission from the hospital superintendent, they only allow visitors on Sunday," Ursula said.

"I've already spoken to her, and she says it's no problem. Be well." Murphy hung up.

The receiver fell from Ursula's hand. The dial tone rang loudly from the tiny speaker in her lap.

"Are you finished?" Mrs. Eriksson asked. She had been standing just outside the door.

"Yes." Ursula set the receiver back on the desk. Shame rippled on her face. "I think I do need that help after all—would you be able to call for a nurse?"

CHAPTER 19
October 1950

It was a Sunday, and Ursula, along with most of the adult patients in the hospital, gathered around the TV in the common room. Sister Kenney was scheduled to appear on *Meet the Press*. Because she had such fame in the Twin Cities and at Riverwood, Superintendent Eriksson had made an exception to allow them to turn on the TV. Even the nurses lingered, curious to hear from Sister Kenny.

"What do you think she's going to say?" Ursula asked Phyllis. It was the only question in the room.

"I haven't the slightest idea, but whatever it is, I know she'll have our interests in mind."

"Hmm."

From various articles she had read in the *Star*, Ursula learned about Sister Kenny's legend in bringing her ideas about polio treatment to the twin cities and the institute. Ursula counted herself lucky she lived in Minnesota. The hospital admitted patients from all backgrounds from across the country, and some polio survivors even flew in from around the world to receive treatment here.

On the TV, one of the program's moderators, Martha Rountree, cleared her throat and introduced Sister Kenny and the four male journalists. The room buzzed. The nurse had become a celebrity to the staff and patients. Even Ursula attributed what success she'd had to the Sister Kenny methods.

"Sister Kenny, you are one of the most controversial figures in medical history," Mrs. Rountree began.

Everyone in the room shifted in their seats. Phyllis's eyebrows went up. A patient near the TV turned up the volume. The journalists showered Sister Kenny with questions she easily answered. They asked her about why she did not submit case studies to physicians or medical journals, and Sister Kenny, always concerned about patients getting the best care, attacked some powers-that-be for policies she believed inhibited the patient from good outcomes. Toward the end of the interview, the other host asked, "People who know you say you are a difficult person. Are you?"

Ursula turned to Phyllis, who had covered her mouth in surprise. "How is she going to answer this?" Ursula mouthed.

Phyllis shrugged.

"I am most difficult in anything that concerns the health and well-being of the children of America and the world," Sister Kenny said.

The room erupted in applause, and Ursula could not hear the rest of Sister Kenny's answer. She beamed with pride, delighted to know such a fierce woman was on the side of polio survivors.

"If she's out there fighting for people like us, we can fight for ourselves in here," Ursula said to Phyllis after the applause subsided. "What an incredible force of a woman."

Motivated by Sister Kenny, Ursula worked harder in therapy that week. She was determined to get stronger and to regain her balance so she could walk on her own. In the therapy room, Ursula worried the carnation pendant at her neck with the fingers on her right hand.

She had seen her mother do the same thing when the air raid sirens sounded. The silver had softened in places, the once-scalloped petals now worn down by the traumas of war. If she remained in this place for months, the pendant would surely become smooth as a stone tossed in rapids.

"Ursula, please stay focused," Miss Miller said.

"Yes, sorry." Ursula dropped the carnation from her hand.

"All right, now, let's try this again. This time I want you to stand up, grab the parallel bars in front of you, and once you've gotten your balance, slowly let go of the bars, one hand at a time." Miss Miller demonstrated with her own hands.

"You want me to let go?"

"I do."

"But I'll fall."

"I'll be right here. Now let's give this a try."

Ursula scooted to the edge of her seat, pressed her palms against the armrests of her chair, settled her feet beneath her knees, but hesitated.

"I don't know . . ."

"Yes, that's it. You're set, now press upward."

"All right."

Ursula stood up, but the shock of being vertical made her sway. Her right ankle wobbled, and then she was back in her seat, Miss Miller helping her settle.

"Yes, very good. Rest for a moment, and we'll try again."

Ursula let out a deep breath. Nearly fifteen years ago, the same ankle had wobbled. The bread had flown upward, and then Ursula had landed on the ground, startled. Her ankle had taken on an impossible angle and pain snapped across her body. Her mother had asked her to pick up bread and her father had promised to bring her home a new book. On a spring day, with the invitation of summer in the air, how could she keep from skipping? With her mind on the book, and the sun's warmth on her skin, she hadn't seen the high curb. As fast as she could, Ursula had steadied into an upright position, putting weight on her left leg, but a gentle press down on her right foot summoned the pain again. Was it broken? Or only twisted? And then, the pain morphed into fear. What would her mother say? She was supposed to start camp soon, where she would learn to be a good German girl. With her absentmindedness, with her now weak body, could she even go? Her mother would be so angry. So ashamed.

"Shall we try this again?" Miss Miller was in front of Ursula.

"Yes." She brought her mind back to the therapy room. "That was a long time ago," she said.

"Did you say something?"

"No, nothing."

Ursula followed the steps—scoot to edge, palms on arm rests, feet planted—and soon she was upright again. This time she expected the swaying, and she gripped the bars in front with more force. She took a step forward, then willed her left leg to follow so she stood squarely between the bars.

"Excellent, this is wonderful. Now, try to let go."

"I don't know about that."

"Start with one hand."

"All right, I think I can . . ." Ursula gritted her teeth, prying her left palm from the bar.

"Okay, good. Now the other one."

"I don't think I can do this." Ursula's right ankle quavered beneath her, the high curb from all those years ago loomed in the therapy room. No, she could not give up. She would not shame her mother. She was a good German girl. Her right hand left the parallel bar.

"There you go." Miss Miller pulled a stopwatch from her skirt pocket and hit the start button.

Ursula could not believe it. After more than two months assuming her legs wouldn't recover, here she was on two feet, balancing without assistance.

"I'm standing!" Joy rippled around her, as she thought only of the book and the sun on her face from that childhood afternoon. But as quickly as the memory flashed, a switch flipped. Her hands gripped the bars to steady herself. She needed to sit down.

"That was fantastic, Ursula. Twelve seconds."

"It felt like much longer than twelve seconds."

"Next time we'll try for twenty seconds, maybe a half a minute." Miss Miller tucked the stopwatch back into her pocket and helped Ursula into her wheelchair. Then she made a note in Ursula's chart, a grin wide on her face. And for another moment, Ursula let the joy back in, the bright welcoming light an afront to the chaos of being undone.

Back in her room, while Phyllis was still at therapy, Ursula decided she had built up enough courage to write to her mother about her circumstances.

Dear Mother,

There is no other way to share this news, and so I will simply say it. At the end of August, I suffered an acute polio attack and was placed in an isolation unit for two weeks. It was an awful time there and I was very scared at the time, but now I am recovering at a wonderful rehabilitation center. If you can believe it, Minnesota is one of the best states in America for me to receive treatment in what is called the Sister Kenny method. I am lucky to be here. Has news of Sister

*Kenny reached Germany? She is nearly a celebrity in America
and cares deeply about polio survivors. My treatment is slow,
but I am getting stronger every day and hope to go home soon.
Give my love to Father and Aunt Kaethe.*

With love,

Ursula

Ursula set down the fountain pen and sighed. She left out so much,
but the more she included about the reality of her situation, the more
she feared her mother would worry. How was she meant to tell her
she may never walk again? That standing had been accomplished, but
walking still felt like a dream? And how would she tell her she may
never have children? That, because of polio, she may never make it
back to Berlin to visit? Ursula folded the letter, placed it in the envelope and sealed it shut. If only she could seal shut her fears as easily.

On October 10, a day before her twenty-sixth birthday, Ursula
rested in bed after physical therapy and wondered how she would
celebrate. She had asked Superintendent Eriksson to make an exception so Roger could take her out for lunch, but the superintendent
had said it was too dangerous for her to leave. That if she was hurt
outside of their care, Ursula would delay her recovery by weeks or
even months. Ursula had been hopeful, but she really wasn't surprised about the decision. Her legs still had precious little strength,
especially for hours of movement. If she fell, how would she get up?
Roger would have to lift her like a child. Besides, every movement
she made required acute attention. She willed her legs to follow her
thoughts, and by the end of each physical therapy session, her head
hurt just as much as her body.

Nevertheless, the notion of celebrating her twenty-sixth birthday in the hospital was absurd to Ursula. She liked her birthday because it was the one day she could shed a layer of self-doubt and suspend herself in contentedness on a day reserved for her. One day to mark the importance of her life.

Ursula and Phyllis had just finished their lunch and were about to have a celebratory birthday dessert when Superintendent Eriksson's heels clapped toward them on the hard dining room floor.

"Mrs. Gorski, there is someone here to see you."

"Hmm?" Ursula twisted in her seat. Could it be Roger? No, he had promised to visit after work.

"Come with me." Superintendent Eriksson's hands were on the back of Ursula's chair, ready to push.

"I can wheel myself," Ursula said. Then, before pressing her hands into the wheels to back up, she looked at Phyllis. "Don't wait for me, get yourself dessert." Phyllis nodded and gave Ursula the thumbs up, her mouth full of the last bite of her turkey sandwich.

Afternoon sun cast a small female figure in shadow. As Ursula rolled into the lobby, she knew who it was.

"Ursula, happy birthday!" Aunt Rose beamed.

"I wasn't expecting you, what a wonderful surprise." Ursula thought she might cry at Rose's kindness. Roger had been her only visitor since she was admitted over a month ago.

"Roger told me he's coming by after work, but I had to see you on your birthday. It's our tradition! And I've been thinking about you so much. How are you faring? Are they treating you well here?" Rose knelt down, kissed Ursula on the cheek and set a wrapped package in her lap.

"Aunt Rose, you did not have to bring me a gift." Ursula's voice broke a bit as she placed her hand over the flowered paper, a talisman from the outside world.

"Don't forget about the balloons," Rose said. From behind the corner the mail boy came with a fistful of pink and yellow helium balloons. "Please tie them to the back of her chair, I don't want them floating away." Aunt Rose supervised the tying, then looked back at Ursula when they were secured. "Now, I know we won't be able to have those delicious scrambled eggs from our favorite diner, but can we get a cup of coffee?"

"Follow me," Ursula said, as she wheeled herself along the corridor, Aunt Rose at her side and the balloons bouncing overhead.

"This isn't so bad—it looks new."

"It was an orphanage. They renovated the building for polio survivors. We're nearly there, the dining room is just up ahead."

When Ursula wheeled through the dining room doors, patients, nurses, and doctors burst into a joyful rendition of "Happy Birthday." As the song began, a member of the kitchen staff walked toward her with a white frosted cake lit with twenty-six candles.

"Make a wish," Aunt Rose said. Ursula closed her eyes and thought about her family, then wished for a baby. Maybe it was an impossible wish to have, but Ursula did not care. A long puff of air extinguished every single candle and the room erupted in applause.

"Are you going to tell me what you wished for?" It was Roger's voice. Ursula opened her eyes and he was there, in front of her.

"You are not meant to reveal the wish," Ursula said, leaning in for a kiss. "If you do, it does not come true."

"But if it was me you wished for, your wish has come true." Roger met Ursula's lips and kissed her with the kind of longing built up after a long period of separation. She lingered for a second but pulled away, thinking about all the eyes on them.

"Oh Roger! How did you manage to arrange this?"

"You can blame me," Phyllis wheeled next to Ursula, taking her hand and giving it a strong squeeze. "I thought a girl should have a bit of a surprise on her birthday."

"I truly cannot believe it."

"You'll be even happier when you take a bite of that cake," Phyllis said.

"I made it especially for you, Ursula. I know how much you love chocolate," Rose said.

"I have never been more spoiled!"

"Well, we better get it sliced," Phyllis said and motioned to the kitchen staff for a knife. "I've been waiting for my dessert." Phyllis winked at Ursula.

The four of them—Ursula, Roger, Rose and Phyllis—gathered around a nearby table. Ursula unwrapped knitting needles and a Better Homes and Gardens magazine from Rose, a collection of white handkerchiefs Phyllis had embroidered with an ornate 'U' in each corner, and from Roger, a silk scarf the color of aubergines. Ursula showered the group with thank you's.

"Here, this is from my mother," Roger said and handed Ursula an envelope.

"You're joking."

"No, she said to give this to you."

Ursula tore open the flap. A birthday card. On the inside she read, "Ursula, Happy Birthday. Get well soon. Mrs. Mary Gorski."

She shoved the card at Roger, eyebrows up. "This is unexpected."

"I'm baffled as you are."

Rose leaned forward and said, "Mary would never expect you to help, but if you have time, I bet she would love if you made a few blankets for that blanket drive she does every year."

Ursula frowned. There always seemed to be a hook behind Mrs. Gorski's apparent kindness. Then again, Ursula hadn't followed through when Rose had suggested it the first time. This would be an opportunity to build their relationship, even from afar. "I could do that," she said.

"It can't hurt, and she'll be so pleased." Rose clasped her hands together.

"And if you teach me how to use those needles, I might be able to help too," Phyllis said.

"You don't need to get wrapped up with Mrs. Gorski, but that's a nice thought Phyllis," Ursula said, taking a bite of the cake. "Rose, how did you make this so light but so rich?"

"Ahh, that's my secret recipe. Maybe I'll share it with you someday."

"I would love that," Ursula said, licking the buttercream frosting from the fork.

"I'd love to stay and chat, but I have to get to my afternoon therapy," Phyllis said, scooting in for a side hug.

"And I'm afraid I have errands to run," Rose said. "But I'm so glad to see you, Ursula. We can't wait to have you home."

"I cannot wait to be home. Thank you for coming, Rose," Ursula said.

And then it was just Ursula and Roger, the dining room empty. A jolt of desire ran through Ursula's body, a wish they could slide into a dark corner, unseen.

"You look beautiful," Roger said.

Ursula blushed and let him take his hands in hers. "This little surprise will keep me going for weeks."

"When Phyllis called me to explain what she had in mind, I knew you would love it."

"She is a good friend to me," Ursula said, "especially as I've only known her for a month. You make fast friends in here, that's for certain."

Roger nodded, but his eyes were unfocused, as if he were thinking of something else. "I actually have something I need to talk to you about," he said, then took a deep breath.

"What is it? Has something happened to my family?" Ursula's pulse quickened.

"No, no, nothing like that." Roger hesitated, then finally spoke again. "You know that promotion I was meant to get?"

"Hmm, I think so?" Ursula relaxed into her chair, relieved that whatever Roger was going to tell her had nothing to do with her mother or father or Aunt Kaethe.

"The one I talked to you about in August?"

Her mind shot back to those weeks of hot and sticky and weak legs and falling. "Oh gosh, Roger, I don't remember anything from August."

"They gave it to the owner's son."

"No! How could they? None of them work as hard as you do!"

Roger shook his head. "I talked to them about it. They told me how much they appreciate my work, but said the decision was final."

"I'm sorry," Ursula said.

"The thing is, Ursula, the bill came in from your first hospital. My veteran's insurance covered some of it, but I'm going to have to use some of the money you've been saving to . . ." He trailed off, looking at her nervously.

"The money I'm saving so I can go see my family?"

Roger nodded mutely.

"No, Roger. You can't. There must be another way." Frustrated, she pushed the empty plate away from her on the table. She thought of the money she'd been squirreling away. Before getting sick, she had been three quarters of the way to her goal.

"I don't have another choice. I already had to give my mother extra money this month." He stared down at his lap, fiddled with the napkin he'd placed there. Ursula knew he had been helping his mother out with money, but didn't know it would cut into their ability to pay the hospital or would deplete all she was saving to get home.

"Can you ask for a raise? More hours? Anything?" The chance to go back to Germany was slipping away. The chance to hug her mother, tell her how sorry she was for leaving.

Roger was quiet for a moment, then looked up to meet her eyes. "I'll see what I can do. I don't want you to worry too much about this."

"Roger," Ursula said, leaning in, "You have to do something. It isn't just about me visiting my family. I heard there was a patient discharged early because he couldn't pay his bills. I cannot believe I'm saying this with how much I'd love to be home, but I'm not ready to leave yet, I need more time. I need to learn to walk with my sticks, I need to . . ." Ursula wanted to explain how she still needed to learn stairs, how to stand for long periods of time on her own, and even how to bathe on her own. But she trailed off, afraid of alarming Roger. Afraid of voicing how much she needed to stay at Riverwood if she were to have a life of her own again.

"I understand," said Roger. Ursula could only hope he truly did.

CHAPTER 20
November 1950

The physical therapy room thrummed with repressed frustration. A woman across the room sobbed, collapsing back to her chair. A man to Ursula's right cursed under his breath. He had fallen a second time. Ursula paused to steady herself against the possibility of the same fate. The surprise birthday celebration had re-energized her, but the conversation with Roger about his mother and the hospital bill weighed her down. Routine exercises seemed harder; her legs were more stiff than usual.

Miss Miller had encouraged her to picture the movements before trying them. So Ursula traced it all mentally. Feet planted, knees loose, but ready, hips engaged, a fluid motion up, up, up. Her legs shuddered as she willed her body to move. But in her mind, she soared. She returned to the airplane over the Atlantic, looking out at the ocean far below. *I could never have pictured this.*

The scent of exhaustion brought Ursula back to the therapy room.

"This week we'll focus on more extended time walking," Miss Miller was saying. It was Monday, the day to set goals. Ursula both feared and loved Mondays. The goals were challenging, more chances to fail. But they also meant she was closer to getting better, closer to going home.

"What does that mean? More walking?"

"I want you to walk the length of the parallel bars, turn around and come back," Miss Miller said, tracing the trek with her eyes.

Light perspiration appeared under Ursula's arms as she followed Miss Miller's gaze. It irritated her how new challenges brought on nervous sweat.

"Are you sure I need to go that far today?"

"I am." Miss Miller's voice was firm. "You've been doing very well."

"But, I don't..." Ursula said, then hesitated. "I don't want to fall, and I only managed two steps last week."

"Falling is a part of the process. You know that. Let's try a few more steps. See how you feel."

Ursula repeated the upward movement in her head. Feet planted. Knees loose. Up, up, up. "All right, I am ready."

"I'll be right here beside you, focus on one step at a time."

Whenever Miss Miller said "one step at a time" Ursula cringed. It seemed like such a cliché. She wanted therapy to be as nuanced as her experience of getting to know herself in this changed body. But no, therapy was regimented. A process collapsed into steps that simplified rather than expanded the possibilities of who she could become. If her body obeyed, the end prize was to walk again. But would she be a whole person again? That was still in doubt.

"I think I need to sit down. My right ankle is wobbling and my left leg feels weak," Ursula said.

"Can you take one more step? You're almost there," Miss Miller said, pointing to the end of the bars.

Ursula tried to wipe the grimace from her face, but her liquid and collapsing legs made it impossible to tame her expression. She could not go one step farther.

"Please, my chair. I think I'm going to fall," Ursula said, willing Miss Miller to move faster.

"Ursula, don't let the fear of falling stop you."

Another phrase she detested. *The fear was real. The therapists knew the fear was real. Why did they have to say it like that?*

"Miss Miller, it's not the fear, my legs are tired. Exhausted in fact. I am exhausted." Ursula wanted to be back in her room, reclining in bed while she fought off the aching waves in her muscles.

Miss Miller finally relented. "Okay, I guess I've pushed you far enough. We can start again tomorrow."

From the comfort of her chair, Ursula wheeled herself to the elevator. At least her arms were strong. She waited for the chime and when she was alone with the doors closed, let out the sob she'd been holding in.

Later that week on Thursday afternoon, Ursula had surprised herself, walking to the end and back, her legs strong below her.

"This is terrific work, Ursula." Miss Miller made additional notes in her chart, then looked up. "I knew you could do it."

"Sometimes I think you know me better than I know myself."

"I think we should try the crutches again. Let's see if you can take a few steps on those." Miss Miller pointed to the tools leaning against the wall. Ursula eyed the two metal rods with cuffs that landed at, and stabilized her forearms. On each crutch, a round piece of metal stuck out just below the cuff so she had a place to hold onto. At the bottom of each rod a rubber crutch tip helped her remain steady.

"Shouldn't that wait until Monday, when we start something new?" She wanted to feel good about her steps, not risk failure with a new task.

"You're strong today, let's try it again. Step by step, remember?"

"Yes, I remember." Ursula sighed.

"Steady now, steady."

Ursula slid her hands through the loops at the top of her crutches and grasped the hand holds. As she stood, she grimaced, then collected her balance at her feet, pausing to confirm the strength from earlier. It was still there. Her right foot advanced, then her left, then her right again. Her left came to rest beside it.

"Oh my!" Ursula regrasped the holds on the crutches as she straightened her spine.

"Wonderful work, just wonderful."

"I never thought . . ."

"Thinking is what can sometimes hold us back."

"Don't I know that." But now maybe that thinking could take her forward.

Returned to her bed on the second floor, Ursula vibrated with energy. She could not believe how much progress she had made over the past few days. Wheels squeaked as the volunteer mail boy took the cart in and out of rooms. Ursula counted back weeks in her head, realizing it was still too soon for a response from her mother. Oh, how she would love to tell her mother about this week's victories.

"I have a package for you," the young boy said from the doorway. He pulled a small brown parcel from the mail cart, handed it to Phyllis, then continued down the hall. Phyllis flipped the package over in her hands until she found a corner to tug on. A letter fell out, along with something wrapped in tissue paper. Ursula shifted onto her side and craned her neck. She was strong enough to maneuver her body while in bed and grateful for the freedom. Grateful she didn't have to press the call button above her head.

"What is it?"

"Why don't you get out of bed and come see for yourself?" Phyllis said with a playful, but challenging look in her eyes. "You're doing so well in therapy."

"I can see just fine from here."

"Have it your way, then," Phyllis said. She had been encouraging Ursula to walk more outside the therapy room.

"I cannot afford to fall, you know that, Phyllis." A bad fall might mean weeks or even months added to her rehabilitation schedule. It would mean more time separated from Roger. She was already home-sick, and missing him.

"I know, I just think it would do you some good to move around more, just as it has done me good." Phyllis pulled a garment from the white paper. A silky knee-length slip fell onto her lap. "Oh gosh, it's beautiful."

"Who would send you a slip? Is it from your sister?"

"No, my neighbor, Lucy." Phyllis ran the delicate fabric through her hands. Tears appeared on her face.

"Are you okay?" Ursula wished she could get closer to comfort Phyllis.

"I'm going to get out of here, Ursula. I am. I am going to wear this slip the day I leave." Phyllis wiped the moisture from under her eyes. "This has really given me a lot of hope."

"May I read the letter she sent?"

"Sure, but you'll have to come over to get it, or you can call for the nurse. My legs are too tired to get out of bed right now," Phyllis said.

Ursula wanted to feel the silk in her hands, to touch something so delicate and fine after months of stiff white sheets and scratchy wool. She scooched her body to the side of the bed and swung her feet over the edge. The floor was cool on her soles. She reached for her sticks propped at the head of her bed and managed to stand. She wavered but stayed upright. With her arms positioned in the cuffs of her crutches she shuffled the few feet to Phyllis's bed.

"I guess I can do this on my own." Ursula wanted to stop worrying so much. She wanted to trust her strength more.

"You sure can."

Phyllis handed Ursula the letter.

Ursula was suddenly very alone as she read it. Why had she wanted to read words from a stranger? She handed the paper back to Phyllis and said, "She sounds like a wonderful neighbor."

"She really is." Phyllis folded the note and placed it on top of the slip.

"I look at you and think you're so strong," Ursula said, her voice quiet. Phyllis seemed wise to Ursula, as if she were much older than her thirty-one years.

"Me? Well, that's nice of you to say. I need to get strong so I can go home to my children. But look at you! Standing with those sticks!" Phyllis reached to squeeze Ursula's hand.

Ursula kept her hands on her crutches, but grinned at Phyllis.

"What I can't understand," Ursula said, "is how I went from never thinking about moving my legs, to thinking about every movement I make." Ursula's legs weakened and she eyed her bed. It was only a few feet away, but she worried she might collapse.

"I keep having dreams that I can walk again," Phyllis said. "For those brief moments, I can still feel it, what it was like to walk on my own without help."

Ursula did not hear any discouragement in Phyllis's voice, only her desire to get better.

"May I see the slip?" Ursula wanted to feel the smooth fabric under her fingers.

"Of course." Phyllis handed Ursula the slip, pointing to the final needlework near the bottom. "She added my initials."

"She has such a fine stitch." Ursula was holding the fabric closer to her face so she could get a good look at the handiwork when she collapsed, falling forward onto Phyllis's bed. "Oh gosh, I knew I was overdoing it."

"Are you okay?" Phyllis was startled.

"My legs couldn't hold me up anymore. Could you call the nurse? I don't think I can get up," Ursula mumbled into the sheet. *Dumme Gans*, stupid goose. Ursula was lying face down across Phyllis's legs with her own legs sprawled like anchors behind her. She was more embarrassed than hurt. Phyllis pressed the call button and Ursula was relieved when she did not recognize the nurse who arrived. It would have been embarrassing to have Nurse Ballard see her like this.

"Are you going to be okay?" Phyllis asked, once Ursula was resettled in bed.

"I shouldn't have gotten up," Ursula said, deflated.

"Don't be silly. You're tired of lying here, just like me." This was the first time Ursula heard defeat in Phyllis' voice, and it startled Ursula enough to change the subject.

"So, you were telling me about your neighbor," Ursula said.

"She taught me needlepoint. We stitched together during both of my pregnancies, especially toward the end when I was swollen and tired."

Then Phyllis kept talking. About how keeping her hands moving made her forget about her swelling belly. About the baby blankets and christening gowns now stitched with her children's initials. Ursula just listened. She knew becoming a mother might be hard. They'd certainly had no luck so far. But it would be impossible if she didn't get better. So instead of resenting Phyllis, she vowed to use her as inspiration. She would walk out of here, too.

CHAPTER 21
December 1950

Outside, the wind sounded across tree branches like a bow being pulled over the strings of a violin. It was meant to be below zero that night, a strange occurrence for early December. From her bed, Ursula watched people shuffle around outside in long coats, warm hats, and scarves. She imagined their eyes watery with cold like hers had been on gusty winter evenings in Berlin, or Minnesota nights when she had to take Vic outside.

"Ursula, are you there?"

Startled, Ursula looked over to see Phyllis in the doorway, standing with her crutches.

"How are those sticks going?"

"Great actually. I'm glad to be on my own two feet and out of that wheelchair." Phyllis pointed one of her sticks at her chair against the wall. She had made quick progress, her legs less damaged by the virus than Ursula's.

"I hope I'll be able to give mine up soon, too," Ursula said, but she knew it could be many more months. Ursula could now walk with her crutches for about ten minutes before needing to sit down. Phyllis could manage twenty minutes, enough time to go downstairs for a coffee.

"You're tougher than me. I know you'll walk out of here," Phyllis said. Concentrating on her steps, she walked deliberately across the room and sat in the chair next to Ursula's bed.

"What had you so lost in thought?"

"Oh gosh, nothing. Sometimes my mind wanders off to places I'd rather forget."

"I understand that," Phyllis said.

"But you're always so cheery. I wouldn't think you have a dark thought in that head of yours."

Phyllis made circles with her wrists to loosen the stiffness from maneuvering with crutches. "I guess what I think about is that now, no matter what happens in the future, I will always be wary of my body failing me. And I feel too young for that. How are we supposed to go on living? Be good women, good wives?"

Ursula blinked at her friend. "What are you saying? This kind of talk is not like you."

"Do you believe in the 'for richer or poorer, in sickness, and in health' lines from your wedding vows?" Phyllis asked, tilting her head.

"Of course I do," Ursula said, but she wondered about the sicker part. Could she be a good wife to Roger if she could barely take care of herself? A tree branch thwacked against the pane of glass. Air whistled through the gaps in the window frames.

"Gosh it's windy out there," Phyllis said.

"It reminds me of winter in Berlin. One day during the war I stepped outside of work for a moment just to get away from the hemmed in feeling I got around all those people. As I stood kicking the snow with my shoes, I remember thinking about how parts of the world kept moving even though other parts were frozen. How long could we go on like that? How long could the world be at war?" Ursula pulled the blanket on her lap up around her shoulders.

"If it makes you feel any better, I had similar questions," Phyllis said.

"For me, as simple as it sounds, the change in weather carried hope."

"Do you feel hopeful now?"

"I don't know." Ursula paused. The sky darkened with thick midday clouds. "The war was something that happened around me. As a child, my parents attempted to shield me from it. But this disease is different. It's happening to me."

"To us," Phyllis said.

Ursula nodded.

They had been sharing a room at Riverwood for more than four months. Phyllis knew some details about the war, but Ursula thought maybe it was time to share more. The room went quiet. Ursula took a deep breath and started at the end, because she didn't know how to start from the beginning.

"After the war ended, the streets in Berlin were filled with Americans and Russians. Most of us girls were happy to see the Americans. They weren't all good, that's certain, but the Russian soldiers were scarier to me. They looked for women to bother. To attack, even. I had to constantly watch my back, talk myself out of dangerous situations." Ursula took another deep breath.

"If it's too hard to talk about, you can stop. You don't have to tell me," Phyllis said.

"No, it's all right," Ursula said. Maybe it would help to get these memories out of her head and into the air. Maybe they would evaporate there. "At the time, I was living with my friend Rita and her family in Berlin. By a stroke of luck, their house was still standing. It hadn't been bombed out like most of the houses on the street. One day we heard screams coming from the house next door. We knew people were there, living in the basement; it was all that was left of that house. Two Russians were trying to rape a girl, but she fought back, and they pushed her down the concrete stairs. We found out later she had hit her head and died. That could have been me or Rita, or anyone I knew."

"Oh, Ursula, I'm so terribly sorry. What an awful thing to witness," Phyllis said. She inhaled, the breath catching in her throat as she placed her head in her hands.

"I'm just glad someone will listen," Ursula said, her head beginning to throb. The war was trapped inside, it filled her up in a way she couldn't pour out. Some days the war never entered her mind and other days it was all she could think about.

"Go on if you can, if you want to . . ." Phyllis said as she quietly leaned the sticks against the chair's armrest.

"I suppose my misery takes you away from this hospital for a while," Ursula said, suddenly angry. Here was Phyllis with her perfect family and her newfound success with crutches. What could she care about all Ursula had gone through?

"That's not fair, Ursula. I'm trying to be a good friend to you and you're not giving me a chance."

"Here's your chance. Listen, and then stop asking me about this," Ursula said, her voice curt. Shame crept up her limbs. She hadn't intended on taking her frustrations out on her closest friend at Riverwood. But the realization had come to her that she would have no chance to replace these horrible memories of Berlin with brighter experiences. The chance to go back to visit her family was now gone, the money she'd saved used for hospital bills.

Phyllis nodded, her face had gone pale.

Gusts of wind banged tree branches against the windows, but Ursula could still hear her heartbeat in her ears.

"Sometimes you could appease the Russian soldiers with watches. They loved watches! You'd see them walking around with five or ten up their arm, like trophies."

"Did they take any from you?" Phyllis asked.

"I had three in the suitcase I kept with me with all my belongings, but they never took them. During one encounter, I gave them my big alarm clock, but they just threw it against a wall."

"Before that, before the Russians came, did you know the war was going badly, that the Germans were losing?"

"I listened to the Allied broadcast on the radio," Ursula said and leaned in. "Carefully of course, because it was risky. But I knew the Germans were losing. And then when the Russian soldiers burst in and wandered through the halls of G-Tower we knew it was over. Berlin was in ruins."

Phyllis shook her head.

"Afterwards, we were ordered to clean the streets and bury the dead. Many people were left where they died. I didn't have the stomach for it, but my friends dug the graves and said short prayers. It became routine." Ursula looked outside again, but she no longer saw the trees, her vision clouded with shame for being incapable of burying people, for not being able to look death in the face.

"I think I need a cup of tea," Phyllis said, as if she had read Ursula's mind. "Here in the States, we followed along with the news. It was all we talked about. But hearing what it was like over there from a friend, well, it brings another perspective."

"Thank you for listening to me," Ursula said, feeling a comfort from Phyllis calling her a friend, especially after she'd lashed out at her. "Now, if you can give me a hand with my chair, I think I'll be able to get out of this bed on my own."

Phyllis wheeled Ursula's chair close to the bed and locked the brakes.

"If you slide off the edge of the bed, your feet will almost be on the floor," Phyllis said.

"Let me know when I'm close." Ursula wiggled her bum to the edge of her bed, helped her legs over the side and felt the tips of her toes sweep the floor.

"Almost there."

Ursula slowly stood up and balanced herself using the bed, faced away from Phyllis while she swung the chair behind her.

"You can sit," Phyllis said.

They took the elevator downstairs. The last of the afternoon therapy sessions had finished and patients were in various states of healing. Some were walking on their own, albeit with lopsided gaits. Others were moving along on sticks like Phyllis, and some, like Ursula, were in wheelchairs. In the dining room, Ursula wheeled and Phyllis hobbled to an empty table near a window. Outside on the snow-covered grounds, a bit of light tried to cut through the gray clouds.

"Would you mind if I took a seat?" A voice rose up from behind them. Ursula looked up. It was Roger.

"What are you doing here?" Visitors were usually only allowed on Sundays and this was a Tuesday afternoon. She hoped he wasn't bringing bad news. A few days before, Roger had called to share how he was working extra hours to help his mother and be sure the hospital bills could be paid. What if those hours weren't available anymore?

"She's had a tough day," Phyllis said, "but now that you're here, I'm sure she'll brighten up."

"That's my girl," Roger said, and placed his hands on Ursula's shoulder to give them a rub. Ursula liked when Roger could loosen her up.

"But what *are* you doing here?"

"It's a surprise. You'll find out soon enough." Roger winked and sat down next to Ursula. "So you two are having tough days?"

"I'm exhausted." Ursula palmed the brake of her chair. She had spent the last few weeks in therapy learning how to walk with crutches for more than ten minutes at a time. It depressed her that she couldn't master what used to be such a simple task.

"My session went great," Phyllis said when Roger glanced her way. "I'm moving around pretty well on these sticks."

"Show off." Ursula tried to keep her voice light and playful, but her nerves were frayed.

"You sound like two bickering sisters." Roger said. He grinned as he spread his arm over the empty seat next to him. Ursula wanted to ask him why he was grinning. She wanted to ask him why he was even there. But then his eyes cut to the dining room entrance and his smile spread even further across his face. Superintendent Erickson was standing in the doorway.

"Pardon me, I have an announcement to make!" The room quieted. "We will have a party complete with a band next Saturday evening. I'd like to thank Mr. Roger Gorski—Mrs. Ursula Gorski's husband—for volunteering his group of musicians. More information has just been posted on the community bulletin board. Friends and family are welcome."

Ursula looked at her beaming husband. "So, this is the surprise! How wonderful!" Her anger from earlier emptied from her body like air leaving a balloon.

"I thought you all could use some fun," Roger said.

"Oh, Mr. Gorski, what a wonderful gesture," Phyllis said, shaking her shoulders as if she were dancing. "I am in need of a good distraction."

"We have a great show prepared for you, and we'll even take a few song requests, so you better have those ready," Roger said.

"So you're telling me that while I've been stuck in here, you've been banging on those drums of Pete's and playing that squeaky trumpet that you had tucked in the closet," Ursula said, amused. The two Gorski boys had played in their high school's band, but she had no idea Roger had started up again.

"I have to admit that it has been too quiet around the house. I thought, why not join a weekend band?"

"Why not indeed!" Phyllis clapped her hands together.

"It's a bit of fun. I'm trying to keep myself busy while Ursula has been here working on getting better," Roger said. Guilt crept over Ursula. She knew it wasn't her fault for falling ill, but imagining Roger alone at home without her made her anxious, as if she was being left behind.

"I bet the lead singer is dreamy," Phyllis said like a teenager admiring her favorite band.

"Well, I guess you'll just have to see." Roger winked at Phyllis, and Ursula wondered who the band's lead singer was. Could it be Roger himself?

"You have a handsome husband at home," Ursula said to Phyllis.

"A girl can admire a man's good looks." Phyllis winked at Ursula.

"Well, ladies, I've got a big show to get ready for," Roger said. He leaned in to kiss Ursula.

"Thank you," Ursula whispered in his ear before his lips met hers.

"For you, anything," Roger whispered back, then met her lips with a fierce kiss.

"You two love birds!" Phyllis smiled.

"See you both Saturday," Roger said as he stood up. Ursula watched him walk through the crowded room. Her heart ached for him, her family, for her old life. Ursula reached across the table and squeezed Phyllis's hands.

"Don't stop being you," Ursula said. Phyllis handed Ursula one of her embroidered handkerchiefs. Ursula dabbed the corners of her eyes.

"Should we go upstairs and choose a dress for next Saturday?"

"Yes, I would like that." The tension from their conversation about the war melted away. Ursula and Phyllis wheeled and shuffled out of the café. The excited chatter of the other patients lifted the mood of the hospital. They all had a party to get ready for.

The staff had cleared a large space in the dining room and set up a small stage—a platform that sat about a foot off the ground. The band, all dressed in suits and bow ties, tuned their instruments, strumming the strings to test the pitch. Roger sat behind a drum set, and gently tapped out rhythms on the tom-tom, traps, and snare drum with an occasional thump of the large bass drum. Ursula waved coyly from her chair. Roger grinned, set down his drumsticks, and came to say hello.

"Hello beautiful," Roger said, as he kissed Ursula. Against her flame of red hair, Ursula's burgundy dress and deep red lipstick painted her into an autumnal show of color.

"I miss you so much," Ursula said in his ear. She yearned for his touch, embrace, and caress. These brief moments were not enough.

"I miss you, too," he said and then kissed her again and smiled. Then to Phyllis he said, "You're looking well." He was always polite around Phyllis, who smiled and batted at the air, as if she wanted to send away the compliment. Ursula was glad Roger liked Phyllis. She had a feeling they would spend a lot of time together once they were finally released from the hospital.

"Are you still taking requests tonight? Phyllis and I came up with a few ideas." Ursula wanted them to play "If I Knew You Were Comin' I'd've Baked a Cake." They had been listening to the lively song on the small radio in their room, clapping and singing along. It was absurd and made Ursula titter.

"I might be able to pull some strings," Roger said, and then chuckled to the band. "Guys, you think we could play a few requests tonight?" Heads nodded on the stage behind Roger. The plucking and tuning slowed.

"Looks like we're going to get started, gotta run," Roger said.

On stage Roger moved with confidence, an ease Ursula recognized from the day they met. The band had given him a distraction in her absence, but it made Ursula uneasy. What if he didn't need her anymore? *That's ridiculous.* Ursula chased away the thought. She wanted to enjoy herself, not be overcome with her "what ifs."

Midway through the set, they played a song Ursula recognized from the night at Schiek's nightclub. She had been tucked in close to Roger gliding across that parquet floor. A terrible sadness overcame her.

Ursula turned to Phyllis. "What if I'm never able to dance with Roger again?"

"Why would you say something like that?" Phyllis said, half whisper, half hiss. "You're ruining a perfectly good time." She shook her head. "Really, Ursula, can you try to simply enjoy the music and ignore those thoughts running around in your head?"

"But what if I can't dance again?" Ursula crunched the folds of her dress in her fists.

"That's up to you. I have every intention to dance again." Phyllis reached for her sticks attached to the back of her chair. "As a matter of fact, I might try it now." Phyllis stood up—slow and steady—and swayed gently to the music. She had donned a navy-blue dress and mauve lipstick. It looked as if she was standing on her own, the sticks hidden in the folds of her dress.

Soon other patients stood, too, but Ursula didn't move. She didn't trust her legs tonight. If she managed to stand and then fell, she would be mortified in front of Roger. She wanted him to see her confident and strong, not on the floor in a heap of taffeta. A tear trickled down her face and she regretted their decision to sit in the front row. If they had opted for the back, she could have stayed hidden. She could only guess how many patients were on their feet behind her, swaying to the music. Comparing speeds of recovery was a dangerous and infuriating game, but she couldn't help herself. She loved to dance, and this moment, which should have been magical, was suddenly awful.

When the song stopped, Phyllis sat down.

"What a thrill!" Phyllis said. Her face glowed. "It was almost like old times. Waiting on the edge of the dance floor, hoping to be asked to dance. I only wish David could have been here, but he couldn't get a sitter."

"It's too bad he couldn't be here," Ursula said. "You probably could have actually danced." She heard the jealousy in her voice and it annoyed her. She should just appreciate how far she had come, not compare herself to others.

"Oh Ursula, just focus on your recovery, not mine," Phyllis said, as if reading Ursula's thoughts. She kept her eyes on the stage, tapping her fingers on the armrest of her chair.

Ursula didn't know what she expected to hear from Phyllis. She wanted Phyllis's empathy but recognized every patient in the hospital had challenges to overcome. She caught Roger's eye and he winked at her as he swished his brush on the snare to the sultry beat of Dean Martin's "Buona Sera." Ursula smiled in spite of her suddenly terrible mood. If only Roger knew how hard it was, how much she missed her old life, how much she understood the world she had built with Roger on Colfax Avenue was forever changed. By the wink, Ursula guessed it hadn't sunk in for him yet. He didn't realize that when she was released from the hospital, she would rely on him for everything.

"Buona Sera" ended and the bandleader announced a short break.

"What do you think? We might be good enough for Schiek's," Roger said as he came off the stage. He was practically giddy.

"You were wonderful. I'm so proud," Ursula said. But her mind flashed to an image she couldn't bear: Roger and his band playing while she watched from the edge, unable to dance on that beautiful parquet.

"And are you ready for a special song?" Roger asked. He turned to the band behind him who had returned to their positions. "Guys, how about we play a little Glenn Miller for my wife?"

A cheer rang out as Roger darted back on stage.

This time Ursula put aside her anger and frustration, and just like in the therapy room, just like the days she got out of bed on her own, with her crutches for support, she stood up in one swift motion. She shook her hips and stamped her crutches until her face hurt from the joy of sinking into the music.

CHAPTER 22
January 1951

Ursula was restless and bored as she waited for the call for dinner. She had spent the week relying on her wheelchair, her right ankle swollen from overwork the week before in therapy. It was already beginning to darken, and Phyllis had fallen asleep with Hemingway's *Across the River and into the Trees* open across her stomach. Ursula hated to wake her, but they usually went down to dinner together. When her roommate let out a loud snore, Ursula couldn't wait any longer. She'd go read the paper until it was time to eat. She carefully moved into her wheelchair and quietly rolled out of the room. When she reached the wood-paneled library, she found the pages of the *Star* loosely shuffled together. Ursula placed it across her lap then wheeled to the sunroom to scan the headlines.

Reading the paper had become Ursula's way of maintaining a connection to the outside world. Her eyes darted across the large font. "More Unease About Korea and Possible War." "Curbs on Communist Activity." Having grown up in an anti-communist family, the curbs were one thing she could agree with. She looked for Cedric Adams's column "In This Corner." He sometimes wrote about the hospital and was steadfast in supporting the work of the March of Dimes. In a recent article, he'd written about the Heart Home project. The writer had organized a Penny Parade to help a sightless mother and her four children, one of whom was stricken with polio, build a new home. Ursula remembered the photos: a simple one-story home, another of the mother playing a beautiful upright piano, the family enjoying Easter dinner from Curly's Theater Café. It gave Ursula hope. If this woman could lead a rich life, so could she.

Ursula startled when Superintendent Eriksson stuck her head in the room. "Dinner will be ready soon," she said. "Best get yourself ready."

She set the paper on a table nearby and took the elevator to her room, where she found Phyllis reading again.

"This letter came for you." Phyllis pointed to an envelope on the table across Ursula's bed. Ursula hesitated, then rolled closer, but even from far away the penmanship gave it away. Her mother had finally written.

Dear Ursula,

Upon reading the news in your letter, I took to bed for a few days. My only daughter sick and after everything we have been through! How is a mother meant to help her child when she is so far away? My words here could never be enough. I have many questions for you, but will spare you as I know how I've upset you in the past.

Your father and I have spoken about coming to America but we do not have the means to travel such a far distance. And with the restrictions placed on us because we're in East Berlin, well, all of this may be more difficult than we initially thought.

Your father blames himself for this—you leaving, and now this awful polio. He thinks he could have convinced you to stay here if he hadn't been taken away. But I was the one who

was here with you in the kitchen that day. I have only myself
to blame. But you were young and stubborn like I was at your
age. You wanted more than I or your father could give you,
more than Germany could give you.

I should have given you my carnation pendant necklace
so you would have something of me with you. An impossible
stand-in I know. It's lost now (you know it belonged to my
grandmother?).

Ursula paused. She traced her fingertips over the pendant at
her neck. She would have to tell her mother she took the family
heirloom. The day Ursula had fetched bread and sprained her
ankle as child, she had returned home fearful her mother would
be upset. Instead, her mother had placed her foot in a cold pan
of water to reduce the swelling. She had cooed and fussed over
Ursula. If only polio could be treated with cold water and a mother's loving touch. Ursula would reply and tell her mother not to
blame herself. She had chosen to leave Germany. Her feet had
guided her up the stairs to the airplane, had taken her over the
ocean and into Roger's arms.

She folded the letter, tucked it back in the envelope, and stuffed
it into the drawer of her bedside table. It was no use, though. Her
mother's words couldn't be hidden away.

"Are you all right?" Phyllis looked up from her book.

Ursula let out a long sigh.

"Upsetting news?" Phyllis motioned toward the drawer where
Ursula had stashed the letter.

"My mother finally wrote."

"And?"

"There's nothing I can say or do to give her any peace," Ursula said. Though she knew what she really wanted was peace for herself, hope life would work out.

"What do you mean?"

"My mother never wanted me to leave, but I did. I chose to come here for what I thought would be a better life," Ursula said. She pulled open the drawer and took out the letter, wanting the paper her mother had touched to be against her skin. "And now, here I am trying to figure out what will become of me."

"Aren't we all."

"But at least you have your family," Ursula said.

"You have your family, too."

"You're a mother. You have your children. What will I have when I leave here?" While she yearned for Roger and the life they had, she still dreamt of telling her mother she was pregnant. No matter how difficult their relationship had been, she knew her mother would rejoice in that news.

"Ursula, you are too hard on yourself. I have never met a more stubborn woman. I wish you would find some way to forgive yourself."

Silence fell between them.

Ursula put her hands on the wheels of her chair, and shifted toward the door. She pushed her hands over the rubber until she picked up speed. *Only myself to blame. You wanted more.* The words in her mother's letter billowed in an invisible cloud behind Ursula. Could she leave her own guilt behind? Get over her fears, worries and doubts? Phyllis was right, she was stubborn. But she was also resilient. She called over her shoulder and down the hallway to Phyllis: "I'll race you to dinner!"

Ursula reached the elevator and slammed her finger against the button, but the car must have been in the basement, and the delay meant Phyllis caught up with Ursula.

"You're awfully fast when you want to be," Phyllis said, panting a bit.

"You managed well on those sticks." Ursula eyed the crutches in Phyllis's hands. The stability cuffs reached her strong biceps.

"Are you sure you don't want to talk more?"

"I'm sure," Ursula said, as she rocked back and forth, the wheels sliding gently beneath her hands. "You told me exactly what I needed to hear."

The elevator door pinged open, and they got in to descend to the first floor. In the dining room, Ursula and Phyllis found two empty spots at a long table. Chairs sat at odd intervals to accommodate wheelchairs.

"They made me walk up and down stairs today," Phyllis said.

Now Ursula understood why Phyllis had fallen asleep before dinner.

"How did it go?" Ursula locked her wheels. Miss Miller had told her she'd be trying stairs soon, maybe in a few weeks once the swelling in her ankle had gone down.

"Fine, I guess. I had to stop a lot to rest, but managed." Phyllis motioned with her hands how she took each step. "Oh look, they have chicken noodle soup for dinner. I hope they have butter to spread on the bread."

One of the women on the kitchen staff ladled soup into patients' bowls.

"I could give up soup forever—the war ruined it for me," Ursula said. But she was hungry, so she plunged her spoon into the broth and raised it to her mouth. The steam ran across her face, leaving tiny beads of moisture on her cheeks. With one soft puff of air across the top of the utensil, the soup was cool enough to eat.

Ursula reached the bottom of the bowl when a woman across the table interrupted the sounds of slurping. "Have you heard? They are looking for the polio mother of the year! And I want to win."

Everyone gave their attention to Irene, a sometimes bridge partner of Phyllis and Ursula. Her features reminded Ursula of the porcelain dolls she had as a child: delicate yet authoritative in their beauty. Irene was pretty and cheerful, and she had navigated her recovery with adoration from the other women at Riverwood: steadily and virtuously. She was exactly the kind of woman who could be polio mother of the year.

"What happens if you win?" Ursula wanted to know if there was a prize.

"You're mother of the year, of course!" Phyllis said and looked at Ursula as if she should have known.

"But is there a prize?"

"Mother of the year is the prize. Someone from Riverwood won a few years ago, so I'm hoping I have a good chance," Irene said.

Ursula thought it all seemed silly, like a made-up way to make polio-stricken mothers feel better.

"Oh." Ursula set her spoon into her empty bowl. She was angered by the idea of a prize for mothers, as if overcoming polio was easy for women without children. "What about women without children?"

"I don't think they have an award for that." Irene's mouth became a graceful pout.

"Irene, some women are not blessed with children," Phyllis said.

Ursula was glad for the interjection.

"I'm sorry. That was thoughtless of me. I'm sure it's hard for those women, too," Irene said. She pointedly avoided eye contact with Ursula.

The heat of shame rose on Ursula's cheeks. Beyond getting pregnant, she had no idea what she wanted from motherhood. She saw how

Phyllis kissed her children's cheeks, hugged and encouraged them when they visited. How her friend Bea had so naturally caressed her belly while sitting across from Ursula at the café. How Sally kept the peace between Elizabeth and Chris. She had plenty of role models. Which one should she be? Who did she want to become?

Ursula pressed her napkin to her face and hoped it would go back to its normal alabaster color. She needed to stop thinking so much about motherhood as it only led to confusion and regret. She purposely turned to Phyllis.

"Tell me more about the book you're reading," she said.

And soon Phyllis was prattling on about Hemingway and what he thought about the war and how he was such a marvelous writer. Ursula watched Phyllis's hands move elegantly as she spoke and became lost in their movement. At least she'd gotten her mind away from the dangerous loop of unanswerable questions.

CHAPTER 23
May 1951

O n a Tuesday morning in mid-May, Roger arrived at Riverwood with a modest bouquet of red roses, smiling ear-to-ear. Today Ursula would petition the court for citizenship. It would be her first time outside the hospital gates since she had arrived in August, more than nine months ago. The affidavits of her two witnesses—Rose and Phyllis—were snug in the envelope in her hand while she waited for Roger in the lobby of the hospital. She shifted on the bench and repositioned her sticks between her knees so they wouldn't fall to the floor. Her wheelchair sat perpendicular to her. She had decided to rely on her chair until she arrived at the court building where she would have to tackle stairs on her sticks.

"Your chariot awaits, my future American," Roger said. He wore the same suit he had donned for his band's performance—grey, double-breasted gray, anchored by dark-brown leather shoes. He had swapped his trendy black bowtie for a more modest one with navy blue with gray geometric shapes. To Ursula he looked distinguished—a perfect tone for a visit to the court.

Ursula scooted into the chair and Roger placed her sticks in the loop on the back.

"I'm nervous," Ursula said as Roger wheeled her to the car. He had borrowed Pete's sedan as the truck would be too difficult for Ursula to navigate. "What if they find problems with my papers?"

"I'm sure that won't happen," Roger said.

"But we had so much trouble getting the government to approve my paperwork to come to America," Ursula said. Filling out the current forms had brought back frustrating memories of delays in Berlin. "I know that was years ago, but I can't help but remember it."

"You already did the hard part—getting here, to America," Roger said. He helped Ursula into the passenger seat and handed her the crutches. "Give me a second. I need to get this chair into the trunk."

Ursula nodded and closed the door. She clutched her sticks between her knees, already anxious about tackling the steep stairs at the federal building.

Roger was in the driver's seat now with the key in the ignition. "Let's get going because afterward I'm taking you out for lunch."

To Ursula, the city looked the same. Tidy rows of houses gave way to the Minneapolis skyline. A part of her wanted it all to look different, changed because she had changed.

They parked close to the entrance where the federal building loomed over them.

"You ready?" Roger stood next to Ursula.

"I'm ready." Ursula took her eyes up the rectangular stones stacked in front of her. She took a deep breath, and let it out. "Just like in therapy—slow and steady."

Ursula lifted her sticks so they were on the next step. She flexed then loosened her leg muscles, then lifted her right leg, then her left. At each step she stopped to regain her balance before moving her sticks up again. At the top she cheered. She didn't care if anyone looked at her. She had done twenty steps. More than any she had ever done in physical therapy.

The grand staircase led to a busy lobby with offices along corridors. A court clerk took Ursula's completed paperwork and explained she would receive information in the mail about her hearing before a judge, the last step in the citizenship process.

"See, that was straightforward," Roger said.

"Let's go to the diner down the street like you promised." Ursula's stomach gurgled. She was hungry but also nervous. She had seen the brave face Roger wore as they ascended to the building's lobby. As they were leaving, a janitor noticed Ursula's crutches and asked if she would like to take the freight elevator. Ursula immediately said yes and thanked him. Roger followed quietly.

At the diner, Roger ordered a grilled cheese sandwich and Ursula chose a BLT. She loved the crunch of the toast, bacon, iceberg lettuce, and beefy tomatoes slathered in mayonnaise. She tried to ignore the patrons staring curiously at her sticks.

"I heard your therapy is going well, that you might get to come home soon," Roger said. He took a big bite of his sandwich, the cheese oozing out the sides. "Superintendent Erikson gave me the great report."

Ursula nodded, though she was still cautious. Even a small setback could mean more weeks in the hospital.

"I'm doing my best, but it's hard. When I get back to the hospital, I will have to rest and will probably have to rest tomorrow, too." Ursula took another bite of the sandwich, chewing slowly as she realized Roger would never fully understand how difficult this was for her. "It took all of my concentration to get up those stairs today."

"But you're doing so well! You managed them just fine." Roger made climbing motions with his fingers.

Ursula thought his fingers were doing a better job on the imaginary stairs than she had on the real ones. Those were a hard, glossy marble perfect for a slip and fall if she had not placed her sticks and feet correctly.

"There is still a lot of work to do. I might never be able to give up my chair." Ursula motioned to the sedan parked outside, the chair folded up in the trunk. Her legs trembled under the table.

"Just you wait and see. You're going to come out of this as if you never had polio," Roger said. His naiveté astonished Ursula. She stopped chewing for a moment and when she swallowed, the sensation made her ill.

"I wish that were true," Ursula said and held his gaze. She needed him to understand the severity of her situation, of their situation. Once she was released from the hospital, she would rely on him every day. He would have to stand in for her current team of doctors, nurses, and physical therapists. Ursula hoped he was up to the task, wanted to believe he would come through for her. She forked a mayonnaise-covered tomato slice that had fallen out of the sandwich.

"We have gotten through tough times together. I know we will get through this. I know we will," Roger said.

"Of course we will," Ursula said, but she was not certain. They finished eating and Roger paid the bill. When Ursula tried to stand up, her legs wobbled. The twenty stairs at the federal building had done their work on her calves and thighs. Even her arms were weak. She gritted her teeth, gripped her sticks, and willed herself to walk the length of the diner to the car.

Roger motioned for Ursula to go ahead of him, which was almost worse than following slowly behind him. She was on display now, eyes wandering over her and flitting away as if she hadn't seen them. Whispers caught in her ears and further unsteadied her legs.

Ursula had not fully considered her legs in this way before, how they carried her, moved her toward some futures and away from

others. At Riverwood, because everyone was in a similar predicament, lingering eyes didn't force her to think about how her body
would be understood, taken in. All her life she had expected her legs
to be there, reliable, unannounced.

Now eyebrows raised in concern, and high-pitched comments
landed without warning. *Maybe you should sit down. Do you need
help?* Ursula lifted her tired feet, a slow shuffle toward the door.
Outside she gulped in the spring air, relieved to be out of sight.

Roger opened the car door and Ursula thumped on the seat, her
tailbone smarting from the landing. She handed him the sticks, and
pulled the door closed. With her right hand, Ursula pressed against
the inside of her knee, then forced her leg straighter, lining up her
foot with her knee. If only her mind could line up with outside
impressions of her.

Ursula let out a sob as Roger slid into the driver's seat and put the
key in the ignition. He reached for her hand. They rode in silence
back to the hospital. She wanted to disappear.

A week later, Dr. Johnson popped his head into the room and Ursula
realized Phyllis might be going home. She rolled onto her right side
so she could watch their conversation.

"You've made good progress, Mrs. Sundberg. We are recommend-
ing one more week, with a discharge day of next Friday," said Dr.
Johnson.

Over the past two weeks, Phyllis had been able to move about
without the use of her sticks. She couldn't go far, but her ability to
walk alone was remarkable. Ursula was elated for Phyllis but her own
progress on the sticks was slow. She struggled with the small set of
stairs in the therapy room as if her ascent at the federal building had
been a dream.

"This is wonderful news! I cannot wait to get home to my kids and David," Phyllis said.

Dr. Johnson consulted his paperwork. "We'll talk through your transition and your follow-up appointments in the coming days, but overall, I'm pleased with your recovery."

"I didn't think I would be able to walk again on my own. I'm truly grateful," Phyllis said.

Dr. Johnson turned to leave, then stopped. "I will warn you though, some of our patients have a difficult time trying to get back to their lives. At least you've made a friend in here," he added, motioning to Ursula.

"I would never have made it through without her," Phyllis said.

When the doctor left, Phyllis turned to Ursula, her eyes bright. "Can you believe it?" she asked.

"I can't. I mean, yes I can. You've been doing so well," Ursula said, but the news had yet to sink in. She didn't want to be in the hospital without Phyllis.

"You're not excited for me?" Phyllis asked.

"I am." Ursula tried adding a dose of energy to her voice. She was making this about her instead of being happy about the good news.

"Oh Ursula, I know how much you want to leave, too, but you won't be long. They'll discharge you soon. I know it," Phyllis said.

"I wouldn't want you to have to spend another minute in this place," Ursula said, untangling herself from her selfishness.

Phyllis nodded, then the smile on her face faded a bit. "We've been in here for so many months that I'm scared to leave. That's the truth of it. How will I actually cope at home?"

"Your family will help," Ursula said. She realized the news had not sunk in for Phyllis, either.

"They've already done so much for me. I need to be able to run my home. Be a proper mother to my son and daughter and be the wife my husband married." Phyllis ran the tips of her fingers over her wedding band.

Ursula tried to think of a way to get Phyllis back to her earlier elation. "You'll do fine," she said. "Why, I'm sure you could be polio mother of the year!"

"Are you being serious?"

"I am," Ursula said. She meant it.

"Who would nominate me?" Phyllis asked, a smile returning to her face.

"I would."

"But you never liked the idea of it."

"Maybe if they had one for polio *woman* of the year as well," Ursula said and imagined being awarded the prize.

"Stop making me laugh," Phyllis said, clutching her belly. Then she walked across the room and sat on the end of Ursula's bed.

"I wonder if they make you compete in your bathing suit, like those ladies on the Miss America competition?" Reading about those women made Ursula feel jealous, their youthful beauty paraded on a stage.

"If they did, I wouldn't do it. Nope, no way. I'm too modest. It would be embarrassing." Phyllis put her hand up like a stop sign.

"I might. Picture me with my sticks walking across that stage. It would be—"

"Ridiculous!"

Ursula tossed her hair and struck a pose. They both laughed.

"What am I going to do without you?" Ursula's smile vanished.

"You'll be out in a flash," Phyllis said.

"I sure hope so," Ursula said.

"Don't forget that I arrived three weeks before you did. I had a head start in that physical therapy room," Phyllis said.

Ursula nodded. She didn't think it would be just three weeks, but the thought made her hopeful. "So, what's the first thing you're going to do when you get home?"

"I'll kiss my kids and David. Then I'll clean. I can't imagine what the house looks like with him in charge," Phyllis said and shook her head.

"Clean? You're not going to clean," Ursula slapped her palms against her lap. "You should do something more fun than that."

"It does sound terrible, doesn't it? How about this? I'll go for ice cream with David and the kids. All we've gotten here is vanilla and I just love mint chocolate chip."

"It would be strawberry for me," Ursula said, thinking about licking up trails of pink ice cream running down a cone.

"You won't believe me when I say it," Phyllis said, "but I've learned a lot from you, Mrs. Ursula Gorski. I want you to know that. If you think you can get rid of me, well then you're mistaken."

Ursula's eyes stung, and her throat tightened. But Phyllis started crying first. She scooted across the bed and hugged Ursula. Their bodies shook as they wept together.

"I'm forever grateful that you were my roommate for the last nine months," Ursula said, sniffling. Her heart swelled and she took a deep breath.

Phyllis smiled, but her cheeks were red, eyes puffy. She dabbed her face with a handkerchief, one embroidered with her initials. The neat letters in blue were surrounded by a trail of lazy flowers skirting the edges of the white fabric. From her pocket, Phyllis pulled out another handkerchief and handed it to Ursula just like Phyllis had the day Ursula arrived. They dried their tears together.

CHAPTER 24

June 1951

Ursula eyed Roger as Nurse Ballard gave him a final reminder of instructions on how to support a polio survivor in the "normal" world. He nodded solemnly as the nurse pointed out items in the small booklet open in his hands.

The staff said repeatedly over the week leading up to her discharge that it would be easy to become discouraged by the challenges in the outside world, and she would need to develop a layer of armor.

She flipped the pen in her hand, then signed her name at the bottom of the papers on a clipboard in her lap. In the end, state funds, Riverwood donors, and the March of Dimes support had helped them cover the cost of treatment. Ursula was humbled by the generosity and how the staff committed to her recovery regardless of her economic status. Regardless of her fears of being unable to pay the final bill.

Ursula eyed Roger, who smiled in her direction. She was suddenly shy around him, like when she had first arrived in America. They would be starting over again under sadly different circumstances.

"I've signed all the papers," Ursula said.

"Are you ready to walk out of here?" Roger asked. He was jovial, almost levitating as he glided across the lobby toward her.

"Right now, I feel more comfortable in my chair. At home I'll have no choice but to walk." She had foolishly held onto the hope she would walk out of the hospital and leave her chair behind. Now hopefulness seemed ridiculous and stupid. She needed the wheelchair. She needed the crutches. She needed Roger to accept those facts just as she had.

"Good luck, Mrs. Gorski. We're going to miss you," Dr. Johnson said. The staff who knew her well had come to see her off. A rush of gratitude overcame her. During her bluest moments they had kept her going, encouraging her when she didn't believe she could take another step.

"If you need anything, you can always call," Miss Miller said as she embraced Ursula.

"Thank you. You saved my life," Ursula whispered.

"You're a courageous woman. I know you'll do well out there." Miss Miller kept her voice low so only Ursula could hear her.

"Time to go." Roger said, taking the handles of Ursula's wheelchair and wheeling her to the truck.

"Roger, I want to do this part myself," Ursula said.

During recent therapy sessions, she had practiced the necessary motions. Now Roger stood by. She instructed him to stand behind her, put his hands near her waist in case she fell backward. With a few pumps of her calves, she was up and then onto the seat, looking over the hood with a deep sense of accomplishment.

Roger lifted her chair and sticks into the truck's bed and slipped into the driver's seat. "Ready?" He asked.

"Let's go home."

CHAPTER 25
July 1951

Over and over again, for two weeks after arriving home from Riverwood, Ursula read the note Roger had taped to the polished oak door: *Do not enter under any circumstances. Surprise will be revealed in due time.* She was stumped as to what Roger had concealed in the empty nursery.

"Roger, what on earth have you done in here?"

"The wait is nearly over. I just need you to close your eyes."

Ursula squished her lids together and for extra measure placed her palms over her face. "Is this good enough?"

A laugh jumped off his lips. "More than good enough."

Ursula heard the door squeak on its hinges. Rogers hands were on the handles of her wheelchair and she was moving forward, into the surprise.

"Okay, you can open them."

Ursula blinked her eyes open. Her mouth involuntarily hung open too.

Roger squatted next to Ursula, peering up at her, "Well, do you like it?"

"I don't know what to say. It's beautiful."

Quiet settled over them while Ursula examined the transformation in front of her. On the far wall, Roger had placed a refinished desk with her typewriter and a lamp. The desk was missing a chair, which he had placed off to the side. A round table that would likely seat four wheelchairs anchored the middle of the room, and a blush-colored two-seater sofa sat under the window.

"You painted in here too?"

"I thought you could use a nice bright space—so I played it safe with white. You can add your own color with your knitting and crocheting projects."

"I suppose I never liked that bright yellow anyway."

Ursula saw a shadow pass across Roger's face. He pressed his lips together.

"How long have you been working on this?" She wanted to stay in the joy of the desk and typewriter and table, not think about what a still-yellow room could mean for them.

"Ever since we petitioned the court for your citizenship. I thought you would need a room of your own in this house, somewhere just for you. It has sat empty for so long."

"I am truly overwhelmed." Ursula thought she might cry.

"I hated seeing you so upset on the way back to Riverwood that day. I just kept thinking 'what can I do to help'? I've felt so useless out here, unable to make anything better while you were stuck doing all the work."

"Roger, you've been thoughtful and supportive—you came to see me as often as you could. Your band even played for us!"

"Sure, but all of these hours by myself with you in there. It made me a bit . . . gosh, I don't know. Anyway, later at work that week a customer brought in a desk and said that we could keep it or sell it, so I asked the boss if I could buy it at a discounted price. When I explained what I was going to do with it, he agreed."

"Really? Why would someone just give that away? And how

generous of your boss." Ursula wheeled herself closer and ran her fingers over the polished surface. "The finish on it brings out all the wood grains."

"The best part is that I inset the typewriter on this sliding wood tray so it will come to you." He slid the typewriter in and out in proud demonstration. "You don't have to leave your chair if you don't want to."

"How did you work this all out?" Ursula pulled the machine toward her so it hovered over her lap. She pretended to type. It was indeed set at a perfect height.

"Superintendent Eriksson let me take a few measurements of a wheelchair similar to yours. I did it before you could see what I was up to."

Ursula glanced at Roger. His hands were on his hips now, he was relaxed as he admired his work. "Thank you, Roger. This is the kindest thing anyone has ever done for me."

"Even kinder than a man promising to marry you and bringing you to America?" A huge smile erupted on Roger's face.

"Nearly." Ursula laughed as she pushed the typewriter back into the desk and rolled to the sofa and around the table to the door. "You've gotten the measurements just right. I haven't knocked any of the furniture with my chair."

"I was hoping you'd say that. I spent quite a few hours on the layout."

"And what is this?" Ursula stopped at the door to admire what was once a coat rack.

"I rigged it up so you have a spot to store your crutches. Like I said, I wanted you to have a place of your own—"

The doorbell interrupted them with a bright chime.

"Oh gosh, someone's already here," Ursula said. Roger had

organized a "Welcome Home" party for Ursula to coincide with the Fourth of July. Everyone had been invited. Pete, Sally, and the kids. Mrs. Gorski. Aunt Rose. Phyllis and her family. And Bea, too.

"I bet it's my brother and his family," Roger said as he slipped by Ursula to open the front door.

Ursula heard children's voices on the front step. She sped to her ramp off the side entrance to the kitchen.

"Well, look who's home!" Pete said, standing at the bottom of the incline with Vic tugging on the leash in his hand. Because Roger was at work so much, Vic had been staying with Pete's family. Ursula coasted down and swept the furry creature up on her lap. She hadn't realized how much she missed the little pest.

"Hi Ursula!" Sally shouted over the barking as she closed the car door. "Vic here seems quite excited to see you."

Vic's enthusiastic licks sent Ursula into a round of giggles. Contented, she petted him until he calmed down.

"What do you think of this ramp?" Pete motioned with his hand.

"It's perfect." Ursula admired the wooden landing that led to an incline to the right and a set of stairs just off the front. It had looked strange when she arrived home, but now she couldn't imagine the house without it.

Pete repeated the story she had already heard from Roger. "Once I heard stairs were causing you some trouble, we came up with a plan. You see I broke my leg when I was a teenager—a stupid bike accident—and I was in a cast all summer on the sofa. Stairs had been the damnedest things on a pair of crutches."

"You don't need to explain yourself. I am just so grateful." She ran her hand over Vic's silky fur while she stuffed Pete's words—"stairs were causing you some trouble"—into the back of her head.

"We're so glad you're home," Sally said, standing next to Pete with her hands full. "But the kids are going to miss that little dog. Now all I hear from those two is 'when can we get a dog, Mom?' I told them they can come play with Vic at your house."

"They are welcome anytime," Ursula said. "Now let's get that food inside." Ursula twirled at the base of the ramp, and when Pete offered to push her up, Ursula nodded. The incline was steeper than the ramps at Riverwood and she would need a few more months to build up strength in her arms to wheel herself upward.

"Auntie Ursula, Auntie Ursula!" A bubble of voices came from the kitchen.

"Chris, Elizabeth, how are you?"

"We love your dog," Chris said, his hands on his hips.

"We love him so much and he loves us too," Elizabeth said, copying her older brother.

"Vic loves both of you, too, but he has to stay here," Sally said.

"Can I get a ride in that thing?" Chris pointed to Ursula's chair.

"Christopher! Do not be rude to Aunt Ursula."

"It's fine, really," Ursula said to Sally. "Chris, take Vic for me and get his leash off, and then we can go for a ride around the house."

Chris did as instructed, then carefully stepped up into Ursula's lap.

"Can I come too?" Elizabeth asked.

"Let me give Chris his turn, and then I can take you."

"Are you sure?" Sally asked.

Ursula nodded heartily. "Hold on!"

"Ooo!" Chris screamed with delight as Ursula wove in and out of rooms. Elizabeth ran behind.

"Watch out you two," Ursula said to Pete and Roger as she spun around the table in her new room, back into the living room, past the dining room, and back into the kitchen.

"My turn! My turn!" Elizabeth practically pushed her brother out of Ursula's lap, then they followed the same route through the house.

"I think that's enough for now kids," Sally said. She was in the kitchen, arranging food, paper plates, and napkins on the counter. "Go find Vic, I'm sure he'd like to play."

"We can go again later," Ursula said as the kids tore out of the room.

"You really didn't have to do that," Sally stopped counting napkins and looked at Ursula.

"I loved it. They are such a joy." A tingling sensation came over her as she glimpsed the life she wanted—the house full of family, a family of her own. "And I'm happy that they aren't afraid of my chair. Adults have a difficult time with it."

"Oh, I suppose I . . ." Sally's eyes traced the floor, then she found her voice again. "I heard Roger made a surprise for you."

The flash of Sally's pity made Ursula want to recoil. She realized even among family, she would need to tune into each person's feelings. She would need to moderate their discomfort before her own.

A car horn sounded on the driveway.

"I'll go see who it is," Sally said.

"No, it's all right, I'll go." Ursula narrowed her eyes as if to say "I'm not helpless" and Sally backed off.

Outside, Phyllis came up the ramp on her crutches. "Well, aren't you spoiled! Look at this, just like we had at Riverwood."

"No chance of me being homebound now. Gosh it's good to see you."

"How long has it been now?"

"Nearly two months!" Ursula counted the weeks on her fingers. Too many weeks to be separated from her best friend.

"Has it really been that long?" Phyllis bent over and kissed Ursula on the cheek.

"Yes, it really has. Now come in, come in."

"Kids, David—I'll be inside."

Ursula introduced Phyllis to Sally, and they got to work—a final mix of the potato salad, onions diced for the brats, and a dusting of powdered sugar for the brownies. The inviting hum in the house filled Ursula with contentment. As they finished in the kitchen, smoke from the barbeque drifted in through the open windows. Ursula rolled to her perch at the top of the ramp. In front of the garage, with cans of Old Style in their hands, Roger rotated brats on the grill while Pete gave instructions.

"Ursula?" A voice flew up the driveway.

"Up here," Ursula shouted, admiring the comradery between the two brothers

"They let you out of the hospital," Mrs. Gorski said at the bottom of the stairs. "That's good."

"Indeed, they have." Ursula shifted her feet on the foot rests. She wasn't quite sure how else to respond. To Ursula, "Let you out" sounded like she had been imprisoned. Maybe being in there for so many months had felt unescapable, but Ursula would never let Mrs. Gorski know that.

Mrs. Gorski eyed the stairs and ramp, then said: "The boys made this for you, huh? Their father taught them how to build, but they could never match his talent."

"I've heard he was quite the woodworker."

"Where are my grandchildren?" Mrs. Gorski eyed the stairs again but opted for the ramp instead.

Pete called to his mother over the noise of the hissing grill. "See, its even good for you and your bad knees."

Ursula saw Roger smirk, then he looked at her. "We'll be in soon, just need to get these last few brats cooked."

"Ursula, there's someone on the phone for you," Sally poked her head through the crack in the door.

"Coming," Ursula said, eager to separate herself from their mother-in-law. Inside, Ursula set the phone in her lap, stretching the cord as long as it would go. In the doorway of her new sanctuary, she pressed the receiver to her ear.

"Ursula? Is that you?" Bea's voice sounded against her head.

"Bea, how wonderful to hear your voice." It brought Ursula back to her former life. She hadn't lost everything.

"I'm so sorry to be calling last minute, but one of the kids is sick with the flu. We're not going to make it to the party today, unfortunately."

"Oh no. That's too bad."

"A few children from our neighborhood got sick last summer with polio. And now we're concerned about another outbreak. Most of those children recovered, but a few were . . ." Bea didn't finish.

"It's probably just the flu, like you said. And you're right to stay home, no need to get anyone else sick," Ursula said. Her stomach recoiled like it had earlier with Sally, but this time it was from the physical memory of being sick, of not knowing what was happening. The fear that had outlined her limbs, ready to color her whole body.

"I can't wait to see you, though. We have so much to catch up on," Bea said and then shouted something inaudible. She had muffled the receiver with her hand.

They hadn't seen each other since before Ursula got sick. They had exchanged a few letters, Christmas, and anniversary cards while Ursula was at Riverwood, but that was it.

"I can try you later—how about next week?"

"I don't mean to be rude, but one of the kids is screaming again . . . we'll talk again soon. Cheers." Bea hung up.

Ursula mumbled goodbye into the phone.

"Sally said you were in here." Rose stood in the doorframe. "Everything all right?"

"I'm glad you made it," Ursula said, then hesitated. She wanted to explain the recoil in her stomach, how quickly fear could find a place inside her body again. It was one thing to share her feelings with Phyllis, but another to explain them to someone who wasn't a polio survivor. "It's fine. My friend Bea just canceled—sick kid."

"I'm sure you were looking forward to seeing her," Rose said stepping into the room.

"I was," Ursula said. The urge to open up to Rose crested, but instead she handed the phone to Rose so she could put it back on the hallway table.

"This is better than Roger described," Rose said when she returned. "You know, he wouldn't even let me have a peek."

"He has been guarding this door ever since I got home! This is truly the most thoughtful thing he's done for me, second to that ramp."

Rose looked like she wanted to say something, paused, then walked to the sofa against the window and sat down.

"Were you going to say something?" Ursula was relieved to have the attention on Rose for a moment.

"Over Sunday lunch one afternoon, Roger was telling us about your progress in therapy, how you were doing on your crutches. The mention of crutches sent Pete complaining about that time he had to go around on them after he broke his leg, and then the two boys came up with the ramp. I honestly couldn't be prouder of them."

Ursula nodded, not letting on that she had heard this story several times already. "It was such a surprise! I wasn't expecting to come home to see it there. You know, somehow that ramp has made me feel more a part of this family."

"You don't have to explain that. I see a bit of myself in you, and how hard it is to find your place in a family. I struggled for a long time with my husband's family—"

"There you both are," Roger said, poking his head into the room. "Lunch is ready, come eat."

"We'll be right there," Ursula said.

"Ursula, before we go, I need to tell you something else," Rose said.

"What is it?"

"Mary won't tell you this because she is too stubborn, but she's grateful to you for making those blankets for mothers in need."

"That's a surprise," Ursula said, elated the knitting work she had done after physical therapy in the afternoons at Riverwood had earned her some respect from Mrs. Gorski.

"It was brave of you, knitting blankets for other peoples' children when you've struggled so much to have your own."

"I needed something to keep these idle hands moving." More than anything, the knitting projects kept her from feeling trapped in her chair when she was too tired to move.

"Ursula! Aunt Rose!" Voices rang from the kitchen.

"We better get going," Rose said.

"Yes, we better." Ursula happily returned to the hubbub of a full house, her family and friends spread around her. Even Mrs. Gorski.

After everyone had gone, and dusk settled over the house, Roger came up behind Ursula and tugged at the zipper on her dress. She was at the kitchen table, sitting over a rum and Coca-Cola.

"What has gotten into you?" Ursula noticed he had turned on the radio, and now jazz swirled around her.

"Ten months of being apart."

Ursula wheeled out of the kitchen, following Roger. When she got to the threshold of their bedroom, she stopped and wondered if she would be able to love him like she used to. But Roger had no doubts, his zipper bulging in front of Ursula's face as he lifted her from the chair. Entwined, Ursula clung to her husband's neck as he lowered her onto their bed. She pulled down the sleeves of her dress, but realized it would be too difficult to remove. So instead, she gathered the skirt around her waist while Roger lowered her underpants, kissing her legs as he slipped the fabric past her feet. The feeling of his lips on her legs sent a shiver through her body. Ursula was suddenly nervous, as if she had never had sex before, but she wanted to keep going. She still clung to the hope she could get pregnant, have a baby. But she also wanted to do what she had longed for all those months in the hospital—feel Roger inside her, feel how close they could be to each other. Roger unzipped his trousers and like teenagers about to get caught, they made love half-dressed. For the first time in many months, she did not feel broken.

PART III

CHAPTER 26
May 1957

Ursula made it a practice to start her day in the office Roger had so lovingly created. It was her space to control. It was clean and orderly, the two lessons formed in the League of German Girls she allowed herself to maintain. She was an American citizen now, so best to keep those obsessions between the four walls of her sacred room. She liked to stay neat with her knitting, too, a habit learned when she was forced to make socks for soldiers. Efficient, tight—but not too tight—loops. How quickly she could wrap the yarn over the needles. She no longer knit socks, but the neatness of her stitches was second nature now, so she could sit in her room and let her mind wander as she knit and purled her way through blankets, scarves, and shawls.

The day Roger had shown her this room he had been so proud. Ursula had seen how much he loved her, how he would not abandon her, how he was ready to accept the life they had in front of them. Maybe he couldn't clearly articulate those feelings, but the act of creating this space was enough. In the days and weeks afterward, Ursula would sit on the office sofa and cry as she imagined what the room would have been like as the nursery. The crib would go where her desk was now, the Moses basket next to it. She would keep the sofa as a place to nurse, or a place to sit while the baby rolled on a blanket on the floor in front of her. She would have asked Roger for a changing table—one customized to a perfect height. Perhaps she would have asked him to refashion a desk so she could sit while she released the diaper pins, moving the soiled fabric to a nearby bucket. She had watched Phyllis do this for her children. The tenderness of her touch, the way she bubbled raspberries on her children's bellies as their bare legs kicked with enthusiasm. The yellow walls would have been painted over—they had long ago agreed it was a hideous shade, even for a baby. Ursula still didn't understand what Sally had been thinking.

But it was not a nursery. It was an office. And most mornings, if she wasn't knitting on the couch, Ursula used the space to read or write. Doing so helped her focus on the life in front of her. She might pound out a letter to her mother at the typewriter, or dash off a quick note of encouragement to a fellow polio survivor on the stationery with the elaborate U in the header. She might clip recipes from the newspaper or magazines and send them to Bea. She could count on her friend to call and let her know how the brownies with walnuts or porkchops with raisins turned out.

After lunch, Mrs. Ohlin would often stop by. Her earlier distrust of the woman had mellowed and an understanding had grown between them. It could even be called neighborly. They spent time talking about Mrs. Ohlin's lush garden, her active children, or what was happening at her church. It was a welcome distraction. Ursula could listen without giving too much away about how stiff her legs were in the morning, how it took her at least ten minutes to get out of bed. How after Roger left for work the house was always too quiet, so she left the radio in the kitchen on for the whole day.

Riverwood had taught her how to persevere and also, perhaps, to move forward. It didn't happen all of a sudden—the letting go of old expectations—but one year folded into two, and then three, four, five, and six. Time eased, and at some point, Ursula accepted that what she had always yearned for—what she had built an altar for in her mind—might be beyond her reach. But she still imagined what it would be like. All of the mothers in her life had come together around that altar and shown her how it might be. She would leave her own mother's harshness behind, and she would be tender, but firm, like Phyllis. She would be fiercely committed to her family like Bea. She would be a little bit nosy like Mrs. Ohlin, just enough to keep the child out of any trouble. There were other details, like the doll she would buy for a daughter—because in truth, she had only ever pictured a daughter. A son occasionally buzzed around her head, but then he buzzed right out and she gazed on her little girl. A girl who had her brown eyes but Roger's curly chestnut-colored hair. A girl who was maybe just a bit taller than she was, but not as tall as Roger. A girl who had her sense of adventure, her desire to explore the possibilities life could offer. A girl who wouldn't have hesitated to fly across the ocean for a new beginning.

And even though Roger never agreed to see Dr. Hunt, Ursula forgave him. She remembered Dr. Hunt explaining how doctors were still experimenting, learning and trying to understand infertility. Ursula decided to accept the emptiness of her womb as her own. It would have been easy to keep blaming Roger, to keep resentment between them. But she couldn't sustain the conflict. It wasn't worth having a wedge between them.

When she'd come home from Riverwood, Ursula knew life would be different. Everything would have to be relearned. Cleaning the house. Maneuvering in her kitchen. Navigating in the neighborhood. She wouldn't have time to indulge any self-pity. But she hadn't counted on all the repressed emotion, all she still carried. Those relentless thoughts about her family, the guilt of leaving them, the constant trying and failing to have a baby. There were the "what ifs"—could staying out of the pool have prevented polio? In her office, over the years, she eventually let it all go. She looked back at the days after the war and saw a different person. She was young and naive and maybe stupid, but she was a person who always found a way forward. Ursula could not, would not, give up on that courageous aspect of herself.

Ursula set down her needles—it was time for a new shade of yarn. But before grabbing the next color, Ursula thumbed her carnation pendant. It offered reassurance, the knowledge her mother had worn the necklace, that it had touched her skin during the longest, most dangerous air raids, had fallen into the hollow of her chest as her bones protruded from beneath her skin from hunger. On days when Ursula wanted to be near her, to feel her unwavering strength, she paused to caress the silver, reminding herself of where she came from.

Ursula let the flower fall back to her chest, and reached for a new skein from the batch of yarn Rose had dropped off a few days ago. She admired the light frosty pink then began circling the long strand from the skein into a ball. Rose had been asking her to teach the women's group at church more complicated knitting patterns and suggested socks. Ursula had refused. Socks were for soldiers and she wouldn't return to that time in her life. But now she reconsidered. Maybe she could would teach the ladies how to make baby socks, instead. She had seen a simple pattern in *Better Homes and Gardens*. From her magazine rack beside the sofa, Ursula flipped through old issues until she found it. With the pages open next to her on the cushion, and Vic sound asleep at her feet, she reviewed the photos and read the instructions. Yes, she thought, baby socks were nothing like soldier socks. And perhaps teaching others could be one more path in her new life.

From her perch in Roger's truck, Ursula admired the dark blue stretch of water as they rounded Lake Harriet. Simply being near the natural pool calmed her, relaxed her. Even though she knew there wasn't a direct connection with contracting polio in pools, polio would unfortunately be associated in her mind with swimming indoors. She was glad the disease also hadn't clouded her love for the Twin Cities' lakes. She was glad to be getting outside in the air after practicing the baby sock pattern all week. She could clear her mind and rest her hands.

Roger parked the car near the band shell. He had memorized the easiest route for Ursula to navigate in her wheelchair or crutches. All around them, electric green buds pushed through stiff bark on the trees, and tulips yet to bloom surfaced from the ground, reaching toward the warm spring sun.

"Can we stop for a moment? I want to sit." Roger motioned toward a bench and sat down, plopping the picnic basket on the ground in front of him. His face was red, dotted with perspiration. He took a handkerchief from his pocket and wiped the beads from his brow.

"Are you feeling ill again?" Ursula asked, worried he was coming down with a cold. He had bouts of illness now, as regular as Ursula's cramped, stiff legs. Roger claimed it was stress. Ursula thought it might be something more.

"Tired, dear," he said.

"You always work too hard," Ursula said and reached for his hand. "I know we've been planning on seeing my family next summer, but maybe this summer we could go up north like Phyllis does with her family. Just for a weekend. It sounds beautiful up there." Ursula pictured hundreds of Lake Harriets laced in the northern forests. Phyllis always seemed more content after a week in the woods. Maybe it would have the same quiet effect on Roger.

"I would like that, but I don't know." Roger sat up straighter and put his hand over his chest.

"What is it?" Ursula leaned forward.

"I don't know where we'll find the money." His voice caught in his throat. "You know I'm still helping my mother with bills."

Ursula no longer had the energy to be upset about his mother and the bills. She had adjusted to the fact Roger would never see his mother struggle. And how could she fault him for that? She had sent her own family money for years. If her mother sounded even a bit distressed in her letters, Ursula pinched from the weekly grocery budget to send them money. She tracked SuperValu's advertisements and bought in bulk, and Roger had never noticed the difference.

"Could Pete help for once?"

"You know I can't ask him. He's got his family, kids to feed," Roger said. His eyebrows knitted together, deepening the wrinkles on his forehead. He played the perfect older brother, always protective.

"You really don't look well," Ursula said, concerned this was more than Roger's routine cold sweats, more than the stressors of everyday life. Ursula wished he would see a doctor, stop being so stubborn. His discernment for his family's circumstances stopped at his own health.

"I'm just tired." The color had drained from his face, he was perspiring even more. Ursula pulled the handkerchief from his hand and dabbed his forehead.

"Maybe have something to eat?" She sat back, but Roger didn't move.

He took a deep breath, pointed to the wicker basket. "What's in there?"

Ursula reached for the basket, then held out a few options. Roger selected a ham sandwich and an apple. Ursula took the remaining sandwich

"Maybe you're right, maybe we could go up north for a weekend," Roger said, taking the apple first and biting into it. He chewed slowly as he ran the white cotton over his face again. "I could work a few more Saturdays this month."

"Are you sure? It was only a suggestion . . . I don't want to add more pressure." She paused. "And I do want to see my family." She adjusted the bread so the ham would stay between the two slices of bread.

"We can find a way to do both," Roger said, pausing to chisel the apple core with his teeth. He would eat the whole thing and toss the stem, which baffled Ursula. She was happy to leave old wartime habits behind.

Roger spun the apple stem in between his fingers. "I don't think I've ever said this," he said, "but I do feel guilty for taking you away from your life there."

"You didn't take me away, I wanted to leave." And that was the truth—Ursula had wanted to leave even if it meant enduring the long-term separation.

"I know, but you left behind your life, your family."

"That was years ago, but . . ." Ursula stopped, holding Roger's gaze. "Promise me that you won't let anything jeopardize the journey next year."

"Nothing will stop us," he said, between bites of his sandwich. "I absolutely promise."

As they finished their lunch Ursula watched the lake glisten in the sun and the spring grass poke through the earth. Roger stretched his legs out on the wooden bench, positioned his head on a balled-up cloth napkin and fell asleep. A light snore buzzed on his lips, and a deep sense of peace fell over Ursula like a cozy blanket.

As Roger slept, Ursula turned her wheelchair to face the lake and saw next summer's homecoming unfold before her. Her mother would smile but not cry. Her father would sob. Aunt Kaethe would shriek with excitement. On her fingers, she counted the months until she would be on an airplane over the Atlantic. Until she would pass through the door of her childhood home and take a deep breath of lavender, and then remove the carnation from her neck and place it again around her mother's. Not long after she left Riverwood, she had written to her mother about the necklace, how she took it, but would eventually return it. In a long reply, instead of being upset, her mother had been grateful. She had written that after the front door had closed the day they argued at the kitchen table, once the tears had stopped, she wished she had given her daughter something, anything.

A dog barked loudly nearby, and Roger startled awake.

"How long did I sleep?" Roger rubbed his sleepy eyes as he sat upright.

"Maybe twenty minutes? I did not want to wake you, you looked content." Ursula spun so her chair was perpendicular to the bench.

"Should we go around the lake?" Roger said.

Ursula watched his eyes follow the ribbon of path framing the water and nodded. She leaned toward the bench to lift the basket, tossing in the used napkins, careful not to disturb the untouched coffee cake.

"Ready?" With the basket nestled in her lap, she unlocked the brakes on her chair.

"Give me a minute," Roger said. Beads of sweat appeared on his forehead again. His face flushed. A strangled noise came from his throat. Startled, Ursula rolled backward, her hands instinctively catching the wheels and flipping the break levers.

"Roger, what's wrong?" She pushed her chair up to him so their knees touched. She swung the basket to the ground and grabbed Roger's hands.

"No, no. Don't make a fuss. Maybe a bit more shut eye will help." Roger leaned back, crossing his arms over his chest. He heaved loudly. Then his eyes popped open with fear.

"Roger!"

"I can't, I can't." He choked on his words and his arms went limp by his sides.

"Roger, what's wrong? What is it?" Ursula shook his knees, then whipped her head around, hoping to see someone. A man walking the dog that had barked so loudly a few minutes before came toward them on the path.

"Help! We need help!" Ursula watched the man pick up his pace and come toward them.

"Ma'am, what's the problem?" In one motion, he took off his hat and motioned for his dog to sit.

"My husband. He's not well." Roger blinked in front of her. "Roger, can you hear me?"

No response.

"Sir, please call for help, there's something wrong with my husband."

"I'll call for a doctor," the man said and ran off, his dog obediently by his side.

Ursula rolled back an inch or two so she could put on her brakes, then stood and shuffled to sit next to Roger on the bench. Adrenaline had kicked in and she transferred herself easily from one seat to the other. She dabbed his forehead. "A doctor is being called," she said. "You are going to be fine, everything is going to be fine."

Roger nodded, but the movement was so slight Ursula couldn't tell if he had heard what she said. She put her hands on his cold, damp face and pulled him into her. Roger slumped over her lap, the weight of him urgent.

"No! No, no, no. Roger, wake up!" Ursula wished she could carry him, pick him up and run to the nearest hospital.

And then they sat, and Ursula stopped tracking time. She stroked Roger's face. The face that had been so kind when she first stepped on the American base in Berlin. The face that had welcomed her through sleepiness when she landed in Minneapolis. The face that had furrowed with concern when nurses wheeled her into the polio insolation unit. The face that had brightened with joy when she was released from Riverwood. The face that had filled with pride as he showed Ursula her newly decorated office.

The rescue squad arrived a few minutes later and started to move Roger onto a stretcher. As they did, Ursula looked again at Roger's face, now pallid and motionless.

"You have to help him, please help him," she said. Roger's helplessness filled her with alarm, an eerie reminder of her own journey on a gurney.

The man with the dog trailed behind the rescue squad and kindly helped Ursula into her chair. He wheeled her over the cracks and bumps in the walkway and Ursula begged him to go faster, to keep up with Roger on his gurney. The man was running now, the wheelchair jolting over the uneven path and his leashed dog sprinting behind them. Just as the ambulance doors were about to close, Ursula caught sight of the soles of Roger's shoes, worn at the heels. She let out a wail that sent the man's dog into wild howls. And when the wailing subsided to deep gasps of air, the man offered Ursula a ride to the hospital. She again urged him on. Faster, faster.

In a bay in the emergency room, Roger had a sheet draped over his body.

"What have you done to him?" Ursula tried to pull back the fabric, but her hands shook.

"I'm so sorry, Mrs. Gorski. We suspect your husband had a heart attack," someone said.

"No. No. No." The word rushed from her mouth. The world blurred. Everything went black.

For five days leading to the funeral mass and burial, Ursula detached from her life. Mimicking how she used to live so she could get through the days. It was as if she had been shelled from the inside, the bombs splitting her apart. The numbness so deep she was too shocked to speak. Her voice stayed trapped in her chest as tears fell in beads from her face. Phyllis coaxed food into her, reminded her to rest. Mrs. Ohlin kept watch with gentle knocks on the door a few times a day, and this time she was thankful for her neighbor's kindness. Rose took on the remaining arrangements when she collapsed in the kitchen on the day Roger's body was transported from the morgue to the funeral home. For Ursula, knowing he was not coming home dealt a finality she could not bear.

From her position at the head of the grave, rows of flat white stones spread out before Ursula. She took a small step back to keep her crutches from sinking into the wet spring ground. Her vision clouded white with the stones, their endlessness. They were arranged with such precision they could have been needlepoint stitches organized on a large hoop that was the Fort Snelling National Cemetery. Their order on any other day would have calmed Ursula, but today she could not forgive their cold sameness, an erasure of the people underneath them.

Ursula pressed her eyes closed. When she opened them, Mrs. Gorski came into focus on the opposite side of the grave. Pete's arm wrapped around his mother's shoulder, Sally and the kids surrounding him. Aunt Rose was on Mrs. Gorski's other side. Phyllis and her family gathered near Ursula. The priest stood on the long side of the rectangle, Bible tucked against his chest under his crossed arms. Farther behind were a few men in uniform. Roger's boss. A few of his colleagues. Mrs. Ohlin, too.

"Let us bow our heads." The priest started to pray, but Ursula's mind wandered. She counted the losses. Her childhood obliterated by war. Berlin left in ruins. Family thousands of miles away. Motherhood an abandoned dream. Mobility greatly diminished. Husband gone. Roger had been her hope. They were building a life together to help her forget her other losses. But now those losses were like trees felled in a forest, chopped into pieces and stacked up to be burned, fueling the flames of her sorrow.

Soon, rifles behind her were fired, the formal military sendoff. The rhythmic staccato caused a surge in Ursula as if she had been pulled through a window and was back on the streets of Berlin, running for cover from Allied fire. She opened and closed her eyes a few times. If she could see what was in front of her, she might get through the day.

After the burial, after the people had gone, after someone rearranged her refrigerator with casseroles that would take weeks for Ursula to eat alone, she sat in the eerie quiet of her living room. Grief washed over her body and combined with the chronic ache of polio and the acute pain of loss. How would she cope and live this life alone? Before coming to American she'd always thought the war would be the worst thing she would have to overcome. Did a difficult beginning set the stage for an even more challenging middle and end?

Ursula rose from the sofa and shuffled to the phone to call Phyllis, the only person who truly understood the magnitude of what she felt.

"Would you be able to stay the night?" Ursula asked, her voice hoarse. "I don't know if I can be in this house alone." The burial had made it real. Roger would never walk through the door again. She felt guilty for asking Phyllis for more help, but the pain of isolation was worse.

"Let me get the kids to bed, and I'll be right over," Phyllis said, her voice strong and calm.

"I cannot explain to you what this feels like." Ursula's voice bordered on the edge of a sob. "How will I get through this?"

"Like you've gotten through every day before this one."

"This feels different," Ursula said, and she heard a child shriek in the background.

"That's Emma. I need to get her into the bath. We can talk about all of this later. I'll see you soon." Phyllis hung up.

Ursula pressed her back against the wall and cried, the phone still cradled in her hands. She had been safe, cared for, and loved by Roger. And she always knew he didn't see her as a barren cripple, but as the woman he'd fallen in love with in Berlin. That underneath the polio survivor Ursula was there, the woman he loved.

As May faltered into June, and Ursula's days, then weeks, heaved with sorrow, she confronted the reality of being a widowed polio survivor. She was ill-equipped to navigate her home without help. To navigate her life without help. She had allowed herself to become too reliant on Roger, had fallen away from a regular exercise routine, had lost some of the mobility in her legs. All the tasks Roger had done—laundry, errands, driving her to the grocery store or to see Phyllis—were now in her hands. If she wanted to survive, she would need to help herself.

She could not rely on the kindness of strangers for the rest of her life, or even for the summer.

Mrs. Ohlin had come by every morning since the funeral to make sure Ursula had gotten out of bed and eaten breakfast. Ursula had not expected Roger's family to come to her aid, as they had their own lives to tend to. But Aunt Rose stopped by with dinners a few times a week, communicating her sympathies through meatloaf and strong embraces. And Phyllis, without hesitation, came whenever Ursula called. With each of Phyllis's visits, though, Ursula sensed a hint of reluctance. It wasn't that her best friend didn't care about her. It was more that Phyllis was stretched enough caring for her own family. Ursula was determined to find a way forward that meant she could ask less of those around her, and ask more of herself.

Ursula first considered hiring a neighbor girl for help but she had no idea how much money she had. Managing their finances had been another one of Roger's responsibilities. Mrs. Ohlin's son, Henry, volunteered to look after Vic, letting himself in the side door and taking the elderly dog to the yard a few times a day. He bragged about the Boy Scout troop badge he had earned. The upholstery shop where Roger had worked had raised some money for her, but those funds had been used to pay for the funeral.

As Ursula considered her plight, she smoothed the newsprint with her palms on the kitchen table. She traced her eyes over the article she'd just read about a three-month outpatient program for polio survivors at the Sister Kenny Institute. The program offered assistance to survivors who needed ongoing treatment. It was nearby. And it also offered financial support. And suddenly a future of independence spooled out in her mind. The program could teach her to drive. Then she could buy a car so she could take herself to and from therapy. She could ferry herself all over the Twin Cities, maybe get a job. She could have some version of life again, even if it wasn't what she had imagined years ago gliding over the Atlantic.

CHAPTER 27
July 1957

At the Sister Kenny Institute, Dr. Vargas's office was small but neatly appointed. A collection of medical textbooks and knickknacks adorned his large mahogany desk. The doctor swiftly stood up from his desk when Ursula came through the open door in her wheelchair. She had thought about using her crutches, but when Phyllis had picked her up that morning, she reminded Ursula of what a long day it would be, so Ursula had just hooked her crutches to the back of her chair. People at the institute might need to look at them, see her walk with them.

After introductions, Dr. Vargas sat back down and folded his hands on the desk. "Tell me why you would make a good candidate for this program."

Ursula explained everything from the initial onset of polio, her treatment at Riverwood, six years of atrophy. That what she needed now was to become more independent.

"And your husband, is he able to help you with your care?" Dr. Vargas glanced at the ring on Ursula's hand.

"He died a few months ago," Ursula said. She instinctively covered her chest with her arms, her heart beat wildly against her ribs. "A heart attack."

"Ay, my deepest sympathies Mrs. Gorski," Dr. Vargas said, his face solemn.

"This is why I have to get better. I have no one else to rely on but myself."

Dr. Vargas nodded, then explained she likely had power in her legs that she had not used in many months. With regular exercise, her strength would return.

"Do you have any other particular goals for the program?" he asked.

Ursula nodded. "I need to learn to drive, well, relearn. I drove before my polio attack."

Dr. Vargas immediately approved her for treatment, and said Ursula likely qualified for financial assistance. He also prescribed a new set of crutches, as the ones she'd used for years now had warped cuffs and dry and cracked rubber tips. Ursula could not believe her luck. After all the grief of the past two months, a lightness filled her body as she turned the wheels of her chair under her palms and went to the gym.

In the open, bright room, a technician asked Ursula to walk a few steps with her crutches so he could asses her current mobility. Then he helped Ursula get acquainted with her new exercises. The parallel bars Ursula had loathed at Riverwood took on a new shine in this environment. She was relieved to see similar equipment dot the space—not every movement would have to be learned from scratch. The technician demonstrated the exercises, and the muscles she would need to engage for the first few weeks of treatment, then asked Ursula to try a few. From her wheelchair, she flexed each leg so it stuck out from her hip at ninety degrees. She alternated legs, the fatigue setting in fast, as a chuckle erupted from her belly and then she couldn't stop laughing. It was as if a valve had released and she could see herself as the Ursula she had always been: a woman who sought adventure, a fierce friend, talented knitter, lover of movies and music, and someone who would not give up. *I'm going to lick polio,* Ursula thought, more determined than ever.

After a month of driving instruction, Ursula decided to buy a new car. Being behind the wheel again had come back to her faster than she thought, and the modified pedals in the institute's special car helped. Without the modifications, she couldn't move her leg fast enough to hit the brake, though, so she needed a car that could be modified to suit her needs.

A few weeks before, Rose had suggested she sell the truck to Pete. Ursula thought this was perfect. She wanted to see Roger's prized vehicle leave the driveway with someone who loved him. So Rose came back the next day with Pete, who handed Ursula an envelope of cash, more than she anticipated. He explained it wasn't charity, not at all. Roger had provided for the family for so long—especially for their mother—and the best way for Pete to honor his brother would be for him to help Ursula.

Between the unexpected money from Pete and the remainder of Roger's insurance benefit, Ursula could buy a car and more. She had calculated the cost of the mortgage, utilities, and groceries. She had added in gas and car repairs. It would be tight, but she could make it work. The money could see her through for a few years. Plus, there was still the nest egg of savings to go to Germany. When she jotted down the number, she had to stop her calculations for the day. She needed that money to live. Losing Roger meant losing the chance to see her family again.

Ursula heard Phyllis honk from the curb. She grabbed her handbag with a healthy chunk of her savings nestled inside.

"Which car place are we going to?" Phyllis asked as Ursula settled in after placing her crutches across the back seat.

"I thought we could go to the Ford dealership near the institute."

"Really? I heard that man can be difficult," Phyllis said, her nose scrunched.

"No one is going to stop me from getting my independence back. Besides, I saw this beautiful Ford advertised in the *Star* and thought if I can find a way to have that car, I will!"

"Well, let's go see what he has to offer," Phyllis said, cracking the windows as she backed out of Ursula's driveway. Warm air blew through their hair as they cruised, just like two young women who'd never been touched by polio enjoying a beautiful summer day. Ursula needed that boost of confidence. She had never bought anything of this magnitude and she was surprisingly nervous. Sure, traveling to a new country alone had been scary, but she'd had Roger waiting for her.

When they arrived at the dealership, Ursula surveyed the cars on the lot—a country sedan, a Crown Victoria and a few Thunderbirds. She walked haltingly along on her sticks, eyeballing the various models. Phyllis was close behind her on her own crutches when a short round-bellied man approached them.

"Can I help you ladies with anything?"

"I'm here to buy a car," Ursula said. She kept her voice strong and steady.

"Where is your husband?" He swiveled his head as if Roger was lurking behind her.

"I'm here to buy a car, not talk about my husband," Ursula said. She had no interest in explaining anything to this man. She simply needed him to sell her a car.

"Ladies don't buy cars. Come on inside. You can give your husband a call. Tell him to come down here, and we can make a deal." He pointed to the entrance of the small office.

"My husband is dead. He will not be coming down here."

"Please, my friend is still grief-stricken," Phyllis said to the man.

"Phyllis, it's fine," Ursula said. She didn't want anyone to feel sorry for her.

"My sympathies," the man said, face flushing a bright red. "What type are you looking for? I don't have anything special for cripples."

"My legs are a bit slow, but I am not a cripple." Ursula's left thigh vibrated under her skirt and she stamped an invisible polka-dot on the pavement, hoping to regain her balance. She needed to make a decision quickly or the power in her legs would go.

"How about this beauty?" The salesman gestured to a sedan with rust at the edges of the doors.

"I prefer this one." Ursula placed her hand on the hood of a blue Ford in front of her. "How much do you want for it?"

"Let's go inside out of the sun," Phyllis said setting her eyes on Ursula.

"Thank you," Ursula mouthed to Phyllis, grateful that she'd noted her shaking leg.

They trailed the man to his office and rested in the seats opposite his paper-littered metal desk. He jotted down a number and set it in front of Ursula. It was higher than the total amount of cash Ursula had stashed in her purse. She thought about life in Berlin after the war, how she'd have to haggle over every bag of sugar, every pair of shoes. She now needed this car as much as she'd needed sugar and shoes. And Ursula knew if he brought the price down a bit more, she would have enough left over to modify the pedals. Ursula found a pen, wrote her own number on the scrap of paper, and pushed it across the desk. The man looked her in the eye for a long moment, then nodded. Then she counted out the cash, signed the paperwork, and finally grasped the keys like a token of triumph, the metal cold in her palm.

Once the salesman was out of sight, Ursula held the keys out to Phyllis. "Can you drive me to the shop down the road? I'm going to need them to install a special set-up so I can work the pedals."

"You're incredible, you know that?" Phyllis took the keys, shaking her head.

"That was nothing, just a bit of wartime smarts I had forgotten I had."

The two of them got in the car, and Ursula twisted the radio dial. When she heard Elvis's "All Shook Up," she cranked down the window and sang at the top of her lungs.

CHAPTER 28
September 1957

On the first day of German class, Ursula stood nervously at the front of the modest room at the institute. Fifteen students looked back at her. It was a mix of Sister Kenny Institute patients, medical students, and nurses. Someone coughed, another person shifted in their chair. Ursula did not have time to indulge her nerves. She had gone to the library, studied books on language instruction, and put together enough lessons for twelve weeks. She needed this class to go well.

If the class went well, the institute would continue to offer it, and, more important, continue to pay her. She needed the money, for the mortgage and more. She could not bear to leave the only home she ever knew in Minneapolis. She had thought about looking for another typing job, but navigating stairs, curbs, and sidewalks would leave her exhausted. Everything took her twice as long. Dr. Vargas had suggested she approach the institute about teaching a German language class when he heard about another polio survivor teaching French, and the powers-that-be were kind enough to let Ursula try.

"Welcome to German for beginners," Ursula said, trying to put authority into her voice. "I'd like each of you to introduce yourself and explain why you want to learn to speak German. Let's begin here, at the front." Ursula pointed at a woman her own age she'd seen in the gym doing exercises. One by one, the students spoke, sharing their names and reasons for wanting to learn German. Then the last student spoke from the back of the room.

"My name is Mateo Fabricio Peralta. I want to learn German to better understand the philosophy of Karl Marx."

Ursula stiffened. She was in no mood to debate socialist politics. She just wanted to get through her first class without a major mishap and go home to rest.

"I believe you learn more from someone in their own language," Mr. Peralta continued. Ursula couldn't decide if she liked his verbosity or not, but thought she understood what he meant.

"Yes, it is possible for things to be misunderstood in translation," Ursula said, remembering her first years in America when there were words and phrases that did not translate well from German to English.

"Languages bring out different ideas, feelings," Mr. Peralta said, his eyes earnest.

"That's a very nice thought but I suggest you take that up with a philosopher. I am here to teach you German." She took a deep breath, wanting to regain control. "Let's begin our first lesson."

For the next forty-five minutes, Ursula explained present tense, moving between the blackboard where she wrote blocky letters in German and the desk where she sat to take pressure off her legs. She was surprised by how the language stuttered on her tongue. She'd rarely spoken it since she'd been in America, only using German in letters home. Her student's faces showed no signs of doubting her fluency, though.

At the end of class, Mr. Peralta stopped by Ursula's desk. She noticed his smooth olive complexion, then caught herself. It was the first time since Roger died that she had observed another man so closely. She stepped back from the desk, uncomfortable.

"You agree?" he said, as he drummed his fingers on his chin. "We must learn concepts in the language they were written?"

"I agree that we both made it through this first class." Ursula flipped her wrist to catch the time on her watch. It was almost eight thirty. Her legs ached, and she wanted to watch the nightly news. "I hope you enjoyed the lesson. I'll see you next week."

"You know I am a student here?" Mr. Peralta asked. "I am learning the methods of the Institute."

Ursula shifted on her stick. She had not recognized him without his white coat, the standard uniform at the Institute for doctors and physical therapists alike.

"Yes, I think I have seen you before. I am a patient of Dr. Vargas. I receive outpatient treatment here."

"Everyone knows Dr. Vargas! I am studying with him. I will bring these treatment methods back to Argentina," Mr. Peralta said, ebullience in his voice.

Ursula gave him a half smile. "I often wonder why anyone would come to Minnesota. It's so cold here, but I suppose there are a few good things. Without the Institute I would be, well, I don't really know where I'd be. Anyway, it's nice to meet you. I must get home." Ursula pulled her wool coat off the back of her chair, resting her stick against the desk, but it fell to the floor as she stuck her arms through the sleeves. Mr. Peralta swept down to retrieve it.

"I am a gentleman, Mrs. Gorski," Mr. Peralta said, offering Ursula her stick. "I will walk you to your car now."

"Mr. Peralta, there's no need. My car is parked near the door. I will be just fine." But a part of Ursula wanted him to accompany her, she liked the attention. And it was refreshing not to explain polio to him.

"You will make me look like a *maleducado*." When Ursula raised an eyebrow in confusion, he explained the word meant badly mannered. He slapped a palm against his thigh and laughed. "Now I am teaching you a few words."

"All right," Ursula said, attempting to appear reluctant. But she liked the way he joked. It was sincere, almost innocent.

A few students lingered in the lobby. "Have a nice night, Mrs. Gorski," they said, waving politely. She waved back with the tips of her fingers. She didn't want to lose her grip on the stick. Ursula pushed open the door and felt Mr. Peralta behind her, holding it open. She took the stairs with determination. Slow. Steady.

"How will you get home?" she asked when they reached her car.

The sun had slid just beyond the horizon and touched everything with ombre light. Pinks turned to purples, which turned to blues.

"The streetcar," Mr. Peralta said. His face was warm in the light.

"You be careful," Ursula said, but didn't want to say goodbye just yet. Intrigue crept inside her—who was this man?

"The streets of Buenos Aires are more dangerous, if I may say."

"Oh, I hadn't thought." Ursula didn't know much about Buenos Aires, only that many former Nazis had fled to Argentina and now carried on normal lives, as if they hadn't left her homeland in ruin. As if they weren't war criminals. Ursula hoped Mr. Peralta had nothing to do with them.

"Minneapolis is *quieto*—I think I say it right—compared to my home."

Getting English words and grammar wrong or misunderstanding the meaning of a word had frustrated Ursula when she first arrived in America. She appreciated his willingness to sink into the language, swim around in it.

"You mean quiet or calm?"

"Ahh, calm. Yes calm."

"It is *quieto* when you first arrive," Ursula repeated his word, trying it on her tongue. "But then you realize there is a whole community here with many things to do."

"I hope to know those many things," Mr. Peralta said, displaying an eager smile.

"It has been nice talking with you, but I do need to go."

Mr. Peralta opened the car door, and as Ursula gently lowered herself onto the seat she caught his scent of citrus and pine. "*Buenas noches, señora*," he said, as he shut the door and turned away.

Ursula started the engine but didn't pull away. She watched Mr. Peralta's tall frame walk away, catching under the streetlamps like staccato spotlights. There was a brief flash as he stopped to light a cigarette, like a firefly darting across a dewy lawn. Ursula was intrigued by him, but that was all she could allow herself. She put the car in reverse, pulled out of the parking lot, and drove home.

CHAPTER 29
October, 1957

Sun pierced the early morning skyline, and Ursula's breath lifted like fog. She was starting her birthday on her favorite bench at Fairview Park. Grief had kept her from the spot all summer. It was her place for hope, and she'd felt none.

Today she left Vic sleeping at home as she couldn't manage him and her sticks, but regular physical therapy made the small slope relatively easy to climb. She had parked her Ford as close as she could to the bottom of the incline, on the street near the paved sidewalk. Now at the top, she plunked her bum on the wooden slats of the bench.

Over the past few weeks, she had become more intrigued by Mr. Peralta. He continued to press his theory about language and expression. He walked her to her car each Tuesday night after class, and she did not protest. He had a charm Ursula could not shake off.

Thirty-three. Thirty-three. Thirty-three. Ursula said the words out loud. She was alone on the hill, probably the only person in the entire park at this hour.

The day before, Rose had called and asked to take Ursula to the diner for a birthday brunch. It was their annual tradition, and Ursula never passed up a chance to see Rose, even though the visits had dwindled. Though they saw each other less, the warmth between them remained.

Shock held Ursula tightly over the summer and into September but released enough for her to piece together what had happened and how she might keep going. If she concentrated on physical therapy she could get through the day, then the week. As her stretching and straining muscles pulled against bones, as her knees slackened, as the swelling in her ankles subsided, she knew she could continue her life. If she could see physical changes, she assured herself she could manage her mind as well.

But what to do with Mr. Peralta? His charm latched onto her like fallen wisps of seeds from the cottonwood trees in her neighborhood. She should just brush it off, but Ursula could not bring herself to do so. For the few hours they spent together in class on Tuesday evenings, and then as Mr. Peralta walked Ursula to her car, she found herself identifying his charms. His gentle mannerisms, curious questions, and observations. The soft welcoming tone of his voice. The way he rolled his *R*s in English when he said her last name.

When Ursula was in the midst of her first crush, she had asked her mother how she met Ursula's father. He was a persistent man, she had said, and she swatted away his advances, as if he were a fly. Ursula and her mother were in the kitchen at the wooden table—it was large then, the leaves not yet firewood. The image of her mother's hand swatting at her father's head made Ursula laugh. "A fly? Father a fly?" They had buckled in laughter until they clutched their sides and coughed.

Mr. Peralta certainly wasn't a fly. Ursula liked his polite curiosity, though he must have seen the ring she still wore, seen she was married. *Was* married. Should she tell him about Roger dying?

Ursula took a deep breath and refocused on the skyline. She wished she could have brought Vic along to talk to. Having the dog with her always made her feel less alone. She palmed the sticks leaning next to her on the bench, the reliable metal and rubber that got her around. She placed her arms through the stability cuffs, counted to three, and stood. In a few hours, she would meet Aunt Rose for brunch, and then Phyllis said she would stop by in the afternoon with the children. Today, Ursula promised herself, she would enjoy her birthday.

CHAPTER 30
November 1957

Ursula threw the car back into drive. This time she would get up the damn hill. Over the summer and into autumn she had done well, learning how much force she needed on the gas and brake pedals, how to shift her legs around to prevent cramping.

Now the Minnesota winters made what had been an easy task difficult, as the back tires slid on the icy road beneath her. Ursula's pulse quickened and the windshield fogged with her fast, forceful breaths. With an abrupt turn to the right and a steady foot on the gas, she managed to navigate the crest of the residential street. She came close to swiping another car as the rear end of the sedan fishtailed, but Ursula dared not stop to catch her breath and at the top of the hill kept moving forward.

The Vargases had invited Ursula for dinner. Dr. Vargas insisted Ursula would get along well with his wife, who was lonely in this new place and hoped to make friends. The doctor briefly explained after one of their appointments that his wife had been reluctant to come to Minnesota, but he insisted polio survivors in Argentina needed better treatment. The Sister Kenny Institute had created an educational exchange program for Argentine doctors and technicians. His wife had left her friends and family behind to accompany her husband on this three-year assignment. She had also left behind her beloved pottery studio.

Ursula could relate to the pain of leaving family and friends—at the very least her knitting and crocheting didn't require a potter's wheel or a kiln. She had turned down a few dinner invitations from the doctor, but he persisted and Ursula finally said yes.

"This weather is terrible!" Mrs. Vargas said, rolling her *R*s as she ushered Ursula inside off the screened-in porch. The Vargases were renting a house in St. Paul, just over the Minneapolis border.

"Yes, I hate driving in it," Ursula said. She had learned early on in Minnesota that weather was always a topic of discussion. It was amusing to hear Mrs. Vargas adopt this custom.

"I'm glad you accepted our invitation. I have found these days empty, not like at home where I have so many people to see and things to do."

"When I first arrived—"

"Isabel, we can talk more in here." Dr. Vargas interrupted the women. "I want to introduce Ursula to our special guest."

As they rounded the corner to the dining room, Ursula saw the back of a dark-haired head. She pulled at Mrs. Vargas's sleeve.

"Dr. Vargas didn't tell me anyone else would be joining us tonight." She wanted to be polite, but she had the urge to rush to the door, back to her car, and out onto the wintry streets.

"He is a friend. You will like him."

"A friend, hmmm," Ursula said, but her hands were sticky with sweat. Had she misunderstood Dr. Vargas's invitation? She was here to get to know his wife, to perhaps make a new friend. She was not here to be introduced to a man. With her left hand Ursula flattened her best dress, a modest navy-blue outfit she had sewn over the winter before Roger had died. She had only worn it a few times, and now she wished she had put on something else, something that didn't remind her so much of him.

"Maybe you know Sr. Mateo Peralta?" Sra. Vargas asked.

"Oh my, I was . . . I didn't know." Ursula's heart beat like it had on the crest of the hill, and her right foot nearly fishtailed, her heel snapping outward. She fought to regain her balance, taking a step forward with her left foot.

"Mrs. Gorski, this is a surprise for me, too," Mr. Peralta said. He rose from the table and kissed Ursula's hand with a gentle bow of his head. "A beautiful surprise."

She wanted to raise her left hand to her cheek. She had a habit of checking her level of embarrassment below her fingers, the degrees of warmth a measure of her emotion. She slowed her breath and aimed for a polite tone. "It will be nice to spend time together when neither of us is working."

"Ursula is right, we have been working very hard at the Institute. Tonight, we enjoy!" Dr. Vargas said as he helped Ursula with her chair. Then he proceeded to take drink orders and the party began.

Ever since they had first met, Ursula's curiosity about Mr. Peralta had steadily grown. She'd already decided he was not a fly to be swatted away, and now, as dinner proceeded, she realized she quite enjoyed his buzzing, especially in this lively group. All formalities were dropped—"no need for me to be a doctor now, call me Arturo." Conversation flowed across the table, Spanish mingling with English as Ursula tried to keep up. Isabel talked about her pottery and gushed when Ursula shared her needlepoint and knitting hobbies. They had more in common than Ursula had anticipated, even though she guessed Isabel was ten years her senior.

They finished a delicious dessert—*dulce de leche*—when Isabel asked, "Mateo, when are you going to find an apartment?"

"I don't know," Mateo said. His tone was suddenly abrupt.

"You arrived in August, no?" Isabel tilted her head, then said to Ursula, "He lives in a hotel. A long-time hotel?"

Mateo nodded, shifting silverware across his plate.

"I'm sure you miss home. I think hotels can be sad places," Ursula said, but realized she had never stayed in an American hotel. She had no idea what Mateo was experiencing.

"I only sleep there. I am at the Institute or the university studying most days." Mateo tilted his empty wine glass and Arturo poured him more. Then Mateo asked Ursula, "And you live here?"

"In St. Paul? No, in north Minneapolis in a small house."

"Are you, how do you say, alone?" Mateo lifted his brow.

Ursula sat up straighter. The direct question startled her.

"I admit I had a very tragic spring," Ursula said. She hoped her short explanation was enough so she could avoid putting her grief on the table like a main course.

Sensing Ursula's discomfort, Isabel suggested they move to the living room to play charades. Mateo started clearing dishes, but Isabel shooed him away.

As Ursula helped with what she could in the kitchen, she thought about Mateo, how many months he must have been in that hotel. It sounded so uninviting, and he'd seemed reluctant to talk about it when asked. An idea flashed: her second bedroom. Technically, it was empty. She could clear out her typewriter, move her yarn, make it comfortable for someone. If she took on a boarder, she could easily cover her mortgage. She wouldn't have to stretch her budget so far, her worries about the future would be eased. She dropped a serving spoon, and it hit the floor with a loud clatter.

"I'm sorry," Ursula said.

"No, you will not be sorry. You are kind to help." Isabel lifted the spoon from the maple and wiped away the residue. She plopped the utensil in the soapy water. "I told Mateo not to ask about your situation. He did not listen."

"That was kind of you, but . . ." Ursula stopped when she realized Mateo was in the doorway, an empty bottle of wine loosely gripped in his hand.

"I heard a crash," Mateo said, his face a half-moon of concern. "And I came for more wine."

Mrs. Vargas pointed to a cupboard. Mateo found another bottle and left.

"He is a kind man, Ursula," Mrs. Vargas said, but did not elaborate.

Over charades, they laughed at each other's dramatic pantomimes. When it was her turn, from her perch on the sofa, Ursula lifted her arms into a peak above her head, modeling the steeple of a church.

"*Iglesia*," Mateo said, jumping up from his seat and pumping his fist. He had won again.

Ursula laughed, a loud cathartic laugh. How long had it been since she had felt this way? It had been six months since Roger had passed, but Ursula couldn't ignore the feelings that had been ignited for Mateo since she met him in early September. It was a small flame, a tingle of excitement mixed with possibility.

"Let's play another round," Ursula said.

CHAPTER 31
March 1958

Ursula settled into a comfortable rhythm: outpatient therapy, teaching German at the institute, and knitting classes for a group of women at Rose's church. Her outpatient program ended after three months, but the fear of atrophy motivated her to continue therapy twice-weekly. She saw the Vargases every other Saturday for dinner, and Mateo usually joined them. They always ended the night with a game of canasta or bridge. Phyllis came by the house with the kids a few times a week. While the kids played with Vic in the yard, Ursula and Phyllis could catch up over coffee. Yarn strung Ursula and Rose together. Rose liked to drop into Ursula's class at church even though she complained she "wasn't much of a knitter." Bea spent more time in England every year, taking her children to visit her severely arthritic mother. Ursula and Bea got together when they could, but they had grown apart while they tended their own lives.

With savings and money from teaching, Ursula estimated she could stay in her house through the summer. She circled the last day of August on the calendar, a reminder that after that date, she would have to decide between skimping on groceries or paying the mortgage. She flipped to December, and circled the 31st. She would have to find a boarder by December. Skimping on groceries would only work for so long.

The first anniversary of Roger's death was in a few months on May 20. She had circled that day, too, but left it blank, unable to find the words for the thumping wrongness lingering around the edges of her body.

Roger would want her to do what was best. He would want her to keep their home for it represented everything she had lost during the war: security, comfort, and predictability. After years of building her life in Minneapolis, she did not want to bring back the worst memories of Berlin. It only took a second to bring back images of sleeping in abandoned basements, asking friends of friends if they had extra room, sharing cots in shifts. Yet here, years on, she still couldn't quite bring herself to ask Mateo, now a friend, if he was interested in being her boarder. Another man in the house meant betraying Roger by moving on with a new part of her life.

Phyllis had settled across from her in the worn, goldenrod-colored sofa Roger had reupholstered years ago in expensive fabric left over from one of his customer's projects. Ursula resented it now. It represented all the work he had done, work she was convinced had led to his heart attack. She cursed the sofa under her breath.

"My sister is watching the kids today, and I couldn't be happier. Do you know what it's like to look after four rowdy children?"

"They are wonderful kids, Phyllis. You're raising them so well." A small half-knitted cardigan lay in Ursula's lap.

"You get to see them when they are on their best behavior. They love you, and they love coming over here." Phyllis pulled a needle through a handkerchief, then took a puff of her Lucky Strike and sent the smoke gently out her nose. She hadn't been able to smoke in the hospital, but she'd taken up the habit in earnest in the years since.

Ursula took up her needles and started a new row. Ice cubes clinked in Phyllis's glass as she took a sip of iced tea.

"You've been quieter than normal today," Phyllis said.

"I have a lot on my mind," Ursula said. She watched Phyllis set down her needlepoint then take a final puff and grind out her cigarette. She didn't want to talk about everything on her mind. Not during a nice visit. But Phyllis had her "You can talk to me" look on her face now.

"There's something bothering you. I know you too well for you to hide things from me." Phyllis tapped on her cigarette pack and pulled out another one.

"How many fresh starts does a girl get in her life?" Ursula finally said. She motioned for the cigarettes, suddenly feeling an unexpected craving. She lit it, but let it hang, glowing in her fingers, as she continued. "I've lived through enough already. Look at me. A crippled widow."

"I know you've had a terrible year, but you've seemed better lately," Phyllis said. "Not on cloud nine, but better."

Ursula took a drag on her cigarette, then coughed and set it aside. Her urge was gone, and it was a good thing. Smoking was a habit she couldn't afford. "It's money. I'm running out."

"But last summer when you bought the car you were flush," Phyllis said, blowing smoke out her nose. "I will never forget the image of all that cash laid out on that man's desk. I had never seen so much money in one place. How could you be out of money?"

"When I had the mechanic make adjustments for my legs it cut into my savings."

"Oh gosh, they always charge so much. David complains anytime he has to take the car in."

"Yes, well, I did the numbers again today . . ."

"You're so resourceful Ursula, I wouldn't know where to start with running the house. David does all of that."

"Roger used to do it all."

Silence stretched between them.

"I'm sorry," Phyllis said, bringing a palm to her forehead.

"I know you didn't mean it that way."

"I just forget sometimes, and I shouldn't."

"You have your own family to worry about. You don't have to worry about me too. But . . ." Ursula paused, deciding if she should share more. "Maybe you can help me figure out how I can keep this house."

"Huh?" Phyllis leaned forward, her eyebrows raised.

"From what I calculated, I can stay here through the end of August, maybe December if I can move some money around. Save on electricity. I have a few tricks."

"Oh Ursula. I didn't know."

"How would you? I don't make a habit of telling people," Ursula said, regretting her decision to tell Phyllis. She didn't want her friend to worry, to be a burden to her with another responsibility.

"Are you sure you've counted correctly? I think I'd mess up the math, it was never my strongest subject."

"Yes, I counted correctly."

"We could go over the numbers one more time together?"

The phone rang, interrupting them. Phyllis stood up to answer it, as she often did. Ursula moved too slowly for the pace of modern technology.

"It was David," Phyllis said, "asking me what was for dinner. I need to get home. I'm so sorry, let's talk more about this later. We'll figure this out."

A response snagged in Ursula's throat. She was afraid of explaining her idea to Phyllis. Even her best friend would think inviting a man to rent a room in her house was a mistake.

The front door opened. A "see you soon" floated through the house and then there was the sound of Phyllis starting her car. Ursula was envious Phyllis had a husband to go home to. Someone she could rely on. She ached for Roger, for the way he had taken care of her.

The cigarette in the ashtray had burned down to the tarry end. Ursula shuffled to the kitchen sink where she snuffed out the embers under the faucet, stifling a cry. Survival against all odds forced clarity, even if the picture—a single man living with a widowed, disabled woman—meant breaking social norms. She would ask Mateo to rent the room.

CHAPTER 32
July 1958

"Mateo, I need to ask you something," Ursula said. She was sitting in the driver's seat of her car looking up at him after German class. She had talked the institute into letting her teach a summer session. Every time she recalculated her expenses, she knew the situation was more and more dire.

"What is it?"

"I know you're still at that hotel, and I'm sure you're tired of it." Ursula shifted her legs in the foot well. She was more nervous than she thought she would be. During the last year they had developed a warm friendship over regular dinners with the Vargases. Their relationship was spattered with flirtatious undertones. Ursula presumed the way he half smiled with his eyes, bowed his head, and helped her with doors was simply part of Mateo's charm. By asking him about the room she worried she would risk their friendship, risk the community she had built with the Vargases. The Argentines stuck together at the institute.

"Are you okay?" Mateo's face twinkled concern.

"I think I have a solution for you. Would you rent a room from me? Instead of renting from the hotel?" There. She said it. Her proposal out in the open.

"A room? In your home?" Mateo's back straightened with surprise.

"Yes, I have a second bedroom that you can rent from me," Ursula said to his chest, his head now above the car. "You won't have to live in that hotel anymore."

Mateo hesitated for a moment. Ursula had caught him off guard. Her mind shifted, and she started drafting the advert she would have to place in the paper. But then Mateo's face was back in front of Ursula's, crouched over the door frame.

"Yes, I like it. I will take the room."

Ursula had been prepared for a "no" or even a "perhaps," but with his yes, Mateo reopened the car door and crouched down so they could talk more. He said he was eager to live in a home, to settle into Minneapolis in a deeper way. They talked about price and he was thrilled Ursula would charge him less than it cost him to stay at the hotel. They agreed on a move-in date.

For the next week, Ursula oscillated between concern and relief. She would be able to keep her home but dreaded the inevitable scandal. Rose would understand, but Mrs. Gorski wouldn't. But Ursula could not waste time on her former mother-in-law and what she might think. She would need to find a way to tell Mrs. Ohlin or gossip would balloon across the neighborhood. And she had waited until the last minute to tell Phyllis, worried her friend would try to talk her out of her plan.

On Saturday, Ursula busied herself in the kitchen, listening to Mateo puttering around in the second bedroom: a suitcase unzipped, the closet door squeaked on its hinges, and dresser drawers slid open and closed. She would be able to pay the mortgage. That simple fact dispelled most of her fears about a man—not her husband—living under her roof.

Ursula washed and dried her hands, trying to focus on dinner. She went to the kitchen table where she could sit and work at the same time. Potato salad and sandwiches would have to be enough. She chopped and diced, then folded together the yellow onion, fresh chives, and potatoes Mrs. Ohlin's son Henry had delivered from their bountiful backyard garden earlier that morning when he'd come to take Vic on a walk. She would need to tell Mrs. Ohlin about Mateo soon, before there were any sightings of a strange man in Ursula's home.

The creaky floorboard in the dining room gave Mateo away. He stuck his head through the doorway to the kitchen. "I help, no?"

He had changed into a fresh white shirt. Ursula would need to tell Mateo about the laundry in the basement, and explain how to use the machine. Since Roger had died, Phyllis had been helping Ursula with the laundry. When she'd been over last week to do the sheets and towels Mateo would use, Ursula asked if the cold, musty space was presentable. Phyllis was vague, so Ursula had descended the stairs with her, one slow courageous step at a time. She cried at the bottom when her feet landed on the concrete. Someone had left Roger's upholstery tools on a rickety wooden table in the corner.

"Yes, you can set the table," Ursula told Mateo. She pointed at the cupboards, explaining where to find the glasses, plates, flatware, and cloth napkins. He moved gracefully around the kitchen with a whistle on his lips. A deep musk with lemon sliced through Ursula's earlier doubt. Something sweet, too. She liked his energy, the enthusiasm that sparked off his body.

"This isn't much, but it's edible, at least, and I didn't have anything more planned for tonight. When it's only me, I have soup and toast." Ursula said.

"*Buen provecho!*" Mateo said.

Across from Ursula, he eagerly folded a helping, and then a second, of the potato salad onto his plate. The sandwiches were gone before

Ursula could tell him it was the cheapest meat and cheese available at the deli. The man at the counter had thankfully thrown in a few extra pieces.

"I emptied a shelf in the cupboard near the sink for you. I thought you might want space to store your food," Ursula said. She hoped he understood he would need to buy his own groceries, make his own meals.

"I feel like I am at home. I forgot about this feeling when I was in that hotel," Mateo said pushing his chair back to stand up. "Now I will clean the dishes."

"You don't have to," Ursula said, but she hoped he would. She liked his helpfulness, that he was willing to do women's work. On nights when Ursula's legs were weak, Roger had done dishes but normally left homemaking to her.

"*No preocupes*. I'll clean, then have a walk. I want to see the neighborhood," Mateo said.

Ursula felt a small rush of panic. She hadn't talked to Mrs. Ohlin yet, and now all the neighbors might see him. But she could not ask him to stay hidden in the house.

"Colfax is a beautiful street with all the trees, and there's a park nearby where you can see the city. It's on Fairview, about a ten-minute walk from here." If he went straight to the park, fewer neighbors would see him.

"A park! I love parks—would you like to join me?"

Ursula paused. She wanted to say yes. Vic needed a walk, and Mrs. Ohlin's son hadn't been by the house that evening. Mrs. Ohlin had called to say something about baseball practice and homework.

"Vic would like it, but . . ." Ursula looked at Vic asleep on the floor in front of the sink. "Maybe it's too far. He's quite an old dog."

"*La próxima*."

"Hmm?"

"Next time."

"Yes, next time," Ursula said, but wondered if he was talking about Vic or herself.

CHAPTER 33
October 1958

Through the summer and into the fall, Ursula and Mateo fell into an informal but respectful rhythm living under the same roof. The outgoing Mateo she knew from German class and dinners at the Vargases was quieter and more reserved in close quarters. She learned Mateo had also grown up Catholic like Roger and abided by a code Ursula had come to know but never fully understood. A code that meant he charmed her in public and respected her in private. Ursula continued her outpatient therapy and teaching classes, but most days she was alone in the house with Vic while Mateo studied at the University of Minnesota and the institute.

"What are you writing about?" Ursula looked up from the half-made blanket she planned to sell at the Christmas craft sale at Rose's church. Mateo sat across from her scribbling notes on a sheet of paper.

"Argentina," Mateo said, his eyes glossy with nostalgia. "I was invited to talk about Argentine culture for a workshop on the progress of education in Argentina. It's being hosted by UNESCO at the university."

"Congratulations, what a wonderful opportunity," Ursula said. She kept putting him together like a puzzle, each piece forming a new picture of him, especially his love of family and passion for his culture. She liked what she saw, but each time she got closer to learning more, he pulled away. His retreat confounded Ursula. Almost a year had gone by since they first met, and it had been a few months since he moved in. She was comfortable around him, and trusted him. Why did he hold back, keep so much inside?

"I am honored to be able to share about Argentina," Mateo said. He twirled a pen between his fingers.

"What are you going to talk about?" Ursula asked.

"*Es difícil.*" Mateo gripped the pen harder. "How do I explain a whole country in one evening?" Ursula understood what he meant. She found even more difficulty describing a place transformed by war.

Mateo took another sip of *mate,* which he'd received from a medical student recently arrived from Buenos Aires. The traditional caffeinated infusion was made from dried holly leaves. Ursula tried it, but preferred black coffee. However, when they drank it together it loosened Mateo's tongue, so Ursula endured the bitter liquid.

"I miss Buenos Aires." Mateo inhaled the leafy brew and leaned back in the chair with a sigh.

"I don't really know much about the city." Ursula wanted him to continue. She set down her knitting and took a sip of mate to keep their conversation going. Bitterness clung to the inside of her cheeks.

"Imagine a street with apartments like books on a shelf, each a different color," he said as he palmed imaginary books in the air in front of him. "Tile under your feet, not like here where you have concrete? Yes, concrete. Big wooden doors. When I open that door to my parent's home, it's cold because of the terrazzo floors and stone walls."

Ursula stilled her hands. The place Mateo described seemed out of reach. She suddenly ached for Berlin and her family in a way that caught in her throat.

"My mother calls me *mi hijo*—my son—but my father is many times silent. His face still, like a lake without wind."

"He is similar to my mother then," Ursula said, hoping he would keep going. In previous conversations about his family, Mateo had hesitated, and stopped. Each time Ursula gathered another detail, though. Enough to sustain her curiosity.

"If your mother has—how do you say, many expectations?"

"High expectations?"

"Yes, high expectations. If I don't finish this education . . . ay, my father will be angry. I have started my medical training many times before."

"You have?" This was new. Mateo had thus far shown dedication to his studies, and a deep interest in his training. Ursula could not square a Mateo who quit or gave up with the Mateo across the table from her.

"Each time I start my studies, life gives me problems. Coming to America is my last chance."

"America was my chance too," Ursula said. "It still is."

"You have a beautiful life." Mateo shook his head, perhaps thinking of his disappointed father. "What am I doing with mine?"

Ursula shrugged, then picked up her knitting needles again. She was annoyed Mateo had ignored her comment about America. He swept by it, focusing instead on himself. She wanted to know more about him, of course. But his abrupt self-centeredness surprised Ursula. Perhaps she'd been like that when she left German at twenty-two. But Mateo was much older. He should have already faced enough challenges to know how to create a life of his own, to let go of his parent's expectations.

Ursula tugged at the yarn and the ball rolled across the table toward Mateo. He wrote Ernesto Guevara on the paper where his notes about Argentine culture should have been, then flipped the ball back to her.

Ursula caught it, then stopped to sip the mate. "What are you writing about?"

"An old classmate. Someone who wouldn't disappoint his father." He lifted his eyes to hers. "You know of Che Guevara, no?"

"I've heard of him."

"If you could have met him when I did. Ay! He wanted to make life better for people. As a doctor, but also as a mobilizer and fighter."

"You knew Guevara?" Ursula was dumbfounded. She had read about him in the newspaper. He was fighting alongside Fidel Castro in Cuba, trying to overthrow the Batista government.

"We both went to the University of Buenos Aires. Once during class, Ernesto argued with the professor about treating the poor," Mateo said, his enthusiasm taking over his earlier shame. "Ernesto inspired me."

"Mateo, this is dangerous. Knowing him is dangerous. The United States opposes the revolutionaries in Cuba."

"Hmm." Mateo stroked his chin. The gesture made him seem aloof, unaware of the consequences of associating himself with a political instigator. "The last time I saw him was in, ahh, '48. How is this dangerous?"

"You haven't lived through political upheaval like I have. I know what is dangerous." The anxiety from her childhood resurfaced, strumming her insides so she vibrated.

"Ernesto took a motorcycle around Argentina, Chile, and then north. He has a path and is following it." Mateo's eyes formed a far-away look, as if he was riding behind Guevara on the motorbike.

"I read the headlines. He's not someone you should associate yourself with," Ursula said.

"I do not worry about these things. It was many years ago that we had class together."

"Mateo, I will tell you again, I have found it's best to leave politics alone," Ursula said.

She looped yarn over the needles again, hoping it would steady her. She had followed the McCarthy trial only a few years before. She knew what some American politicians wanted to do with communists. And before that, conversations about communist infiltrators echoed in the hallways at Riverwood, the patients encouraged by *Counterspy,* a radio drama about turning people in for espionage or subversive activities. She had lived through enough political drama in Germany, but Phyllis liked the radio program and Ursula had reluctantly listened. In her own house now, though, she did not have to listen. She could put a stop to this nonsense.

"My mother told me about his motorcycle journey," Mateo said. Much like Ursula, he received news from his mother in long letters.

"You must tell your mother to keep those stories out of her letters, too," Ursula said. Fear broke through her façade. Her stance had been unwavering for years. She was against the communists, a gut feeling shared with her parents stuck behind the Iron Curtain. McCarthy's hearings had stopped, but their legacy lingered, and she did not want to be accused of harboring a communist in her home. Had she known more about Mateo's deep interest in these topics, she might have found a different boarder.

"You don't understand. Argentine mothers are proud of their sons. I can picture her now, telling Señora Guevara how I will come home to help the polio survivors, how people are learning to walk again at the Institute in Minnesota," Mateo said. He smiled, captivated by his own imagination.

"That is nice, Mateo, but you need to keep this information about the Guevaras to yourself. Do you know the history of America and what they do to communists?" Ursula asked. She was irritated. He did not seem to understand the weight of his words.

"Are you telling me you side with the Americans?" Frustration wrapped Mateo's face.

"I am an American, of course I'm going to side with my country."

"Your country?"

"Yes, Mateo. My country." She held his eyes, needing him to hear what she was saying. "I am a citizen of this country."

He sat back in his chair and mumbled something in Spanish that Ursula could not understand.

"I don't know what you just said, but you really need to stop talking about all of this Guevera nonsense. You're going to find yourself in a heap of trouble," Ursula said. Alarm spread in her voice. "And for your presentation for UNESCO, you should keep to the topics they asked you to talk about."

Mateo leaned forward and scribbled notes, his handwriting rushed. Ursula couldn't make out what he was writing. She feared he would say something during his talk that he wouldn't be able to take back. Something that would get him sent home, back to Argentina. Showing any kind of enthusiasm for communism was dangerous. It might not earn him a spot on a government watchlist like in previous years, but Ursula had enough experience with watching and being watched.

As she watched him continue to write, Ursula turned her thoughts inward. She had to face up to her feelings—her concern about Mateo's political passions wasn't detached. No, her interest in Mateo had grown well beyond his ability to help her cover expenses. Romantic curiosity bubbled in her limbs, popping up against her skin. She'd tried to tamp her feelings, but she needed to face up to her desire to know what might transpire between them beyond friendship. What would it be like to dance with Mateo, to be held in his arms? She had watched his body move across the living room at the Vargases, how he held strength in his back under his gentle, elegant step. She had chased away the image of the two of them enlaced, upset with herself for replacing Roger with another man, even if it was only in her head. Today, though, sitting across from Mateo, she saw her anger about his communist sympathies for what it was—care. She cared enough to be concerned about him, about a future together, whatever that meant.

The mate was cool now, the leaves like wet autumn mush. Mateo picked up the special gourd that held his drink and drew one more sputtered sip through the metal straw that had belonged to his grandfather. Mateo had shown Ursula how the vessel worked, how to pack the leaves and cover them with water. He'd told her stories of drinking mate with those he loved. Maybe Mateo could tell the UNESCO people about mate, how it brought families in Argentina together. How he and his parents and his grandparents would sit and talk, the conversation stirred by the leaves at the base of the silver straw.

CHAPTER 34
October 1959

Ursula and Mateo drove north on Highway 371 toward the headwaters of the Mississippi for a night away from the city before winter set in. She was at the wheel, concentrating on the road. Her red hair was tied in a knot at the base of her neck and a few wispy strands fell across her right cheek. She could feel them but did not want to take her hands off the wheel to slide them behind her ear.

She glanced out the window. The leaves were warm oranges, brilliant reds, and mustard yellows. Ursula was grateful for the cool air. The heat of the summer always reminded her of being diagnosed with polio, and she was happy to have August temperatures behind her. Mateo had suggested a night away as a birthday gift, and she had agreed immediately. Then she had arranged for Vic to stay with Mrs. Ohlin, and packed her suitcase.

Between Ursula's hours in the gym and teaching German, and Mateo's university classes and training at the institute, recent months had flown by. Mateo had stayed on topic at the UNESCO presentation the fall before, speaking only about culture. From the audience, Ursula had harnessed her anxiousness, afraid it would catapult her onto the stage. Mateo had even mentioned mate, showing off his straw and gourd. To Ursula's surprise, the UNESCO organizers invited him to speak again, and he did so in the spring. The public show of trust by Mateo lessened Ursula's fears about him. She still had questions, though.

Not long after Mateo's second UNESCO talk—it was sometime in March—Ursula decided to speak to Isabel about Mateo. A warm friendship had developed between the two women over regular dinners, one that held a different weight compared to Ursula's relationship with Phyllis. She couldn't tell Phyllis about her developing romantic feelings for Mateo, or her fears about his political interest. Phyllis would panic, she would tell Ursula to be sensible about both romance and politics. But Phyllis did not understand how much the war had taught Ursula. She understood how convictions and emotions layered onto people, how you could still find a way to engage with those you didn't agree with, love them even. Isabel, not constrained by Midwest American standards, supported Ursula in a way that Phyllis did not. So, Ursula told Isabel about Mateo's connection to the Guevaras, about his growing interest in communism and Cuba. Isabel concluded Mateo was only trying to impress Ursula, show off his association to a widely known family. Some men are like that in Buenos Aires, she had said.

What Ursula kept to herself that evening with Isabel, what Ursula believed was more important than any of Mateo's political fixations, was how much he respected her. He didn't treat Ursula differently because of her crippled condition. He didn't look at her the way other people did when she walked with her sticks, or rolled down the sidewalk in her wheelchair. This was something she did share with Phyllis, knowing her best friend would understand. More than a decade had passed since her polio attack—apart from Roger, Mateo was the only man who appreciated her.

Ursula never worked out if Isabel had said something to Mateo encouraging him to show his interest in Ursula. In April, though, at home after dinner, Mateo had taken her hand and asked her to dance in the kitchen. When Ursula was close, he had kissed her. Her body had tingled with pleasure. His lips were soft like a ripe pear brushed with earthy mate. She found no bitterness.

"I waited because our situation is complicated," Mateo had said. He said he hoped Ursula was interested in him too.

Their affection grew like wildfire into the spring and through the summer. They kept their displays private for fear of more gossip, but in the house, they were generous with touch. They had not, however, had sex. Mateo still slept in his room and Ursula in hers. She put it down to Mateo's continued insistence their lives were complex, but she hoped this night away would change that. In the woods, they could be in private together where no one would know them.

"Fidel was right to blame the Americans for dropping anti-communist leaflets!" Mateo muttered and shook the newsprint in his hands.

"The Americans and Mr. Castro are not getting along, and each side blames the other. I don't need to remind you of my terrible experiences with the communists after the war." Ursula wished Mateo would stop talking about Cuba. Ever since Fidel Castro had gained more popularity, he was a constant topic of conversation. She reminded herself of what Isabel had said: convictions like these were common among men like Mateo. But she couldn't help thinking about Germany when she was a girl. Before the war, Ursula's neighbors had been swept up in a political fever and became party members who obediently followed the Reich's commands. The similarity between her neighbors' ferocity about Hitler and Mateo's about Castro left Ursula queasy.

"I understand why you don't like communists," Mateo said, his left hand grazing the top of Ursula's stiff, sore leg, feeling his way over the fabric of her dress. "But Fidel is different."

"You're lucky I keep my mouth shut about communism, Mateo. I don't know how many times I must tell you not to talk about these things." Ursula gripped the steering wheel tighter.

"He will change Cuba and fix the country's problems," Mateo said.

"He will not fix everything." Ursula stared ahead at the road, picturing Cuba going the way of Germany. Picturing the magnetized masses.

"*Mi amor*, he is changing Cuba. He is going to change Argentina, all of Sur America." Mateo's words were hypnotic. "He will listen to the people. This is what the people want."

"That's what Hitler said," Ursula said.

"Ay Hitler, *cómo tú sabes* . . ." Mateo said.

"I do know, Mateo," Ursula said.

"*Por supuesto*," he said and resumed reading the paper. His left hand pulled away from her thigh and met the left page. With her peripheral vision Ursula could see Mateo's nose buried further in the black ink, further in the revolution.

It was like when Ursula's father would bring home the first edition. He'd read it front to back and pause on his own writing, double checking for errors. Her father said Ursula needed to learn to think for herself, that facts mattered. Not long after he told her this, Ursula was forced to join the League of German Girls where she was taught to inform on her parents if she heard anything that went against the Führer. She didn't want to betray her parents. But the instruction did make her listen more carefully to what they said.

One day, she eavesdropped on her father discussing the German political situation with a neighbor. "He will do us no good. I don't like what is happening," her father had said.

"You only say that because the party is different. This party is for Germany." The neighbor seemed very sure of himself.

"But how? How is this party for Germany?"

"He will unite us. He is uniting us!"

"If you are relying on one person to unite us, then you are relying on the devil," her father said. "You may not return to my home if you speak these words in my presence again. I respect you, but with regard to this, I will not bend."

Ursula remembered the loud voices, the anger on her father's face. If he was afraid, he did not show it. The neighbor, who had been a friend for many years, had left in a hurry, saying her father would regret his words. It scared Ursula, though she did not entirely understand why. She only knew to keep the fight to herself, locked far away from the League of German Girls.

Now in the car with Mateo, Ursula understood the fear. She understood the consequences of blindly following a dangerous leader, and she saw that kind of devotion in Mateo. It was in the tone of his voice, his fervor, his uncompromising commitment. He disregarded other opinions that might upset his worldview. That was how wars started. Ursula wanted to be upset with Mateo, but then he was smiling at her as if their disagreement had not happened. He placed the paper in his lap and gently guided the errant strands of her hair behind her ears.

"You are gorgeous, like a movie star."

"And *you* are quite charming," Ursula said. Stubborn, too, she wanted to add. They rode in silence for the remainder of the journey. The oaks and maples had given way to thick and green pines, their color deepening as they drove. Sometimes the trees looked black. But then the early afternoon sun would sift through the dense needles, showing their true color.

Signs indicating the headwaters of the Mississippi led them to their destination—a modest log cabin nestled amongst tall firs along the east edge of Lake Itasca. They owed the privilege of their stay to a professor of Mateo's who graciously offered the cabin for the night. He'd planned a getaway with his wife, but she had fallen ill. Ursula and Mateo kept the reservation under the professor's name, knowing the consequences of a woman traveling with a man who was not her husband. With "Mr. and Mrs." on the reservation, Mateo had suggested they pretend to be newly married on their honeymoon. Ursula had agreed. What harm would it do? No one knew them this far north of Minneapolis.

"I'll get the key," Mateo said. He left the newspaper folded in the seat and closed the door. A few mosquitos snuck in and buzzed around Ursula's head. She swatted them away. Outside a few families walked along a nearby trail. As she followed them with her gaze, she mindlessly spun her wedding ring around her finger. She hoped Roger would forgive her.

Mateo returned with the key and a map so they could locate their cabin. "The staff believes our honeymoon story," he said, grinning.

A woman in her late 50s who Ursula suspected had fallen for Mateo's charm waved at their car. Mateo kissed Ursula on the cheek and then waved back. He opened the modest map of the grounds and pointed to the cabin they would stay in. The woman yelled congratulations as Ursula pulled away.

Inside the rustic cabin, Ursula steadied herself on the back of the small sofa. Mateo had flopped in the armchair near the stone fireplace, the tourist pamphlet open in his hands. She liked the ease of his body, the way he didn't think about what his limbs were doing. Pine layered with stale cigarettes rasped Ursula's nose. She was suddenly eager to get outside. "Want to go for a walk?"

"Yes! We must see where this *río* begins," Mateo said, the guide flapping in his hand.

Ursula liked when he mixed Spanish with English. It reminded her of when she became more comfortable speaking English and could sprinkle in German without embarrassment, without feeling she lacked control of the language.

"It says the park was established in 1891, and the *río* travels 2,552 miles to *el golfo de México*." Mateo's eyes moved back and forth over the short, matter-of-fact paragraphs. A few color photos dotted the trifold pages. "We go, yes?" He stood and tucked the pamphlet into his back pocket.

Ursula gathered a single crutch in her right hand and navigated her way out of the cabin. On the small porch, she flipped sunglasses from her hair to her eyes. A camera Phyllis had loaned her was strung across her body. She wanted to document this trip, preserve it for the future.

Soon they found the path to the headwaters. Although Ursula often saw the Mississippi while going back and forth over the bridges spanning its banks in the Twin Cities, this was different. Maybe seeing the headwaters would tell her something she needed to know.

In a clearing ahead of them, small ripples of water cascaded over rounded rocks.

"I thought it would be more dramatic," Ursula said. The air was still and Lake Itasca shone like glass.

"It begins small, then gets bigger." He was reading the brochure again.

"I hope you knew that already." Ursula laughed.

"I did. The Mississippi *es un río famoso*," Mateo said, then pointed at the camera. "I want to take your picture. Stay there and face me. I want to see the river behind you."

"All right." Ursula let Mateo lift the camera off her shoulder. She stood with her back to the water and lifted her lips. This is what it was like to be carefree.

"*Mira qué guapa estás,*" Mateo said as he lowered the camera from his face and stepped closer to Ursula.

"You are very good at giving me compliments," Ursula said, though she always doubted them.

"What are you saying? You are beautiful! Beautiful in all ways." He gestured at her, oblivious to her disability. "Your face, your body, your mind, your voice, all beautiful!"

Ursula laughed. "Perhaps some of those things, but not my voice," she said.

"Even your voice," he said, laughing with her. "Sing for me, my Ursula." Mateo swung the camera over his shoulder and opened his arms out wide.

"No, I will not." She dug her crutch into the ground, suddenly annoyed. His compliments had been endearing at first, but now he seemed to be taunting her.

"You are stubborn like a *burro.*"

"I don't understand that word."

Mateo mimicked a donkey.

Ursula rolled her eyes, shifting her neck to take in the dark outline of the lake transformed to river. Mateo's arms reached around her waist. She snuggled her left hand under his.

"*Te quiero,*" he said.

A breath rose in Ursula's chest. His voice was low, and so quiet Ursula wondered if she had heard him correctly. I love you?

"Hmm?" She rubbed her thumb over the wedding band, wanting to trust the feelings between them.

"I care about you."

"I care about you, too." Ursula shifted back to face Mateo but she snagged her foot on a rock, lurching forward.

"*¡Cuidado!*" Mateo caught her before she fell.

"Gosh, I scared myself," Ursula said, silently chiding herself for not paying attention.

"You are like that river, getting stronger each kilometer," Mateo said.

"You think so?"

"Yes, I do," Mateo said, and together they walked back through the pines.

The resort offered dinner at the rustic lodge where Mateo had checked in. In the wood-paneled dining room, they placed their order with the same woman who had congratulated them earlier. The lie was on Ursula's lips as she asked for a club sandwich.

"I got you something for your birthday," Mateo said.

"Mateo, you shouldn't have gotten me anything at all. This night away was the gift." She meant this, but also wondered a bit about what it might be.

"But I wanted to. I'll give it to you when we get back to the cabin. It's just a little something."

Ursula sighed. "Little somethings" were not something she needed. "You know I don't like too many doodads to clutter up my environment. I learned to be more practical after I was bombed out in the war and moved so many times." Now in the middle of the woods so many years later, it was strange to think of the war.

"You let the war in like water," Mateo said, sitting back in his seat. A shadow darted on his face as the sun lowered through the windows.

"I don't understand what you mean."

"You drank the war and now it's inside of you, making decisions about your life."

"I grew up with the war. I was a child, a teenager. It was my childhood. What else should I have known?"

"In Argentina, we had our problems, too. We lived with the Nazi spies; our government was friends with Germany and Italy during the war. We lived, though."

"Despite my experiences, I lived, too." Irritation crawled up Ursula's legs.

"But do you now?" Mateo pressed on.

"Yes, I do. You, however, seem very preoccupied with politics. I grew up steeped in politics and now I am tired by it all." Ursula glanced toward the kitchen, wishing the sandwiches would arrive. They'd be a distraction from this conversation.

"If you believe in something, you must fight for it," Mateo said, nervously tapping his foot on the ground.

"Mateo, please, no more politics today." Ursula saw the argument in his eyes.

"You cannot ignore what is happening around you."

"And you cannot be seen to be commiserating with communists, or supporting Cuba," Ursula said as she leaned into the table. A family sitting nearby stared. "And you should keep your voice down."

"I can say and believe what I want," Mateo said, his voice louder.

"You are making a big mistake." Ursula dropped her voice to a whisper.

"You don't understand." Mateo shook his head.

"You are not a citizen of this country. You do not have the freedom to say whatever you want," Ursula said. She wanted Mateo to give up his obsession with communism, at least for tonight. "I am a citizen, and I am proud to be, but even I know better than to speak too much about such things."

"I'm sorry, I don't mean to upset you," Mateo said, reaching for Ursula's hands. She took his palms like an olive branch.

"You are only upsetting me because I don't want you to be taken away. I have seen too many people taken away from me," Ursula said. She quelled the fear rising from deep in her body.

The same woman who had congratulated them on their "marriage" brought them their coffee and sandwiches. "Hello, honeymooners! I have your dinner." Ursula and Mateo both smiled politely, and Ursula took a deep breath as she arranged her napkin on her lap. Maybe the food would mediate their argument.

"I miss my family's beef and lamb barbecue," Mateo said before he bit into his chicken sandwich. "My mother makes delicious food. Maybe I will try to make it for you someday."

"I would like that," Ursula said. She chewed what tasted like day-old bread and thought about her mother's braised pork roast and cabbage. They both seemed to be longing for home.

Ursula nuzzled in Mateo's chest as they glided over creaky wooden floorboards later that evening. After the rift between them had dissipated, she had suggested they dance. A small radio over the fireplace blared the hits. Mateo had presented her with a birthday gift. It wasn't the knickknack she'd feared, but a pretty pair of white triangle-shaped earrings etched with her initials.

In the forest next to Lake Itasca, away from the neighbors' judgmental gazes, desire pulsed through her. She placed her lips a breath's distance from Mateo's, like she could fog a pane of glass.

"I love having you close to me," Mateo said.

As Ursula closed her lips against his, he pushed through and his tongue met hers. She was surprised when, after just a moment, he pulled away.

"What is it?" Ursula said. She was certain she had understood his signals. They had come to this remote place for privacy. To be intimate together, or so she thought.

"Why is life so complicated?"

"What are you asking me, Mateo?"

"I have to finish my studies . . ."

"What does that have to do with us, tonight?"

He stepped close so their bodies touched and they kissed again. "I want you. But I cannot become a father. I have too much work to do." He let go of Ursula's waist.

Ursula took a step back, feeling rejected. "There is no possibility of that."

"I don't understand."

"I am unable to have children."

"But polio survivors like you have children."

"It's not that."

"What is it?"

"I don't know, the doctor said . . . it doesn't matter now. You don't need to worry." Ursula wanted to explain her desire to be a mother, her struggle to get pregnant. None of it mattered now, that era of her life gone.

"*Seguro?*"

"Yes, I am sure."

Mateo pulled her back into a light embrace, and they danced to another song. Each time Ursula's legs faltered, Mateo drew her closer. He anticipated Ursula's needs without diminishing her ability to feel desired. With Mateo, she could let go of polio, and she did not have to wonder about his intent. She did not have to swat away his pity, because he did not hold any for her.

"Let's go to the bedroom," Ursula said, lips inches from Mateo's. The brandy he had poured himself earlier was on his breath.

In the bedroom, Ursula lowered herself onto the bed. "Mateo, I want you to undress me."

"I will do anything for you," Mateo said, his voice smooth.

He sat down next to Ursula and she shifted to face him, then reached to slip his shirt off. Bare-chested next to her, Ursula could not contain her longing for him. Their bodies intertwined, clothes tangling and untangling until they were both naked. Ursula felt Mateo against her thigh, she reached for him, his strength.

"Can I come in?" Mateo stopped. He hovered over Ursula, his hands on either side of her shoulders.

"Yes," Ursula said. Her voice caught in her throat, then she laughed lightly at his phrasing, as if he had knocked on a door. Once open, Ursula let go. She let her body rock under Mateo's. His strong legs were against hers, his smooth stomach against her fleshy one. Ursula put her hands on the tufts of dark hair on his chest when her body began to shake. For once the spasms were pleasurable, for once she could let go.

Ursula woke when sun poked through the curtains, casting a rectangle of light across Mateo's face. She admired the black brushstrokes of his eyebrows and the prominent nose pointing toward dusty-pink lips. She liked seeing him this close, with a peacefulness that evaporated his political passions. When she laid a hand across his chest, he stirred and opened his brown eyes.

"You were watching me sleep," Mateo said, rubbing his eyes.

"I was."

"Like a spy."

"Like a lover," Ursula said.

Mateo sat up and kissed Ursula. Ursula kissed him back. She wanted to recreate their night, to linger in that feeling forever.

"It is a pity that we must leave today," Mateo said.

"I could stay here forever with you," Ursula said and let her head fall back into the pillow, realizing the romantic spell would be broken the second they returned to the house on Colfax Avenue.

"Would you like to see the water again, once more before we go?" Mateo rolled onto his side and swept strands of hair away from Ursula's face.

"If I can get my legs warmed up," Ursula said.

"I can help if you want," Mateo said.

"As long as you are patient. My Kenny technician goes slowly but is firm."

"Anything for the most beautiful woman in the world. I am a Kenny technician after all," Mateo said.

"Kenny technician-in-training," she corrected, raising her eyebrows.

"Maybe in training," he laughed, "but I'm very good. Lay on your back and I will work on your legs. You tell me if any of these movements are too painful."

Ursula moved her legs under Mateo's direction, and she had to agree. He was good. She liked how he held her limbs with warmth and gentle strength.

"That's enough. I think my legs are warm. I will try to stand with my sticks." Ursula swung her legs to the floor. The wooden boards beneath her bare feet cool but firm and supportive. She put pressure down, first on one foot and then the other, and with Mateo's help, stood up.

"Before we see the river again, I'm going to get coffee and find the paper." He fumbled for his clothes strewn on the floor then quickly dressed. From the bathroom, Ursula heard the front door shut, but the mingled scents of the forest and Mateo stayed in the air. Lemon, oranges, and the sap of pine. Ursula inhaled and let the night before wash over her again.

CHAPTER 35
November 1959

"I loved the red velvet dress Doris wore," Ursula said to Phyllis. They had just seen the matinee showing of *Pillow Talk* starring Doris Day, and now they were at the café across the street, watching people pass and discussing Hollywood glamour. The day was warm enough for just a light coat, but soon they would need hats, scarves, and gloves—more layers to navigate with crutches.

"You could learn to make that dress. You're so good with knitting, I bet you would be good with sewing, too," Phyllis said.

"It would take months for me to make a dress like that! And when would I have the time?" She thought about squeezing in dressmaking between time with Mateo, physical therapy, and teaching both German and knitting.

"You do have a full schedule," Phyllis agreed. "And it's so good that Mateo gets you out of the house more," Phyllis said.

"It's not about Mateo," Ursula said, a bit offended. "I got myself out of the house once I learned to drive." She tried to channel Doris Day's confidence. Then she eyed her sticks slung over the empty chair, confirmation she had little in common with the movie star. Nausea unexpectedly overcame her.

"You're just like Jan in *Pillow Talk*. Independent, swatting away a man," Phyllis said. A giggle bounced on her lips.

Ursula shrugged and put the back of her hand against her fore-head. "I'm hardly swatting him away. He lives in my house, for good-ness sake. I just wonder if I will ever get married again." Since their trip up north the month before, Mateo and Ursula had continued to argue about politics. What future would they have if they couldn't get past that?

"You will get married again, I know you will," Phyllis said, but doubt hung in the air between them. Ursula told Phyllis about a newspaper Mateo had left on the kitchen table. It was full of under-lined paragraphs and circled headlines, all related to Cuba and the mess the country was in.

"Mateo doesn't seem keen on anything more than what we have now, even though I know he cares about me." Ursula sighed.

"Have you told him how you feel?"

"He knows how I feel," Ursula said. She adjusted the earrings Mateo had given her for her birthday as a waitress dropped off the coffee they'd ordered.

"But have told him you love him and want to get married?" Phyllis reached across the table for a packet of sugar. "It's a big step, and huge commitment. You've only known each other a short time, but I can see how your feelings sped up, with him living in your house."

"I know Mateo better than when I married Roger," Ursula said. "And shouldn't Mateo tell me he wants a future together? I believe he loves me; he seemed quite clear about his feelings when we were up north."

"You're lucky that a kind and handsome man is interested in you, but it's more than being intimate with him," Phyllis said, stirring her coffee.

"I know, Phyllis, I was married for over ten years." Sometimes her friend seemed to forget that. "And now, with the way I get around, men either stare or look right past me. But Mateo sees me. He doesn't see me as my crippled legs."

"I'm glad he's not like most men who feel sorry for us polios."

"You know, if we were in that movie, we'd be lumped in with the 'someone who is a little different' crowd. There's no room for us in the normal world," Ursula said. Anger jolted in her gut and the nausea blipped again. She shuffled her feet, anxious she was coming down with the flu. The flu had been going around at the institute, but she couldn't afford to get sick and miss teaching any of her classes. Maybe getting something in her stomach would help. And she was tired of this conversation.

Ursula slipped her coin purse around her wrist and reached for her sticks. "I'm going to get myself something sweet to eat. Would you like anything?"

"Yes please, one of those." Phyllis pointed toward a piece of chocolate cake in the case near the counter.

Ursula walked to the counter, navigating her sticks between the crowded tables.

"How much for those two?" Ursula asked, pointing at the remaining pieces of chocolate cake left in the case.

"Fifteen cents each, please. I'll bring them out to you."

Ursula handed the man a few coins. She wanted to vomit.

"Why are you so red?" Phyllis asked when Ursula returned to the table.

"I had a sick feeling, but it has passed," Ursula said. She didn't want Phyllis to worry. A moment later, the man delivered the two pieces of cake with a flourish. "*Bon appétit* girls."

"I think I've lost my appetite," Ursula said through another wave of nausea.

"I don't believe you. You love chocolate cake!" Phyllis sunk her fork into the fluffy layers, oblivious to Ursula's hesitancy. Ursula brought a small forkful to her mouth but knew she would be sick. While Phyllis devoured the cake, Ursula stood up and hurried to the bathroom.

Once there, the tile walls closed in on her. She splashed cold water on her face and was transported to the small toilet on the airplane over the Atlantic where she had been sick with turbulence and nerves. She had bet on Roger and the promise of a new life, one in which she was an American wife with an American husband and an American baby. A baby.

In the mirror she no longer saw a scared German girl, but an aged and wiser American woman. She was no longer an American wife, but an American widow, having endured the unimaginable. The final part of her dream might be growing inside of her. A baby? Not with Roger, her beloved American husband, but with Mateo. Ursula could finally become an American mother.

CHAPTER 36
December 1959

On New Year's Eve, Ursula again gazed into a mirror. Her red hair, laced with stray silver strands and pulled into a soft chignon at her neck, complemented the dark-green dress Mateo had bought her for Christmas. She would tell him tonight. She had to. She could not go into 1960 with a secret between them. With a baby between them. As her delicate fingers dusted her lids with eye shadow, eyeliner, and mascara, she imagined the conversation. A deep shade of red lipstick finished the look. But in her nervousness, she had applied it poorly. She wiped it off with a tissue and started again.

"*Amor, nos están esperando!*" Mateo shouted from the front entry.

"I'm coming," Ursula said

With lips confidently puckered, she flipped off the bathroom light, grabbed her coat, and pulled it around her shoulders. With her stick in her right hand and handbag in the other, she carefully set foot on the icy stoop.

"*Guapa,*" Mateo said in Ursula's ear as they approached the Vargases' car.

"Happy New Year!" Dr. Vargas said when they got in.

"Almost. Don't jinx it," Ursula said and snuggled into Mateo's shoulder.

Schiek's Café radiated with energy, the crowd excited to celebrate the end of a decade. Tonight, they would say goodbye to the '50s and usher in the '60s. Gold and silver tinsel hung tastefully around the dining room, while confetti lay on the tables. A waiter handed out hats for men and Happy New Year fascinators for women. The foursome left their winter coats with the attendant and were delivered to their table by a tuxedoed waiter.

"Can we dance?" Mateo asked, and before Ursula could reply, he was guiding her to the dance floor. They glided to the first song, and without sticks, Ursula felt as if she was flying. They danced to a second, then a third. Ursula was so happy she could no longer contain the burning secret. The newly found strength in her legs gave her unexpected courage and confidence.

"Mateo, I have something to tell you," Ursula said into his ear.

"What is it, amor?" Mateo's lips pressed against her neck.

"There's something important we need to talk about," Ursula said. She tried to keep her voice light, but her nerves twisted with energy. It had been easy in the bathroom at home, the rehearsed conversation where she controlled both parts.

"Mateo, Ursula! We are ordering appetizers!" Isabel called from their table interrupting Ursula's plan. When they rejoined the Vargases, Ursula could not concentrate on the conversation. All she could think about was what she would say to Mateo and when. Maybe she should put it off until the morning, but the weight of the news was heavier than before. *I have to tell him tonight.*

Dinner was as delicious as she remembered from the one—and only—other night she'd eaten at Schiek's. She and Roger had gotten into an argument, something about the war and Ursula's family. She wished she could go back to enjoy that night, to tell herself her family would be all right.

The band struck up again, and revelers emptied onto the dance floor. Dr. Vargas pulled Isabel to her feet and Mateo looked at Ursula expectantly.

"I think I'd like to rest my legs a bit longer," Ursula said. She hoped to ring in the New Year on her feet, but was tiring more quickly than expected.

"Then what is it you wanted to tell me?" he asked. He leaned in to brush a stray hair from Ursula's face.

Ursula, caught off guard by the question, hesitated.

"Are you all right?" Mateo asked. "You're pale."

"I'm expecting," she said. The words fell quickly out of her mouth. This wasn't how she'd planned it.

"Expecting? What are you expecting?" Mateo looked confused.

"A baby." Ursula clasped her hands across her belly.

"Amor, I thought you were . . . I cannot remember the word." Mateo pulled back from her, his face a puzzle. "Are you sure?"

"Yes, I'm sure."

"I am confused. You said, remember when we were at Lake Itasca? You said . . ."

"I know, I told you I was barren. The doctors told me I was barren." This was not the full truth. Dr. Hunt had told her Roger might have a problem.

"*Un momento.*" Mateo stood up and went to the bar.

Ursula sat, alone. Did Mateo just suddenly need a drink? Or had he already taken away the future she imagined? She picked up her stick and marched to the bar where Mateo had ordered himself a whiskey.

"Don't you want this? Don't you want to be with me?"

"Shhh." Mateo put his pointer finger to his lips. "This is personal. We can talk at home."

"Just tell me you want this," Ursula said, her legs trembling.

"I want to be with you, Ursula, I do." Mateo kissed Ursula's forehead. "But I need time to think about this."

"What does that mean?"

"I need time. *Un poco de tiempo*," Mateo said. His thumb and index finger created a gap in the air to demonstrate the amount of time, the gap small enough for his silver mate straw to pass through.

"We'll talk in the morning, first thing," Ursula said, relieved.

"First thing," Mateo promised. "Now let's dance. It is a party after all."

They danced until the midnight countdown. Ursula shouted, "Happy New Year" with the crowd. This time next year, she thought, she'd be a mother.

Ursula woke to snow the next morning. Mateo was asleep, his breath rolling in and out like a gentle wave. The chilly room cooled her throbbing thighs and calf muscles, and she rubbed them with the palms of her hand. Slowly her right leg made a stiff bicycle motion, then the left. Ursula repeated the motion until she was loose enough to sit up and place her feet on the floor. She grabbed her sticks from the modified umbrella stand next to the bed and went to the bathroom. Her hair smelt of stale cigarette smoke, making her gag.

Mateo stuck his head through the partially open door as Ursula washed her hands and face.

"Are you sick?" he asked, his face pale with concern. "I heard choking." He said choking in Spanish and mimed the motion with his hands.

"Morning sickness," she said and turned off the taps.

"Oh," Mateo lowered the toilet seat cover, sat down, and pressed his face into his hands. He looked up at her nervously. "Are you sick every day?"

"Mostly in the morning," Ursula said, feeling another wave of nausea. How had he not noticed over the last few weeks?

"Last night I was surprised by the news," Mateo said in Spanish and then English, his mind processing the events in both languages. "I never thought I would be a father."

Ursula wondered if Mateo's relationship with his own father had something to do with his reaction to her pregnancy. From what she had gathered, Mateo was acutely concerned about what his father thought.

"I had always hoped to be a mother," Ursula said, "but after polio and infertility problems, I'd made peace with it not happening." Ursula studied her reflection, makeup smudged below her eyes and lips dry from the cold.

"You know how important my medical training is," Mateo continued. "I cannot do anything to jeopardize that." He paused until Ursula turned from the mirror to look directly at him. "Ursula, I can't be a father. Our dreams are different."

The words hit her like an air raid siren, sharp and intense. Her legs gave way and she fell to the cold tile. Mateo's medical training kicked in, and he helped Ursula to the living room, where she sunk into the sofa.

"You can be a father and study," she finally said. "I will take care of the baby. We can be a family." Ursula needed him to believe in their potential together, to believe in her ability to be a mother.

"It is not so simple. How will you care for a child?" Mateo flipped his eyes to Ursula's sticks.

"You think I haven't thought about it? How difficult it might be for me to raise a child?" Ursula leaned forward, trying to make Mateo understand her urgency. "But we can do it. I know we can."

Mateo looked away as she placed her hands around her belly and imagined the baby's face. A mix of Mateo's strong jawline and her soft eyes and red hair.

"I need more time," Mateo said. He slowly paced the room.

"You said that last night. But Mateo, this baby will arrive in months!" Ursula was afraid of how quickly the days would pass without a plan, without any commitment to the future.

"How would I stay here?" Mateo asked. "There's visa and paperwork. Would they even approve it?"

"They will approve it," Ursula said. If an ex-enemy war bride could become a citizen, Mateo could, too. She'd make sure of it. She would reach out to Bea, to her old citizenship teacher, to anyone who might be able to help.

"But I would be leaving my family in Argentina," Mateo said.

Ursula thought again about her own family, leaving them behind.

"Mateo, I have not seen my family in more than ten years. You survive. You build your life because you have to." Ursula shot him a defiant look.

"When I said I love you, I meant it, but marriage? That's far away." Mateo said "far away" in Spanish, his face hardening.

Even in another language the words were harsh, like she was being clawed from the inside out.

"When will you be ready?"

"I don't know, I hadn't thought about it before today," Mateo said.

Ursula shook her head. After months living together, after their trip up north, he hadn't thought about marriage? Or at least some version of a future together? She had put too much faith in him, but she had allowed herself to fall for a foolish man. A dreamer who believed in Che Guevara, but could not believe in the woman standing in front of him, carrying his child.

"How can that be true? You said you loved me." Ursula paused. "I love you, Mateo! We're not young anymore. Anyone our age would be lucky to find someone to marry." She left out the part that would hurt to say the most. Anyone like her would be lucky to get married.

"This is the first time I heard you say you love me." Mateo sat down next to her on the sofa. "I confessed my feelings in the woods, but you . . ."

"How could you not see I was in love with you. I have been in love with you for months." Ursula was exposed and vulnerable. She wondered if earlier words could have made any difference.

"I need to finish school or my father will be disappointed," Mateo said, changing the subject. A pained expression crept across his face.

"What does it matter what your father thinks? You're a grown man. You can make your own decisions." Ursula's voice shook as it grew louder. "I came to America when I was twenty-two years old. My mother warned me not to leave Germany, but I did." Ursula pictured the cellar she'd lived in for a time, ankle deep with water. She remembered the hunger, risking her life for a potato. Long nights sleeping on the floors of shelters, huddled with strangers for warmth. Her father, imprisoned for speaking out about the communists. A girl pushed down the stairs to her death by the Russian soldiers. Leaving was the easy choice. Saying goodbye to her family was not.

"Maybe your life would have been better if you stayed," Mateo said, as he rested his eyes on her sticks.

"How dare you say that!" Ursula said. Her voice was steely, her body rigid. "How dare you judge the circumstances of my life just because you cannot accept your own."

"I'm sorry . . ." Mateo's voice trailed off. "It wasn't my idea to come here. I made a deal with my father. He said if I finished my training, he would forgive me for my failure to finish medical school."

Ursula's mouth parted but words stuck in her throat. His warm hands wrapped over hers, which had chilled with nervous sweat. She wanted to yank herself away, to be anywhere but in this living room fighting with Mateo. She was angry with herself for falling in love with him, for trusting him, for believing he might offer her a future.

"Ursula, I have to make him proud," Mateo said, choking back a sob. "My father was right. I am a failure."

She needed to affirm him, convince him to stay if only for her sake. She needed this last chance to become a mother. A chance she thought was gone forever when Roger died. Now it was here, inside her, and she could not let it go.

Ursula cleared her throat. "You are not a failure. You're doing wonderful work at the Institute. Don't you see, you can have your own life here? You don't have to live by your father's expectations."

They wrapped their arms around each other, the baby between them. But even so close to Mateo, the room was cold again.

Ursula kept the news about her pregnancy and the argument with Mateo to herself, but after a week she wanted to explode. Mateo sequestered himself at the university and spent extra hours at the Institute. He insisted he wasn't avoiding Ursula, but she had no other explanation for his behavior. Finally, Ursula reached out to Phyllis. She needed her best friend's advice.

"But Ursula, what are you going to do?" Phyllis sat on the living room sofa, a needlepoint project frozen in her hand.

"I don't know," Ursula said. "As naive as this sounds, I honestly had thought Mateo and I would get married eventually. Even before I found out I was pregnant. And now, I don't know . . . maybe he will come to his senses, take responsibility."

"I don't think it's so simple. First, this child has been . . ." Phyllis hesitated, ". . . conceived out of wedlock, which is, well I don't need to tell you how bad that is."

"But if we get married soon, we can figure it out." Ursula clutched her hands around her belly. "I had my doubts about Roger before I married him, but look at the life we had together."

"And how are you going to get married? Mateo is a student. Isn't he supposed to go home after he finishes his training?"

"We haven't talked about that." She paused. "Well, actually we did, but the conversation didn't go far." The unresolved tension between her and Mateo made the hair on her neck stand on end.

"If you cannot get him to stay and help you, whatever that looks like, your circumstances make it very difficult for you to be a mother on your own." Phyllis looked up from her stitching. "I don't need to tell you that."

"Circumstances? How are my circumstances that different compared to yours? We are both polio survivors, and you've managed fine." Ursula was surprised Phyllis wasn't being more understanding. She knew how much being a mother meant to Ursula.

"But I have David," Phyllis set down the embroidery loop and pressed her palms against her thighs.

"What are you trying to say? That I won't have Mateo?"

"No, that's not it. It's just that you've had such a difficult life. And, as your friend, I don't want to see you endure anymore hardship." Phyllis's eyes were wide with concern.

"This is it, Phyllis. This is my chance to have a child. When will I get another? I'm a thirty-five-year-old crippled woman. I'm a widow." Ursula said, laying the bleak facts on the table.

"I understand, but this will be harder than you realize." Phyllis sighed loudly and began to gather her things into her handbag.

"You think I haven't thought about how hard this might be? You think you know better?"

"I've given birth to two children since we were released from Riverwood. I think I do indeed know how difficult it is."

"I was hoping you would be . . ." Ursula could not finish.

"Ursula," Phyllis stopped, and held her eye, "You need to consider your options. There's a doctor I can put you in touch with."

"For what?"

"So, you can remove it, move on."

"You don't think I haven't thought about that?" Ursula wanted to slap Phyllis. "But how can I move on from this baby when it's here inside me?"

Phyllis perched on the edge of the sofa, her handbag clasped in her hands. "Okay, then," she said. "Perhaps you could consider adoption. There are many agencies here in the city that you could work with."

"You want me to give away my baby!" Ursula said. She was shouting now.

"That's not what I meant."

"It certainly sounded like that."

"I'm sorry, I cannot imagine how difficult this is for you." Phyllis stood up and looked down on her friend. Was that pity in her friend's eyes? "Oh Ursula, I've always admired your determination, but in this case, I think you're outmatched by the outside world." Phyllis put on her coat. "And as much as I want to, I can't help you every time you call. I have my own family to look after."

"Just go."

When the door closed behind Phyllis, Ursula burst into tears.

CHAPTER 37
February 1960

The national weather service predicted a foot or more of snow to fall from Saturday morning to Sunday night. Under normal circumstances, Ursula would have been eager to have uninterrupted time with Mateo, but now the tension between them buzzed like the anxious journalists covering the weather. Ursula tried to understand why Mateo was consumed by the deal he made with his father. She thought he could finish school and become a father, too. It would be difficult, yes, but certainly not impossible. Instead, Mateo seemed strangled by his father's wishes, unable to process his own future. And the more Ursula imagined her own future, she came to realize it would be impossible to start a family without Mateo. She needed him. She could not raise this child alone. And until he made a commitment to her and this baby, she could not share her secret with anyone else.

When Mateo arrived home from school on Friday evening with a large bag of groceries, Ursula took it as a good sign.

"I thought we could have a nice dinner," he said, setting the bag on the kitchen counter. "I'm going to cook one of my mother's dishes."

On Saturday, as the snow accumulated outside, Mateo conjured his mother's kitchen from Midwestern cheeses and meats. He shooed Ursula away and she attached crocheted flowers to baby blankets as the aroma of seared steak, oregano, and chili wafted through the house. From the kitchen, she could hear pots clattering on the stove and a whistle guiding Mateo's feet from the sink to the chopping board and back to the stove. It was as if he directed a gastronomic orchestra to summon his mother's kitchen in Buenos Aires. Ursula caught the tune Mateo whistled and hummed along. Tension eased with every note.

"Your father is cooking us a special dinner," she whispered, her hands circling her belly button. She'd seen a pregnant mother do the same thing while sheltering from an air raid in G-Tower. The woman, not much older than she had been, spoke quietly and sang lullabies as she ran her palms over the dirty fabric of her worn dress.

"You will grow up in peace time. Your life will be very different compared to mine," Ursula whispered again.

Ursula shifted on the sofa, placing a pillow behind her lower back. This ache was a new one, different from her exercises at the institute. She thought about how she would be able to balance as her pregnancy progressed. Over the last year, Ursula had gotten good at all her exercises, the technicians often asking her to demonstrate for the other patients. Proud of herself, she always agreed. Now, though, she worried about falling and hurting herself. And she worried about what she would say to people at the institute. It would all be so complicated.

Outside, heavy snow turned the picture window into a curtain of white. The safety of home lulled Ursula to sleep. She woke when Mateo's smooth tenor called her for dinner.

Vic had fallen asleep at her feet. She shooed him away so she could reach for her crutch, then got up from the sofa. In the dining room, Mateo had dressed the table with the embroidered white tablecloth Ursula had received from Pete and Sally as a wedding gift. China from her life with Roger adorned the table and left her breathless. Roger would never have dodged his responsibilities like Mateo. She cursed silently. He needed to come through for her, show courage.

Once Ursula was seated, Mateo brought in food from the kitchen, settled in his own chair, and passed her *carne asada*. She spooned a slice of meat onto the china plate. The dissonance of the situation made her skin crawl. Food from Mateo on dishes from her wedding. Ursula found herself wondering why Mateo had cooked this elaborate meal as he explained the dishes and their meaning.

"At home, my mother would make," Mateo pointed at the main course *provoleta*—cheese oozing in a cast iron pan, "but I could not find the exact ingredients."

"Since this is the first time I've had it, I wouldn't be able to tell the difference," Ursula said, giving him a sincere smile. For the first time in weeks, they were alone together. Ursula needed his attention; she needed him to listen.

"Mateo, we need to talk. I hate to interrupt this wonderful dinner, but—"

"Please, not tonight," Mateo said, his voice sharp.

"Then when? When will we make a decision about our future? The baby will come so soon," Ursula said, impatience colliding with hormones.

"We can talk tomorrow," Mateo said.

"You have been saying that since the New Year." She forced herself not to scream, not to pound her fists on the table. Instead, her voice broke into a frustrated mewl. "You don't get any more time, Mateo. I cannot live like this any longer."

"I am not meant to be a father and husband."

"Is that what you've been worried about this whole time? I'm scared, too, but we'll figure it out together."

Mateo looked down at his plate of food. "If my father finds out I have a child here, he will stop sending money."

"What?" Ursula was taken aback.

"He sends me money every month to cover tuition and board. Without him, what will I have to give you?" Mateo's face burned red.

"You're joking." Her breath quickened and rushed in her ears. The practical realization nearly strangled her. Without the money, Mateo wouldn't be able to continue school and board with her. The visa and paperwork that had seemed straightforward before would be impossible. Her American dream was collapsing. She dug her index fingers into her temples. "What are you going to do? What am I going to do?"

"I don't know. Maybe I can write to my uncle in Cuba? See if he can help? We were close when I was a child. He is always good to me."

"Do you think he would?" Ursula asked, clinging to any lifeline.

"Perhaps?"

"Does this mean that you want to stay?"

"I will write to him," Mateo said.

"You will?"

"I will write him now," Mateo said. His face broke into a smile. He got up to get a paper and pen from his room.

When Mateo was out of earshot, Ursula talked again to her baby. "Everything will work out. We are going to be fine." But she didn't quite believe it.

CHAPTER 38
March 1960

Ursula kissed Mateo goodbye as he studied for an exam at the kitchen table. Books with muscle groups and therapy definitions were open like accordions on the table. As Ursula opened the side door, he stopped and looked up. "Come back here, *mi amor*," he said, grabbing her hand in the small space. Mateo kissed her, enveloping her in a rush of warmth. Things had been so much better since he wrote to his uncle.

"I love you," she said.

"I love you, too," Mateo said back, his brown eyes pools of home.

Ursula drove to the Institute along the slushy roadway, the change of season clawing at the air. She had thought about revealing her pregnancy to people at the institute, but wanted to wait until Mateo heard from his uncle. Only then would she have more confidence in Mateo's intentions.

Once in the gym, the technician modified her exercises and Ursula complained about the extra weight she gained over the winter. The technician didn't question this, and for more than an hour they worked together to loosen and strengthen. Ursula counted her steps from left to right, left to right again. With each movement, Ursula promised herself she would be the best mother she could be, strong and resilient.

On her drive home, as her legs hummed from fatigue, she thought about Mateo's spontaneous "I love you" from earlier in the morning. While they danced around their future, Ursula never doubted his heart. He did love her. But love wasn't enough. Her foot pressed the modified brake pedal, then the gas pedal as she turned onto Colfax Avenue. The dark pavement poked through the layer of snow like a spotted cow.

Inside the house, Mateo's books were still scattered on the kitchen table, but Mateo was not where Ursula had left him.

"Mateo! I'm home," Ursula called. Her voice bounced in the silence, and she tried again. "Mateo?" Maybe he was in the basement doing laundry. Ursula walked to the top of the stairs and called his name a third time, with no response. She checked the bedroom to see if he had decided to nap. She knew this exam weighed on him. He had been up late with his books all week.

After two rounds around the modest house, she confirmed it was empty. Perhaps he had gone to the corner store for more cigarettes. He smoked more when he was stressed. She found a half-full pack on the kitchen table, though, and that was when she started to panic. They had groceries. Ursula had shopped the day before. But maybe he needed another book from the library.

After she made lunch—leftover minestrone soup—she busied her hands knitting a tiny cardigan. By dinner, she could no longer make sense of his absence. He normally told her if he had plans.

Ursula called Phyllis. "I can't find Mateo."

"You can't find him? What do you mean?"

"I arrived home from the Institute, and he was gone. He was here this morning studying for an exam," Ursula said.

"Maybe he forgot to mention he had plans," Phyllis said.

"I thought he could have gone to the library to get another book, but he's never there that long," Ursula said, the panic returning.

"He probably ran into friends," Phyllis said. A child screamed in the background. "I bet they are at the student union having dinner."

"You're probably right." Ursula took a deep breath, trying to steady herself. "It's probably the hormones. They make me panicky about everything." But she knew it was more than hormones. Something was wrong.

"When I was pregnant, I became hysterical at the smallest mishap," Phyllis said, reassurance in her voice. "He'll be home, don't worry."

Ursula ate the last of the lunch soup for dinner because she did not have the heart to make the beef stroganoff they had talked about in bed that morning. In the living room, she turned on the television. As her hands absentmindedly worked row by row, a tiny thump registered from inside her abdomen. Ursula swam with delight. She waited, hoping for another kick.

"He's going to come home, little one," she said. "I know he is."

A week of frantic calls with the Vargases and Phyllis led nowhere. Mateo was gone. Disappeared. Ursula couldn't sleep, and barely ate. If it hadn't been for the baby she would have lived on the adrenaline.

Then, on the ninth day after he left, Ursula noticed a postcard wedged between a letter from the bank and the *Ladies Home Journal*. When she'd first moved to Minneapolis, receiving mail thrilled Ursula. She used to sit on the front steps with Vic, waiting for the mailman and the possibility of an airmail envelope. Now her stomach plummeted when she spotted the postcard with the palm trees and a greeting. "Hello from Miami!"

Miami? She did not know anyone in Miami. Her hand shook as she flipped over the thick paper to see Mateo's loose handwriting. There were only a few sentences, as casual as if Mateo had gone on a business trip and would be home in a few days.

Sorry I did not say goodbye. I'll write from my uncle's house. Con cariño, Mateo.

Ursula read the words again, slowly and carefully. Goodbye was beyond the point, as far as she was concerned. Mateo should be in the house with her now planning for how they would welcome their baby in July. The last place he should be was on his way to his uncle's house in Cuba. Ursula sunk into the sofa and let out a scream so loud the windows rattled. Her body shuddered. The baby flipped, punching her from the inside.

Before the postcard arrived, Ursula had clung to a thread of hope, though she could not come up with where Mateo could have gone. Nothing made sense.

Then she remembered. Phyllis had been to Cuba. David had surprised her with a week-long vacation to celebrate their anniversary not long after Phyllis had been released from Riverwood. Phyllis might know what to do. At the very least, she had been to Cuba. She had walked the streets of Havana.

Ursula tucked the postcard in the pocket of her skirt, found the car keys, and drove to Phyllis's house.

"Ursula? I wasn't expecting you!" Phyllis opened the front door with Emma in her arms.

"I couldn't wait another second. I have to talk with you." Ursula pushed past Phyllis into the entryway. Inside, other kids were screaming, and David was on the sofa smoking and reading the paper. She wondered how he could read in this racket.

"Let's go to the kitchen," Phyllis said, then yelled, "Go play outside!" Ursula sat down, and with one hand Phyllis put the teakettle on the stove. Emma started to cry when Phyllis tried to seat her in the high chair.

"I'll be quick. You are overwhelmed," Ursula said. Emma screamed, then tugged her face into a grin when Phyllis settled her on her lap, instead.

"This is what you have to look forward to," Phyllis said, her tone matter of fact.

"A postcard arrived in the mail today." Ursula took the stiff paper from her skirt and set it on the table in front of Phyllis.

Phyllis read the postcard. "You're kidding" she said. Then she read it a second time, and scoffed at the picture. "What in god's name is he doing in Miami?"

"He is on his way to Cuba to see his uncle in Havana," Ursula said, but out loud it sounded outrageous. Why would he go without telling her?

"Well, this takes the cake. First, he abandons you, and now he's sending postcards from Miami as if nothing is wrong."

"Maybe he'll come home?" Ursula's voice still held hope. "Maybe he's only going to be gone for a few more days? He told me his uncle might help with money."

"Mateo did not have to go to Cuba to get money from his uncle. He could have asked him to wire it, found a way to do it from here. Why does he need money from his uncle anyway?"

"Well," Ursula said, feeling an embarrassed heat creep up her neck, "Mateo said if his father found out he fathered a child, he would be cut off."

"Cut off?" Phyllis pulled the postcard from Emma's toddler grip and pushed it across the table toward Ursula.

"Mateo's father was paying for his tuition and board," Ursula said. She picked up the postcard and stared at the palm trees, their green leaves carefree in the wind. She hated them.

"No matter which way you look at this, it's not good for you,"

Phyllis said. "If he returns—and that's a big if—you're still going to have to figure out what to do with the baby." Phyllis repositioned Emma.

"We can find him! You've been to Cuba. You can tell me all about it. Maybe I can go there to look for him." Ursula did not want to confront the possibility he might truly be gone. She still had time to find him.

"Oh Ursula," Phyllis said, "listen to yourself. I went to Cuba years ago on vacation. What you need, if you really want to find Mateo, is an international detective." She sighed. "And that would be so expensive and probably still pointless."

"I can't just give up. I am this close!" Ursula pinched weeks between her fingers. "I am this close to becoming a mother."

"I'm not saying you should totally give up on finding Mateo, but you have to focus on how *you're* going to survive, too. How you're going to survive with a baby."

"But—"

"But of all the people I know, you will. You will get through this," Phyllis said. As she emphasized "you," her eyes watered with tears. "I'm sorry, this is just heartbreaking."

"Mommy why you cry?" Emma asked, poking at Phyllis's cheek. The tiny voice shattered Ursula's heart. Her innocent question brought a harrowing clarity. She suddenly understood the choices she would have to make to survive.

CHAPTER 39
April 1960

Ursula's rounded belly bumped against the Formica counter. She placed her hands flat on the pristine surface and dropped her head, eyes closed. Cleaning allowed her to let go of her thoughts while her hands worked, and for a moment she had forgotten about her expanding abdomen. She opened her eyes and caught sight of a corner of the floral linoleum floor, stained black for more than a decade. It had happened the evening they had gone to Schiek's Cafe and Roger had spent hours sitting on a kitchen bench, making sure the shine was perfect on his black dress shoes. The polish had splashed onto the floor and splotches remained, even after years of cleaning. Ursula looked away as a knot formed in her throat.

Ursula had been nervous about setting foot in the Catholic Charities building earlier that morning. She'd been shown into an office where a picture of the Virgin Mary hung prominently on the wall, a rosary slung over the corner of the frame. Her mind flashed to Roger's mother, worrying a string of beads between her fingers.

Ursula had thought about not coming. Letting Catholic Charities have a record of the visit seemed dangerous. It brought back the anxious feeling of being watched. It was as if she had turned the calendar to 1943, when she had learned to type and was conscripted into a work program. During long hours at the desk, she tried to stay alert, to ready herself for the comments and questions coming from one of the higherups. "You're a pretty one, you know that? When are you going to make babies for the Führer?" And then he would tell her about his wife, how she might not mind if he helped out the race. She was *that* committed to the Führer he had said. Ursula rejected his advances with caution, until one day he was no longer there, replaced by another man who was less interested in the typists.

Ursula shivered from the memory then set her eyes on the Virgin, considering the way her palms extended outward from under the folds of her robe. For a moment, Ursula thought this faithful woman might levitate off the wall and grasp Ursula. Nestle her in the folds of fabric. Ursula needed a warm, familiar embrace. She suddenly longed for her mother's arms, for her protection from the outside world. Then Ursula scoffed under her breath. She wasn't a girl anymore, far from it.

The woman at Catholic Charities had been pleasant at first, but the cheerful robin's egg blue of her sheath dress was a false welcome. As soon as Ursula shared a few details—keeping the abstract and hypothetical—judgment had hung in the air between them. The woman's skin pinched with concern between her eyes. Ursula said she was simply looking for information about adoption services. She tried to keep her voice calm and steady, as if she was teaching knitting or German.

"If, perhaps, a woman was in a position to place a child for adoption," Ursula had said, hoping to shield herself from intrusive questions. She had worn a baggy dress, but this woman would be a fool to not see Ursula was already very pregnant. "And if this woman needed help," Ursula had ventured on, her voice quiet but steady, "what options would be available to her?"

The small straight-haired women had opened a drawer in her

modest desk, a cigarette dangling at an impossible angle from her mouth. Then she had placed a few pieces of paper on the smooth surface and slid them across to Ursula.

"You are out of options," the woman had said, stating a conclusion Ursula wasn't quite ready to reach. "If you pursue our services, which I firmly recommend you do, I can assure you this child will go to a good home." She had seen through Ursula's earlier hesitation, knew exactly what Ursula was asking.

The words "Surrendering custody of your child" jumped off the page in front of Ursula. The letters were like small knives coming toward her, embedding themselves into her chest. Ursula shuddered.

"I think I have heard enough," Ursula had said, folding the papers and stuffing them into her handbag. She reached for her sticks and as she stood up, controlled a slight wobble of her right ankle. She could not let this woman see any weakness.

"You know, you're not the first polio that has come in here." The woman had extinguished her cigarette in an ashtray and sat back in her chair, flicking her metal lighter open and closed.

Ursula glared at her, the annoyingly pleasant face, this woman who knew nothing about her. It was as if she were challenging Ursula to disagree, or relent, or Ursula couldn't decide what. She would not, however, be intimidated by this woman or anyone else who thought they knew what a woman with polio could or could not do.

At the door, Ursula looked back over her shoulder. "You've obviously never heard of polio mother of the year, have you?"

Ursula drove home in a mental haze, then screamed as soon as she set foot inside her house, throwing her purse against the wall. The thwack startled Vic and he started barking.

There had to be another way forward. A path that did not involve giving away her child.

Now alone in the kitchen, though, Ursula's confidence and conviction about keeping the baby faltered. Could she consider this house a "good" home? Were the four solid walls enough to contain her and the new life she would be—already was—responsible for? She shifted in the chair. Her back ached more with each passing week, an incessant reminder of the impending due date. An incessant reminder that she needed to make a decision. Only a few more months and the baby would take a first breath, fill its lungs with the same air as Ursula.

With some effort, Ursula retrieved her purse from the floor and took out the papers. As she shoved the pages into the trash, a square of thick cardboard fell out—a business card. She bent over, bracing herself against the counter to pick up the card. Mrs. Dorothy O'Connell, it read in simple black font. Case Worker. Catholic Charities. Then a number. Ursula ran her fingers over the print. The words and digits, created a path she did not want to follow. If she called this number, she wouldn't be able to go back.

At her typewriter, Ursula hammered a letter to the ambassador to Cuba. A final plea to find Mateo. Anguish piled up on her face as she sunk her fingers into the keys.

A few weeks later, in early May, a letter arrived from the American ambassador to Cuba. Ursula sat at the kitchen table and placed a silver letter opener under the flap. As the two pieces separated, her stomach lurched. Before unfolding the letter, Ursula took a deep breath, wishing for good news. Though anything would be better than the silence hanging over Mateo's absence.

Dear Mrs. Gorski:

I have received your letter of April 18, 1960, in which you indicate an interest in knowing the welfare and whereabouts of your friend, Mr. Mateo Fabricio Peralta, an Argentine citizen.

Upon my direction, an officer of the Embassy spoke personally with Mr. Peralta at the address in Cuba furnished by you and reported back to me that Mr. Peralta is well and will write to you as soon as possible. He also said that he plans to leave Cuba and return to his home in Argentina.

I trust the above information will prove helpful to you and that you will hear from your friend soon.

Sincerely yours,

Philip W. Bonsal

American Ambassador

Ursula read the last line of the ambassador's letter again. *I trust the above information will prove helpful to you and that you will hear from your friend soon.*

"He's more than a friend, he's the father of my child," Ursula screamed in the empty kitchen, as she defensively placed her arms across her belly.

The news that Mateo was planning to return to Argentina crashed around her in the silent house. It was confirmation of what she already knew. Mateo had abandoned her. Left her behind.

Her whole body ached. Her mind ached. Her heart ached with the desire to bring Mateo back to Minnesota. It was the same ache that had driven her for weeks, ever since the postcard from him had arrived. She hobbled to her bed, took off her shoes and lay on top of the sheets. Then she fell asleep and dreamt of Cuba.

Ursula was last to disembark from the plane. Phyllis was there, walking down the stairs designed for people with working legs. By the time Ursula set foot on the tarmac, she dripped with sweat.

Phyllis managed to hail a taxi. As they passed a promenade near the sea crowded with tourists, Ursula wondered how they would ever find Mateo in this pulsing city. Shirtless boys were sprawled on the sea wall, some on the brink of diving into the water below, fearless.

They turned a corner onto a crowded street with rows of buildings rising majestically on either side, a promise of modernity. People leaned in and out of doorways, windows, and balconies. Then the buildings transformed, the concrete shifting into giant pregnant women staring down at them, disappointed in Ursula. Ursula tried to tell Phyllis it was a stupid idea to come to Cuba to look for Mateo, but Phyllis had disappeared, lost in the forest of giant legs. Ursula called and called for Phyllis, but it was hopeless. Then the legs were buildings again, and out of a slightly open door, Ursula saw Mateo. When she called his name, he disappeared too.

CHAPTER 40
July 1960

The contractions started at 9:37 a.m. on July 6, 1960, more than five months after Mateo had disappeared from Ursula's life. She was in bed, unable to move far on her own, her belly so wide it threw her completely off balance.

"Are you awake?" Phyllis walked into the bedroom. She had been with Ursula for the past week, arriving early each morning and staying until after the late-night news.

"I think the baby is coming." Ursula clutched her stomach, her skin straining to hold everything in.

"Did your water break?"

"I don't know. I think so?" The sheet underneath her was damp. She hadn't been sleeping well in the summer heat and assumed it was sweat. And then the pain shot through her. Ursula gritted her teeth and groaned. This was worse than the hot blankets at the polio hospital.

"I'm going to call the doctor," Phyllis said.

"That's a good idea." Ursula's voice trailed off as another wave of pain collapsed across her body. It ran along her limbs so quickly she didn't know where it began or where it stopped. "And Phyllis, I need you to do one more thing for me." Then she told her friend where she had put the business card for the Catholic Charities case worker. Once they were at the hospital, Phyllis would need to call the number.

At the Twin Cities General hospital, where a decade before she received her polio diagnosis, Ursula was ushered by an orderly into a large room. A nurse motioned for her to change into a gown behind a curtain. This floor was for mothers. The isolation unit where Dr. Anderson had delivered the devastating news was likely gone now with advent of the polio vaccine.

Wiggling in her wheelchair, Ursula struggled to remove her dress as a contraction hit. She moaned in pain, flapping her arms in a useless attempt to get the dress off and over her head. Ursula did not know where her sticks were. Phyllis had them with her when she walked Ursula through the hospital doors, but now Phyllis was gone.

"Hello? Is anyone there?" The room beyond the curtain was still, then footsteps came closer.

"Are you finished?" A nurse asked, pulling back the curtain.

Ursula sensed this nurse was nothing like the kind and helpful nurses at Riverwood. The nurses there had never seemed burdened by their patients.

"I need help getting this off."

The nurse sighed and said, "I should have known you would need help."

Over the next twelve hours Ursula was alone in her bed, shaking with pain. Between contractions she held back tears and tried to make sense of what was in front of her. From somewhere on the ward a baby cried and a mother sang a lullaby. Ursula desperately wanted to trade places with that mother, to hold her baby, to go home to a husband. As the contractions quickened, she cursed Mateo. But she was even angrier with herself for believing he would ever take responsibility. Mateo never had any intention of staying, of finding a way forward so they could be a family.

At dawn on July seventh, almost twenty-four hours after Ursula was admitted, a doctor placed a gas mask over her face. "You're almost there and this will help with the pain." As the blurring vapors took hold, the words "A good home" shot through her mind. She had to take responsibly for this life she was about to give birth to. Her heart shattered into grains of sand as Ursula made a decision about her future. Then everything went blank in a numbing fog.

In the large shared room in the maternity ward, a nurse came in with a bundle in her arms. Groggy, sore, and exhausted, Ursula blinked open her eyes.

"Mrs. Gorski, would you like to hold your baby girl?"

Ursula knew the answer in her heart.

"No," Ursula said, shifting her gaze toward the window. "If I hold her, I will never let her go."

As the nurse left the room, Ursula heard the baby she had just given birth to cry out. Ursula wanted to take her daughter and run. She willed her legs to move, but her entire body was spent from labor. Months earlier, she had imagined Mateo standing beside the hospital bed and cradling their baby, the two of them peering into her blue eyes. I've been waiting all my life to meet you, she would tell the baby, an angelic glow surrounding their family. Even in this daydream, the infant always disappeared as Ursula leaned in to kiss her forehead.

A different nurse walked across the room and stood at the foot of Ursula's bed, making notes in her chart. Then she looked up. "Your baby is settled in the nursery," she said.

"Please, would you take me to see her? I need to see her." Ursula formed her hands into fists under the sheets, channeling agony. She needed to know what she had been carrying was real because she would never feel her baby's soft skin, graze fingers over her pink cheeks, or tickle the bottoms of her feet. She would never hear her say her first word. She would never watch her learn to walk. The "nevers" mounted into a chorus so loud it threatened to split her open. But she could not go back now. It would be impossible to raise this baby girl alone. She had already signed the paperwork.

The nurse helped Ursula into a wheelchair and pushed her to the nursery. When they got close, Ursula locked the wheels and carefully stood up so she could see the rows of infants in their bassinets. With her face pressed against the glass, she searched for her baby girl.

"She's in the back, see?" The nurse pointed.

The baby's dark eyes pierced the room. A tuft of dark brown hair—the same color as Mateo's—poked out from under a pink stocking cap.

"I love you," Ursula mouthed through the glass.

"She's beautiful, Mrs. Gorski," the nurse said.

A smile trembled on Ursula's tired face. She held her voice steady and turned to the nurse. "Am I a mother?"

Ursula knew it was an unfair question. Still, she needed to hear someone say she had become the person she'd dreamed of becoming for all these years.

The nurse lowered her voice as if someone else were listening. "I understand you're not here under the easiest circumstances," she said. "But that does not make you any less of a mother."

Ursula slumped back in the wheelchair, silent tears dropping onto the hospital gown drawn tight over her breasts and abdomen. "Please help me back to my room."

"I'm so sorry, Mrs. Gorski." The nurse unlocked the brakes and the rubber wheels circled on the sterile hospital floor, taking Ursula farther from her baby.

It hit her then, how her own mother must have felt the day Ursula said she was leaving for America. The day Ursula sat across the table from her and made a case for marrying Roger, for traveling across the ocean, for creating a life in a country not spoiled by war. Ursula understood now, the weight of it. Her mother had to contain a volcano of grief inside her body to let her daughter go.

"One day, I will see my daughter again."

AUTHOR NOTE

What We Leave Behind is inspired by my maternal grandmother's life. In the early 1980s, my mother wrote to Catholic Charities hoping to be put in contact with her birth mother. "My heart has written to you several times, but my hand has not," Ursula wrote back. Their friendship blossomed, as did my relationship with Ursula—letters sailed between Minnesota and Arizona, where Ursula eventually settled and lived for the remainder of her life. Ursula was a prolific letter writer and composed memoirs that wrestled with questions of individual agency and resistance during times of great political upheaval. She dreamed of being published, but died in 1998.

Ursula, February 1952,
Courtesy of the author's family archives

ACKNOWLEDGMENTS

This book is a labor of love and a profoundly personal story. I first learned about Ursula as a child. Interest in her life stayed with me through adolescence and adulthood. Her story captivated me, and anyone I shared it with was equally surprised and intrigued. Exploring Ursula's story more deeply originated in a workshop at StoryStudio Chicago.

A huge thank you to Kathleen Furin, my developmental editor, for believing in this book from the early stages when the manuscript was unrefined, but the story flashed brightly in our conversations. Kathleen coaxed the story's potential with exacting questions, care, and excitement.

To Brooke Warner and team at She Writes Press for believing in me and this story. I am proud to be part of their 2023 cohort of authors.

I am forever indebted to the polio survivors who generously offered their hearts and stories. Your experiences profoundly shaped this book.

A deep, and special thank you to Francine Falk-Allen for her careful review of my manuscript, and for sharing her personal experiences living with polio.

Thank you to Sonja Sharp for her incisive feedback on living with a physical disability, and on the challenges mothers with disabilities face in an ableist world.

Thank you to Kathy Miller and Shoshanna Matney for detailed feedback and tough conversations. A special thank you to Kathy, for her careful copy edits (she cared about this manuscript as if it were her own).

Thank you to Ariel Montague for her detailed historical research.

To Jamie Kelter Davis for the beautiful author photo.

To Ilsa Brink for the perfect website design to compliment the book.

To the She Writes Press team for the beautiful cover design, and to Casey and TJ for art direction on the cover design.

Insight and generosity flowed from Susan Wigoda, a dear friend, expert writer, and giver of feedback. She happily read drafts of the manuscript and encouraged changes that made this book what it is today. Rogue Writers to the rescue!

Faithful friends listened to my writerly woes and encouraged me to keep going, including Eni, Melissa, Lydia, Alex, Claire, Kristin, Mireia, Anna, and Hallie (who gets a special thank you for providing insights on Argentina).

This book would not exist without my mom, Cathy. She was by my side, even from a geographic distance, with enthusiasm, curiosity, and meticulous attention to detail. Cathy was the first to dig into the archives at the Minnesota Historical Society and at the University of Minnesota. She has a unique and fearless emotional capacity for her own personal history. Even as I wrote difficult passages of the book, including the ending, she read with heart and interest. Mom, you never turned away when this process became difficult. I am forever grateful.

To my family in the United Sates, Ireland, and Australia, for listening and cheering me on. Thank you again Mom, Dad, Kate, Becky, and Jim.

For lovingly encouraging me to keep going every time I wanted to give up, my husband Michael believed in me when I needed it most, gave me space to process the huge challenge of writing a book, and frequently reminded me: "You love to write. Keep writing." Michael, you sustain me.

ABOUT THE AUTHOR

photo credit: Jamie Kelter Davis

Christine Gallagher Kearney is a Midwest Review "Great Midwest Writing Contest" finalist, and a semi-finalist for Chestnut Review's "Stubborn Artists Contest." She has published in *Wild Roof Journal, Driftless Magazine, ForbesWoman, Fortune,* and *Cara Magazine* and is a former food columnist for the *Irish American News.* Christine graduated with her bachelor's degrees in International Relations and Spanish from Mount Holyoke College, later earning her master's degree in Organizational and Multicultural Communication through DePaul University. She has a career in the corporate world and writes in her off hours. *What We Leave Behind* is her debut novel. Christine grew up in Minnesota, but now lives in Chicago with her husband and dachshund.

SELECTED TITLES FROM SHE WRITES PRESS

She Writes Press is an independent publishing company founded to serve women writers everywhere. Visit us at www.shewritespress.com.

Expect Deception by JoAnn Ainsworth. $16.95, 978-1-63152-060-0
When the US government recruits Livvy Delacourt and a team of fellow psychics to find Nazi spies on the East Coast during WWII, she must sharpen her skills quickly—or risk dying.

This Is How It Begins by Joan Dempsey. $16.95, 978-1-63152-308-3
When eighty-five-year-old art professor Ludka Zeilonka's gay grandson, Tommy, is fired over concerns that he's silencing Christian kids in the classroom, she is drawn into the political firestorm—and as both sides battle to preserve their respective rights to free speech, the hatred on display raises the specter of her WWII past.

All the Light There Was by Nancy Kricorian. $16.95, 978-1-63152-905-4
A lyrical, finely wrought tale of loyalty, love, and the many faces of resistance, told from the perspective of an Armenian girl living in Paris during the Nazi occupation of the 1940s.

An Address in Amsterdam by Mary Dingee Fillmore
$16.95, 978-1-63152-133-1
After facing relentless danger and escalating raids for 18 months, Rachel Klein—a well-behaved young Jewish woman who transformed herself into a courier for the underground when the Nazis invaded her country—persuades her parents to hide with her in a dank basement, where much is revealed.

Portrait of a Woman in White by Susan Winkler. $16.95, 978-1-93831-483-4
When the Nazis steal a Matisse portrait from the eccentric, art-loving Rosenswigs, the Parisian family is thrust into the tumult of war and separation, their fates intertwined with that of their beloved portrait.

The Sweetness by Sande Boritz Berger. $16.95, 978-1-63152-907-8
A compelling and powerful story of two girls—cousins living on separate continents—whose strikingly different lives are forever changed when the Nazis invade Vilna, Lithuania.